The Cat Who Solved Three Murders

L T Shearer has had a lifelong love of canal boats and calico cats, and both are combined in *The Cat Who Caught a Killer*, a one-of-a-kind debut crime novel. The series continues with *The Cat Who Solved Three Murders*.

By L T Shearer

The Cat Who Caught a Killer
The Cat Who Solved Three Murders

L T SHEARER

The Cat Who Solved Three Murders

PAN BOOKS

First published 2023 by Macmillan

This paperback edition first published 2024 by Pan Books
an imprint of Pan Macmillan
The Smithson, 6 Briset Street, London EC1M 5NR
EU representative: Macmillan Publishers Ireland Ltd, 1st Floor,
The Liffey Trust Centre, 117–126 Sheriff Street Upper,
Dublin 1, D01 YC43
Associated companies throughout the world
www.panmacmillan.com

ISBN 978-1-5290-9806-8

1 3 5 7 9 8 6 4 2

A CIP catalogue record for this book is available from the British Library.

Typeset by Palimpsest Book Production Ltd, Falkirk, Stirlingshire
Printed and bound by CPI Group (UK) Ltd, Croydon, CR0 4YY

Visit **www.panmacmillan.com** to read more about all our books
and to buy them. You will also find features, author interviews and
news of any author events, and you can sign up for e-newsletters
so that you're always first to hear about our new releases.

1

The Prius slowed at the front gate and the driver twisted around in his seat. His name was Mo, which Lulu assumed was short for Mohammed. He was in his mid-forties and had been the perfect Uber driver, offering her hand sanitizer, breath mints and bottled water before setting off from Oxford city centre and asking her what music she would like played during their journey. He had looked surprised when she had walked up with Conrad sitting on her shoulders, but if he had any objections at all to riding with a calico cat, he had kept them to himself. Conrad was standing on the seat next to Lulu, his paws up against the glass as he peered at the house in the distance. Lulu could see his reflection in the glass – the right side of his head was mainly black with a white patch around the nose and mouth, and the left side was brown and white.

'Is this it?' Mo asked. 'It looks like a hotel.'

'It does, doesn't it?'

'You said it was a house. But this is where the GPS is bringing me.'

'Then this must be it,' said Lulu.

'Sometimes the GPS is wrong.'

There were two black wrought-iron gates, each almost twelve feet high, and they were open. There were weathered stone turrets either side of the gates set into an eight-foot-high stone wall. A tarmac driveway cut through several acres of manicured lawns, leading to a Georgian mansion with four massive chimney stacks. There were several cars and vans parked outside and Mo was right – it definitely had the look of a hotel.

Conrad twisted around and looked at Lulu. 'Meow!' he said and pointedly looked back at the turret on the right. There was a brass sign set into the stonework: HEPWORTH HOUSE.

'This is definitely it,' said Lulu.

'So this is a house?' Mo took both his hands off the steering wheel and opened his palms wide. 'For one family?'

'My friends don't have children,' said Lulu.

'So just two people live here?' He shook his head. 'Unbelievable. They must be very rich.'

'I think they are, now,' said Lulu.

Mo put his hands back on the steering wheel, turned the Prius into the driveway and drove slowly towards the house, muttering under his breath. Lulu could understand his astonishment. The house was breathtakingly beautiful, and so big that it really didn't make sense that only two people lived there. It was a far cry from the last home that Julia and Bernard Grenville had lived in, a small terraced house in what could only be described as a deprived area of Oxford. The house was nice enough but the area had one of the highest crime rates in the city and during dinner at least half a dozen car alarms had gone off. But that was six years ago, back when Bernard was a struggling antique shop owner and Julia was working as a lab researcher. Things had taken a turn for the better since those days, clearly.

Lulu and Julia had been firm friends for more than thirty years. Their paths had first crossed when Julia had been a forensic investigator while Lulu had been walking a beat in Stoke Newington. The friendship had lasted even though Julia and her husband had left London for Oxford. The invitation to Bernard's sixtieth birthday party had come out of the blue, but Lulu had eagerly accepted – she had nothing pressing to do and was keen to catch up with them. Julia had mentioned that they had come into some money now that her company was about to go public, but clearly 'some money' was a gross understatement.

Mo brought the Prius to a stop next to a gleaming white Bentley. 'Have a nice day,' he said. He looked at the Bentley and sighed. 'Now that is a wicked car.'

'It is, isn't it?' said Lulu. The last time she had seen Bernard and Julia, they were driving a three-year-old Ford Fiesta. She opened the door and Conrad jumped off the seat and onto the ground. Lulu climbed out, picked him up, and closed the door. Mo flashed the Bentley another jealous glance and drove off.

Lulu held Conrad up so that he could climb onto her shoulders and settle around her neck. 'This house is amazing,' he said. Conrad hadn't said a word during the twenty-minute drive from the city centre. Lulu was the only person he ever spoke to; he never said anything other than 'meow' when there was anyone else around. Lulu had come to accept that Conrad could talk, but there were times when she still thought that perhaps she was dreaming and that one day she would wake up. Cats didn't talk, obviously. That was a fact of life. Except that Conrad did. He was an exceptional cat, perhaps one of a kind. He was a calico cat. Often referred to as a tortoiseshell but Lulu never liked that name as Conrad looked nothing like a tortoise. Most calico cats were female, but Conrad was indeed exceptional. In so many ways.

'It's not what I expected,' said Lulu. She looked over at the vehicles parked in a line to their left. One was a Mercedes Sprinter van in the livery of Thames Valley Police, another was a nondescript blue Ford Mondeo which she instinctively recognized as a police vehicle. There was also a white BMW, a grey Volvo and a blue Range Rover, both less than a year old.

'They're scientists, you said.'

'Julia was; she studied forensic science at university but then did a PhD in virology. Her husband is an art dealer. Well, antiques really. But these days he mainly helps her run the company.'

'What does it do, again? This company?'

'Julia did explain but I couldn't really follow it. It's something to do with vaccines but the techniques they use have wider implications for all sorts of illnesses.' She reached up and rubbed him under the chin and he purred. 'I'll tell you what, I'll ask her to explain it to me again and you can hear it from the horse's mouth.'

'See now, I have never understood that phrase. Horses don't talk. Have you ever heard a horse talk? No. So why don't they say "from the cat's mouth" instead?'

'Well, strictly speaking, cats don't usually talk, either.'

'That's true. I am special.' He wrinkled his nose.

'Oh, I would say unique.'

Lulu walked up to the front door. There was a large brass knocker in the shape of a lion's head in the centre, but on the wall to the right was a brass bell push. She pressed it but didn't hear anything from inside the house. 'Do you think it's working?' she said.

'Hard to tell,' said Conrad. 'Maybe the maid has to find the under butler and the under butler has to find the butler

4

and then the butler will have to make his way to the front door.'

Lulu laughed. 'It is a very big house, isn't it?'

'It's enormous,' said Conrad. 'It's a mansion.'

They heard footsteps and then the handle turned and the door opened. Lulu had half expected to be greeted by a liveried butler so she was pleasantly surprised to see that it was Julia. She was wearing a pretty blue cotton dress and had her blonde hair tied back in a ponytail. If anything her hair colour was even brighter than last time Lulu had seen her. Lulu had stopped dyeing her hair years ago and had embraced her greyness, which her hairdresser always kindly referred to as platinum.

Julia's face broke into a beaming smile. 'Lulu, my goodness, you're here.'

'Well, yes. You invited me, remember?'

Julia frowned. 'And there's a cat on your shoulders.'

'Yes, there is.'

'No, there's a cat on your shoulders. Why is there a cat on your shoulders?'

'This is Conrad,' said Lulu.

Julia laughed. 'Your date?'

'Very much so.'

'Meow,' said Conrad.

'Oh my goodness, he talks.'

'Yes,' said Lulu. 'He does.'

Conrad jumped down off her shoulders and landed with a dull plop on the doorstep.

Julia looked over Lulu's shoulder. 'Where's your car?'

'We took an Uber.'

'From London?'

'From Oxford. We came on *The Lark*.'

'*The Lark*?'

'My narrowboat.'

'You sailed from Maida Vale?'

'You drive a narrowboat rather than sail her, but yes.'

'But don't they travel at five miles an hour or something?'

'Between three or four. Pretty much walking pace.'

Julia frowned. 'So how long did it take?'

'Well, we weren't rushing, so eight days.' She gestured at the Sprinter van. 'Julia, why are the police here?'

'I'm so glad you came, Lulu,' said Julia, stepping forward and hugging her. She air-kissed her on both cheeks and then hugged her again. 'It's just that something rather awful happened yesterday.'

'What? What happened?'

Julia put her arm around Lulu and guided her through the doorway. 'I'll make you a cup of tea and tell you all about it,' she said.

They walked into a double-height hall with a sweeping double marble staircase that curved around a chandelier that must have been fifteen feet tall and composed of thousands of pieces of glass. It had the look of a crystal waterfall and it shimmered as Lulu looked up at it.

'This way,' said Julia, taking Lulu down a hallway to the left. The hallway was lined with modern paintings, large canvases with splashes of colour. There were doors leading off both sides. The kitchen was at the end of the hallway; it was ultra-modern, with gleaming white marble and stainless-steel appliances and a huge white oak island surrounded by half a dozen chrome-and-leather stools, above which hung a set of copper pans.

'Oh, this is lovely,' said Lulu.

'Really? I think it looks like a hotel kitchen, ready to serve up two dozen English breakfasts at a moment's notice. Bernard is the chef in the family, I can barely boil an egg.'

'Where is Bernard?'

'Well, that's the thing, Lulu. Look, I really don't want to drink tea – how would you feel about champagne?'

'Champagne?'

Julia opened one side of a large fridge to reveal half a dozen bottles of champagne. 'I really could do with a drink and seeing you after so long would seem to be the perfect excuse. And I have fresh orange juice too if you wanted a Buck's Fizz.'

'I'm always happy to have an excuse for a drink,' said Lulu.

'Excellent.' Julia put the champagne on the island, then took a pitcher of orange juice from the fridge and gave it to Lulu. 'You hold this and we'll go through to the conservatory. And what about Conrad? What does he drink?'

'Water would be great,' said Lulu.

'Tap water?'

'Meow!' said Conrad, looking up at Julia with his bright green eyes.

'I'll take that as a definite no,' said Julia.

'He likes Evian.'

'Well, of course he does,' said Julia. She took a bottle of Evian from the fridge and gave it to Lulu. 'Through there,' she said, nodding at two sliding doors that led to a large conservatory. She picked up two flutes and a glass bowl, retrieved the champagne and followed Lulu through the doors.

The conservatory overlooked the expansive grounds, which included a small lake, a wooden gazebo and several greenhouses and outbuildings. There was a wood in the distance. 'This is just lovely, Julia,' said Lulu, admiring the view. 'It's like a stately home.'

'It's not a home yet,' said Julia. 'But we're getting there.' Two large wooden-bladed fans were turning overhead. There were three rattan sofas with overstuffed floral cushions around a circular glass-topped rattan table. Julia put the glasses, bowl and champagne onto the table and sat down with a sigh.

Lulu put the orange juice and the Evian bottle down and then she sat next to Julia. There was clearly something wrong with Bernard, but she figured it was best to let Julia talk about it in her own time. Lulu had been a police officer in a previous life and had carried out more than her fair share of interrogations. Sometimes it was best to simply say nothing and to wait for the other person to fill the silence.

Julia uncorked the champagne with an ease that suggested she had done it many times before. She poured some into the two flutes and then added orange juice, while Lulu opened the bottle of Evian and sloshed some into the bowl. Lulu put the bowl down in front of Conrad and he lapped at it.

Julia handed a glass of Buck's Fizz to Lulu. 'I'm so happy to see you again,' said Julia. They clinked glasses and drank. Conrad curled up at Lulu's feet and rested his chin on his paws. 'How long has it been?'

Lulu forced a smile. 'Since Simon's funeral, I suppose.' Lulu's husband had died, and not long afterwards she had moved onto *The Lark*. A new start.

'Oh my gosh, yes. It was. I'm so sorry I let things slide,

we were just so busy with the company. We literally haven't had a day off in the last year.' She sipped her drink, then looked out over the gardens. She was clearly getting ready to say something, so Lulu stayed quiet. Julia sighed. 'Something terrible happened yesterday, Lulu. I'm still in shock. There was a robbery here, some paintings were stolen, and a man was killed. Bernard was hurt; he's in bed at the moment.'

'Julia! Why didn't you say something?'

Julia smiled ruefully. 'I'm saying something now. It wouldn't have been right to hit you with it before you'd crossed the threshold, would it?'

'Is Bernard okay?'

'The doctor says he'll be fine. They gave him a scan yesterday and they told him to take it easy, but there's no lasting damage.'

Lulu covered her mouth with her hand. 'Oh, Julia, that's terrible. Why didn't you cancel tomorrow's party? Everyone would have understood.'

'We talked about it, but it was such a terrible thing to happen that we didn't want it to overshadow Bernard's birthday. If we allow it to affect us, it'll affect us for ever. His birthday will always be a reminder that someone was killed in our house – it would be blighted. This way, we just keep that room closed, we have the party, we bring fresh life into the house and we move on.'

'Yes, I suppose so.'

'There is no suppose so, Lulu. It was a terrible thing to happen but we can't allow it to control the way we behave. Plus a lot of VIPs have been invited, people that are involved with our company. We don't want to mess them around by cancelling at such short notice.'

'And the police are okay with that? All those people trampling over a crime scene?'

Julia grinned. 'They weren't happy at all. But Bernard is in the local Rotary Club with the assistant chief constable and he rang him up and explained everything. Bernard's friend fast-tracked the forensic investigation and they should be finished by this evening.'

Lulu nodded, then sipped her drink. 'Could I see the room where it happened?'

Julia laughed. 'You really can never forget that you were a police officer, can you?'

Lulu smiled. 'Guilty as charged. Is the room still being treated as a crime scene?'

'I'm afraid so. The very nice detective who came along said she thought we might have the room back this afternoon, but if you really want a peep, I can show you through the window.'

'No, it's okay.'

'You are so funny, Lulu. I know you really want to have a snoop around, it's your nature. And you can't fight your nature.'

Lulu laughed. 'I'm sorry, you know me too well.'

Julia put down her glass and stood up. 'Come on.' She looked at the glass and smiled. 'On second thoughts, I'll take this with me.' She picked up the glass again.

Lulu looked down at Conrad. 'Come on,' she said. 'Let's go for a walk.'

Conrad got to his feet, stretched, and jumped up onto the sofa. He meowed and then jumped up onto her shoulders. Lulu stood up carefully and Conrad adjusted his position before settling down.

'That is amazing,' said Julia. 'Did it take a lot of training?'

'I got the hang of it pretty quickly,' said Lulu.

'No, I meant . . .' She laughed as she realized that Lulu was joking. 'Right. I walked into that one, didn't I?'

Julia opened a sliding door and stepped out onto a flagged walkway. She turned right and Lulu followed her. 'How many acres do you have here?' Lulu asked as she looked out over the garden.

'There's about five acres that make up the grounds, which is marked by the stone wall. But we own several of the adjoining fields. They're rented out to local farmers.'

'How do you take care of it all?'

'Oh, there's a gardening firm does all the hard work, though Bernard is threatening to get one of those ride-on lawnmowers.'

Ahead of them was a stone barn that had been renovated, with a new slate roof. 'This will be Bernard's studio, when he eventually starts painting again.'

'He was such a good artist, I remember.'

'Past tense is right,' said Julia. 'It's been twenty-five years since he picked up a brush. He could never make any money from it. But if everything goes as planned he'll have time to paint again, and that's where he'll be doing it.'

She turned around the corner and led the way towards a large raised terrace with massive stone urns at each corner. There were steps on three sides leading up to the terrace. In the distance were woods and Lulu saw movement. She shaded her eyes with her hand and realized that there were half a dozen uniformed police officers moving among the trees. 'Julia, what's happening over there?' she asked, pointing at the woods.

Julia turned to look. 'Ah, they're doing a search. That's where the thieves went. I suppose they're looking for clues.'

Julia walked up the steps and Lulu went up after her. There were several trees in large ornate ceramic pots that had been trimmed into the shapes of animals. There was a sitting dog, a dolphin, a lion and some sort of bird. There were strips of blue and white police crime scene tape running between the two urns closest to the building, clearly to stop anyone going through the French windows.

'That is the study,' said Julia. 'Bernard and I both work there, it's one of our favourite rooms in the house. Though whether it remains that way after what happened – well, we'll see.' She smiled grimly.

Lulu walked up to the police tape. One of the panels of glass was broken. She peered through the hole into the room. It was very large and when she saw two doors leading off to the corridor she realized that it was actually two rooms knocked into one. There were desks at either end of the room. The one on the right was glass and chrome with two large Apple monitors, the other was an old oak desk that looked as if it might have belonged in a Napoleonic general's war room.

Conrad jumped down off Lulu's shoulders and landed on the flagstones with a dull thud.

'So this is how they got in?' asked Lulu.

'Apparently, yes. And they left the same way.' Julia waved her champagne flute at the woods. 'They must have run across the lawn to the trees.'

'What's over there, behind the wood?'

'A field. Potatoes. And beyond that is Featherdown Farm. Old Mr Reynolds runs it. He rents the field from us. I forget what he pays but it includes all the potatoes we can eat.'

Lulu looked through the windows again. 'There doesn't seem to be much damage?'

'No, there isn't. Just some blood on the floor.'

'And the man who died – who was he?'

'An insurance broker who was talking about policies with Bernard. They smashed their way in and attacked Bernard and the broker and then escaped with some paintings.'

'Were you in the house?'

Julia shook her head. 'I was at the florist's, discussing the flower arrangements for tomorrow and checking that the cake was okay. In a way it was lucky I wasn't here, but then if I had been here I might have . . .' She shrugged. 'I don't know, I feel guilty about not being here.'

'How many robbers were there?'

'I don't really know.'

'Well, I'm sure Bernard is just grateful that you weren't in harm's way.'

Conrad was pushing his nose against the glass to get a better look into the study.

'He is so cute,' said Julia. 'Does he go everywhere with you?'

'Pretty much.'

'You said his name is Conrad? That's an unusual name for a cat. Why did you call him that?'

'I didn't.'

'Oh, is he a rescue cat?'

'I think actually he rescued me,' said Lulu. She bent down and Conrad jumped up onto her shoulders. 'This terrace is amazing,' said Lulu, trying to change the subject because she didn't want to tell Julia that Conrad had named himself. Lulu had long since become used to the fact that

Conrad could talk, but as he had made it clear he wasn't prepared to talk to anyone else, it was probably information best kept to herself.

'The plan was to have the party out here if the weather was good,' said Julia. 'We were going to have tables out and a marquee on the lawn. But after what happened in the study . . .' She grimaced and left the sentence unfinished.

'I don't know. If you did have a lot of people moving through the room to the terrace, you might erase the bad memories.'

'A man died in there, Lulu.'

'Well, yes. But this is a very old house, isn't it? And in the old days people generally used to die at home. A lot of people have probably died here over the centuries.'

'A fact which the estate agent neglected to mention,' said Julia. She chuckled. 'You're right, of course. We need to wash the bad memories away, and what better way to do that than with a party? Let's see what Bernard thinks.'

2

They went back around the side of the house, through the conservatory and into the kitchen. They left their glasses on the island and Julia led the way down the hallway to the staircase.

'This hall is just amazing,' said Lulu, looking up at the massive chandelier above their heads. 'How on earth do you clean that?'

'Oh, you have to leave that to the professionals,' said Julia.

'Expensive, I'd guess?'

'An arm and a leg,' said Julia. 'It was handmade in Italy, specifically for this space. I dread to think what it cost.'

'You didn't buy it?'

Julia shook her head. 'The previous owner did all the work, to be honest. I mean, we tinkered with the interior design, but it's very much his vision. It's hard to find fault with anything he did. He had a good eye.'

'What does he do?'

'For a living? He runs a hedge fund.'

'And lost all his money, so had to sell?'

Julia laughed. 'No, he made so much money that this was too small for him. He moved to the Hamptons with his husband and they live in a place five times this big.'

'Husband?' Realization dawned. 'Ah, so they were a gay couple. How nice.'

'They're lovely,' said Julia. 'He's offered to let Bernard

and me stay in his new place next time we're in the States. He and his husband are lovely, really lovely. I think the only issue I had was their taste in art. They loved the Old Masters, oils mainly. Whereas Bernard and I go for the modern stuff. Post the Sixties, anyway.'

They went up the left arm of the sweeping staircase. There were large paintings all the way up, modern canvases with abstract splashes of colour.

They turned left at the top of the stairs, where there were more paintings. 'Where did all the art come from?' asked Lulu. 'I don't remember you having all these paintings before?'

'Oh, Bernard and I have always collected art, you know that. We've been buying pieces since we left university. We had to put some of them in storage and this is really the first house we've had that has enough space to put them all on show. And last year we were flush with cash from our pre-IPO investors and Bernard said it was crazy to leave it in the bank when they were paying such low interest.'

'Pre-IPO?'

Julia grinned. 'That's when investors buy into a company prior to the initial public offering. We had quite a large cash injection two years ago – that's why we have the house and many of the paintings. In fact that's how we ended up with the house in the first place. The guys who owned the house were big investors and they had us over here to hear our pitch. We fell in love with it. They invested and we bought the house.'

'Serendipity.'

'That's exactly what Bernard said.'

They reached a white door and Julia turned the handle. The bedroom had been done with an Asian feel, with Chinese chests, a beautiful antique Japanese silk kimono on display on a wall, several jade statues of dragons and horses, and a red and gold abstract painting with stylized Chinese calligraphy. The room was so big that the super-king-sized bed actually looked small. Bernard was lying propped up with three pillows, tapping on his iPad. He put it down and looked at them over the top of his glasses. 'Lulu? How lovely to see you.' He had a large bandage across his forehead and his right eye was badly bruised. 'Is that a cat on your shoulder?'

'That's Conrad,' said Julia. 'Lulu's plus one.'

Conrad jumped down off Lulu's shoulders and landed on a Chinese-style sofa at the foot of the bed.

'Well, you have clearly been in the wars,' Lulu said, walking across the stripped oak floor to sit on the side of the bed. 'What on earth were you doing?'

'I was in the study minding my own business and two heavies wearing ski masks barged in and clubbed me over the head with a poker. And they hit the chap I was with so hard that they split his skull open.'

'But why?'

'Why?' said Bernard, frowning.

'I mean, why did they hit you?'

'Shock and awe,' said Bernard. 'They stormed in, pushed us around, then one of them grabbed a poker and laid into us with it.'

'They came in through the window? The French window?'

'From the terrace, yes.'

'So it was locked?'

'Locked?'

'Well, they broke the glass to get in.'

Bernard laughed awkwardly. 'Are you investigating the case, Lulu?'

'No, of course not.' She patted his leg through the quilt. 'I just want to make sure they catch the bastards that did this to you, that's all.'

'The detective they sent is very thorough,' said Julia. 'She had a forensic team in yesterday afternoon and they've been searching the grounds all day.' She looked at Bernard. 'Lulu said we should definitely have the party on the terrace tomorrow. Exorcise the demons.'

'That's a good idea,' said Bernard.

'Will you be okay to come down?' asked Julia.

'I think so. I'm feeling a lot better today.'

'How many people are coming?' asked Lulu.

'About two hundred,' said Julia.

'Oh my goodness. That's a lot.'

'Quite a few will be business colleagues and contacts. So it'll be tax deductible.'

'Oh, so that's why we're having a party,' said Bernard. 'Nothing to do with my hitting the big six-oh.'

'It's everything to do with your birthday, but we might as well save some money while we're at it. Which is another reason we have to go ahead – everyone was paid in advance.'

'Oh, there was never any question of cancelling,' said Bernard. 'I'm not going to let a couple of thugs ruin my life.'

'Are you sure you'll be okay?' asked Lulu. 'That eye looks awful.'

'It probably looks worse than it feels,' he said. 'They gave me some pretty strong painkillers at the hospital.'

'And they're sure there's no internal damage?'

'The scans were fine. They said I have a very thick skull.'

'Well, we all knew that, darling,' said Julia, flashing him a mischievous smile.

Bernard smiled back, then wagged his finger at her. 'Where are you living these days?' he asked Lulu.

'I'm on a narrowboat,' she said. 'I actually drove it to Oxford from Little Venice. The entire living space I have would fit comfortably into a quarter of this room.'

'Does one drive a boat?'

Lulu grinned. 'One does.'

'And does one park it or moor it?'

'Either is fine. I'm parked at Jericho. I was lucky, a chap was just leaving as we arrived.' She looked around. There were two sliding doors that opened into a dressing area lined with mirrored wardrobes. 'I can't get over how wonderful this house is.'

'We like it,' said Bernard.

'And your painting collection. It's breathtaking.'

'Julia has great taste.'

'Bernard, that's not true!' said Julia. 'He's the one with the good eye. Especially with the newer artists. If it was down to me we'd have pictures of dogs playing poker on the walls.' She leaned over and kissed him on the cheek. 'Now, you get some rest. I'll get some lunch for Lulu.'

'I should be up for dinner,' he said.

'Let's see how you feel,' said Julia.

'Marvellous to see you again, Lulu,' said Bernard. 'And it was an absolute pleasure to meet your plus one.'

'Meow,' said Conrad, who was still standing on the sofa.

'Conrad said the pleasure was all his.'

'What a wonderfully polite cat he is.'

3

Lunch was a selection of Marks & Spencer nibbles and the rest of the Buck's Fizz. Julia served it in the conservatory and they sat on separate sofas. Conrad sat next to Lulu and she put smoked salmon pate, cooked prawns and some Scottish salmon and broccoli quiche on a plate for him.

'It was a lifesaver when Ocado started delivering M&S food,' said Julia. 'Tap tap tap on the mobile and a van pulls up with whatever you want.'

'You never need to leave home,' said Lulu.

'Well, you've taken a totally different approach: you take your house with you. I envy you the freedom.'

'Oh, how can you say that with a house as lovely as this?' said Lulu as she helped herself to some avocado, feta and grain salad.

'Oh, it is gorgeous, I know it is. But it ties you down. I can't just get up and go – but you, you can go almost anywhere.'

'Well, not anywhere. But yes, there are almost five thousand miles of navigable canals and rivers so I am spoilt for choice. I do spend most of my time in Little Venice, though. That feels like home.'

'What about the house you used to live in? That was a lovely house.'

'It's rented out. I don't want to live there again, but selling it just seems wrong. It was where Simon grew up, and I lived there when we were taking care of his mother.'

'Sometimes you have to move on, Lulu. You can't keep looking back.'

'I know, I know.' She picked up a piri piri chicken wing. 'One step at a time.'

'Your problem is that you don't like change.'

'Well, who does?'

'Change is what makes things improve,' said Julia. 'That's why we now have M&S delivered and I don't have to drive into Oxford. And change is what our company is all about. The technologies we are using now to tackle illnesses weren't even thought of twenty years ago. Change has paid for this house and everything in it.'

'Yes, I understand that nothing can stay the same. But life now is just so – complicated. Everyone is on their phone all the time, they seem to live their lives on social media. People are so angry. That's why I love the canals. People are kinder, more helpful, more considerate. They smile and wave and look out for each other.'

'Well, I hope it stays that way,' said Julia.

Something moved outside and Lulu started. It was a woman. A blonde woman peering through the glass. She was wearing black-framed spectacles with oblong lenses and had her hair tied back.

'Oh, that's Inspector Calder. She's probably got some news for us.' Julia stood up and opened the door.

'Sorry to disturb you,' said the inspector. 'I just wanted to let you know that I'm still here with a search team. We've worked our way across the lawn and we'll make a start on the wood. I doubt that we'll get everything done before dusk so we'll be back first thing tomorrow.' She was wearing a high-vis jacket over a dark blue suit.

'Come in, come in, we're just having a late lunch.'

'Then I really won't disturb you.'

The inspector turned away but Julia put a hand out and took her arm. 'No, please, come and meet my friend. And have a drink. You've been out there all day.'

Inspector Calder seemed set to refuse, but then she smiled. 'Why not?' She looked at the jug on the table. 'Orange juice?'

'With a splash of champagne,' said Julia. 'Buck's Fizz.'

'Oh, just the orange juice for me,' said the inspector, sitting down next to Julia. 'I do love a Buck's Fizz but I'm on duty, obviously.' Lulu guessed she was in her mid to late twenties, which was young to be an inspector. It really was true that the police were getting younger. Lulu hadn't made inspector until she was in her thirties.

'This is Lulu Lewis, my very good friend,' said Julia. 'And if you were to have the merest splash of fizz in your orange juice, our lips would be sealed.' She stood up. 'Let me get you a glass. And help yourself to nibbles.'

As she headed to the kitchen, the inspector noticed Conrad sitting next to Lulu. 'Oh, is that your cat?' she asked.

'His name is Conrad, and I rather think I'm his.'

The inspector chuckled. 'I thought calico cats were always female.'

'Conrad is a very unusual cat,' said Lulu.

'He is lovely.'

'Meow!' said Conrad.

'And he talks!'

'Yes, he does,' said Lulu. 'Constantly.'

Julia returned with a flute and poured orange juice into it. She handed it to the inspector and sat down. 'Do you expect to find anything?' she said.

The inspector shrugged. 'Searches like this are always a long shot, but sometimes criminals do drop things.'

Julia held up the bottle of champagne and raised her eyebrows. The inspector laughed. 'Absolutely not,' she said. 'Much as I'd like to, it would be more than my job's worth.'

'So, which direction would the burglars have headed towards, do you think?' asked Lulu. 'Julia said there's a farm beyond the woods.'

'That's right. We think that's where they went.'

'Surely they couldn't have left their vehicle there?'

'Actually, the farmer was out all morning on the other side of the farm. And he lives alone so there was no one around to see them arrive or leave.'

'What about tyre tracks? Any there that shouldn't be there?'

The inspector's eyes narrowed and she looked at Lulu for several seconds before speaking. 'You seem very interested in the investigation.'

'I'm sorry, I didn't mean to pry. It's just I used to be in the job and I can't help myself.'

'Oh Lulu, you're always hiding your light under a bushel.' Julia looked over at the inspector. 'Lulu was a detective superintendent with the Metropolitan Police.'

'Really? That's impressive.'

'Not really,' said Lulu. 'Mainly admin and paperwork.'

'Lulu, really, you need to stop that.' Julia smiled at the inspector. 'She worked on some very big cases. But she always belittles her achievements. I've never understood why. I have to say, if she had pushed herself forward a bit more aggressively she could have been commissioner.' Lulu opened her mouth to protest but Julia silenced her with a wave of a ring-encrusted hand. 'You know it's true, so please don't deny it.'

'Fine,' said Lulu. 'I won't.'

'So where were you based?' asked the inspector.

'Latterly at New Scotland Yard, but I started walking a beat in Stoke Newington and then I had spells in Kilburn and Ealing. Always north of the river, but they moved me around. I retired almost ten years ago.'

'I've worked a few cases with Met detectives,' said the inspector. She ran through a few names, and when she mentioned Phil Jackson Lulu's face broke into a grin.

'It's definitely a small world,' said Lulu. 'Phil I know very well. He was my bag carrier for a while but that was a long time ago. He's working out of Kensington Police Station in Earls Court Road these days.'

'I know – that's where I linked up with him. We had a county lines drug gang from his patch operating in Oxford and he was a big help. A very good guy. He said he was handing in his papers soon.'

'Phil has been saying that for years. His father left him a patch of land in Barbados and he keeps threatening to go and work for the cops there. But his mum is from Galway so he keeps thinking about moving there. And meanwhile life goes on.'

'That's what John Lennon said, isn't it? Life is what happens while you're making plans.' She smiled and nodded. 'So, you're here for the birthday party?'

'That's right, Lulu and I have been friends for more than thirty years,' said Julia.

'But you weren't a police officer, were you, Mrs Grenville?'

'No, I was a forensic scientist. A scenes of crime officer.'

'Oh, you didn't mention it when SOCO were here.'

'My SOCO days were a long time ago,' said Julia.

'Julia is also one for hiding her very impressive light under a bushel,' said Lulu. 'She was one of the best forensic investigators around.'

'Why did you leave?' The inspector picked up a chicken wing and nibbled it.

'I just got fed up with seeing how terrible people can be to each other,' said Julia. 'I wanted to make people's lives better rather than clearing up after them.'

'And you've clearly done very well out of it. You could never have bought a house like this on a SOCO salary.'

'That's for sure,' said Julia.

'Anyway, as far as the case goes, we have dusted for prints but, as Mr Grenville says they were all wearing gloves, that probably isn't going to be much help. We have nothing in the way of footprints, and as Mrs Lewis says, we are checking tyre prints at the farm.'

'Please, call me Lulu.'

'Okay, then I'm Tracey.'

'Well if we're all on first name terms then I'm Julia,' said Julia. She raised her glass. 'Girl power!' They clinked their glasses together.

'What I'm trying to say in my clumsy way is that we're not expecting a quick breakthrough on this case,' said Tracey. 'They wore ski masks and gloves so we have no descriptions to go on, and no prints. Our best hope is to track down the paintings, which Mr Grenville tells me are distinctive and readily identifiable. Mr Grenville thinks they were white, but that's as far as it goes.'

'No one saw them approach the house?' asked Lulu.

'I know the house is big, but we don't have a permanent staff,' said Julia. 'There was a cleaning team in but they didn't see anything.'

'What about CCTV?'

'In the house? No. We have an alarm, but that's it.'

Lulu looked at the inspector. 'What about cameras on the roads? Any chance of using ANPR to track the vehicle?'

'If we knew what sort of car they were using and if they were on a main road, yes, that's a possibility.'

'Have there been any similar break-ins in the area?'

If Tracey resented Lulu's questions, she didn't show it. 'There have been a number, yes. Usually isolated houses that are targeted and usually at night or when the owners are away. The way the police are stretched these days, they know that most alarms aren't even answered and if they are answered it could be hours before a patrol car arrives.'

'But this was in broad daylight,' said Lulu.

'Yes. That's true.'

'And here's what I don't understand. They obviously weren't opportunistic, they couldn't have just walked by and looked through the window. They knew the paintings were here. That surely must mean either that they had been to the house before or that they had information on what was here.'

'Ah, you haven't seen the magazine,' said Tracey.

'What magazine?'

'I'll get it,' said Julia. She stood up and disappeared into the kitchen.

'Does the poker seem a strange choice of murder weapon to you?' asked Lulu.

'I'm not sure that murder was the intent,' said the inspector.

'Who was the victim?'

'Chap by the name of Billy Russell. An insurance broker. It seems to me that if murder was the intent then they would probably have killed Mr Grenville too. I think they just wanted to incapacitate Mr Grenville and Mr Russell and hit Mr Russell too hard.'

Lulu opened her mouth to reply but Julia returned with a copy of a Sunday magazine. 'This was in the local paper,' she said. She sat down and passed it to Lulu. There was a picture of Julia on the cover, wearing a white coat and standing in a laboratory. 'Oh my goodness, a cover girl,' said Lulu. The headline was 'Billion-Dollar Bugs'.

'I was surprised myself,' she said. 'I knew they were doing an article on me, but I had no idea I'd be on the cover.'

'But not Bernard?'

'Bernard always takes a back seat when it comes to promoting the company.'

'And billion-dollar bugs?' asked Lulu.

Julia laughed. 'Journalistic licence. We use microbes in the vaccine-manufacturing process.'

'And the billion dollars?'

'That's the value of the company. That's not all ours.'

'Have a look at the article,' said Tracey.

Lulu flicked through the magazine. The article ran to three pages, complete with graphs and charts that showed how successful the company had been and how it was projected to grow over the coming years. There were more pictures of Julia in a laboratory but there were also several photographs of Julia in various rooms of the house, including one of her sitting behind her desk in the study. 'Ah, I see what you mean,' Lulu said to the inspector. Paintings featured in many of the photographs, so any would-be burglar could see what was on offer.

'Julia had never tried to conceal where she lives, so finding the house wouldn't be difficult,' said the inspector, 'and some of the paintings in the photographs there are very valuable.'

'So they would have known what paintings were here. That makes sense.' Lulu put the magazine onto the coffee table. 'And if they had the address then Google Maps would give them a satellite view of the house and the area.'

'Google Maps is a housebreaker's dream,' said Tracey.

'And these other robberies, they usually took place at night?'

'Yes, or at the weekend when the occupants were away. So no descriptions. And no forensic evidence. They obviously wore gloves. No shoe prints either, so we think they were wearing shoe covers.'

'That's clever of them.'

'Oh, they are definitely a professional gang. On several of the jobs they dealt with quite sophisticated alarm systems.'

'Strange then that this time it was during the day and Julia and Bernard were getting ready for the birthday party.'

'Yes. I thought that.'

'And this is the first time the robberies have resulted in violence?'

'Yes. I did ask Mr Grenville what happened but he's still a little confused. He did take quite a bump to the head.'

'Confused in what way?'

'Well, why did the intruders beat them so badly. Did either of them say anything or do anything to spark the attack? Did Mr Russell lash out, for instance? I'm afraid Mr Grenville doesn't seem to remember much in the way of details.'

'As you said, he was hit over the head,' said Julia. 'He's still in shock.'

'Absolutely,' said Tracey. 'I'll come back and see him in a couple of days; we'll see if his memory improves. I'll also need a list of the paintings that were stolen.'

'Oh, I can give you that,' said Julia. 'We have them all photographed for insurance purposes.'

'How easy would they be to sell?' asked Lulu.

'Oh, not difficult at all,' said Julia. 'Most of them are by well-known or up-and-coming artists. We were hoping to get a Jackson Pollock after the IPO.'

'IPO?' repeated Tracey.

'Initial public offering,' said Julia. 'When we take the company public. We were planning to sell some of our shares and buy some really special pieces.'

'Well if you do, make sure you put in a decent security system,' said the inspector. 'How much attention is given to provenance? Could someone just take a painting into any art gallery and sell it?'

'Possibly, with some of the cheaper paintings. But the more expensive ones would need a receipt at the very least. Of course, there are plenty of private collectors around who don't care about provenance, especially out in the Middle East and China.'

'We'll be looking at that,' said Tracey. 'I've already been in touch with the Met's Art and Antiques Unit and they're on the case.' She finished her orange juice and put the glass on the table. 'And with that I'll leave you,' she said, standing up. 'It's been a pleasure, Lulu. And if you do see Phil Jackson before me, please do give him my best.'

'I will,' said Lulu.

Julia stood up but Tracey held up a hand. 'I'll see myself out, I need to check on the search team.'

'And what about the terrace and the study?' asked Julia. 'Are we okay to go back in there now?'

'I'll have them remove the crime scene tape. Our SOCO people have got everything they need. They were told to pull out all the stops on this one. Apparently the assistant chief constable has taken a personal interest in the case.' She reached into her jacket and brought out a wallet. She opened it, took out a card, and gave it to Julia. 'If you want to get the room professionally cleaned, these are some companies that we recommend. But from what I saw there wasn't too much damage. We'll be keeping the poker, obviously. But everything else is now yours to do with as you wish.' She took another card from her wallet, this one a business card with the Thames Valley Police crest on it. 'This is my number, and my email address. Send me a list of the missing paintings when you have it.'

'I will. And thank you so much. Oh, and what about Mr Russell's car? The grey Volvo. That's not staying here, is it?'

'No, it's not needed as evidence. I'm told that a transporter will be collecting it later today and returning it to its owner. Well, not the owner, obviously. The owner's wife. Widow. Mrs Russell.' Tracey smiled awkwardly, nodded at them both, then left through the door into the garden.

'She seems nice,' said Lulu. 'Very professional, too.'

'A bit young, don't you think? To be in charge of a murder case?'

'I'm sure she has the right experience,' said Lulu. 'Her bosses must think she's up to it.'

'She didn't seem too confident of catching the thieves, though.' Julia took a piece of quiche and began eating it.

'It's difficult when there's no forensics and no identification,' said Lulu. 'Tracing the car the thieves used is the best hope. They may well get the paintings back, but in my experience fences stay pretty tight-lipped.'

'Honour among thieves?'

Lulu smiled. 'Usually more a case of snitches get stitches. But don't worry, they'll put a lot of resources into the case because there was a murder involved. They'll make it a priority. Who was this Mr Russell? You said he was an insurance broker?'

'I never met him,' said Julia. 'Bernard had spoken to him about increasing our coverage. It's been a while since we had our collection valued and obviously it's gone up considerably.'

'Wrong place, wrong time,' said Lulu. 'It's often the way.'

4

After they had finished their nibbles and Buck's Fizz, they went through to the study and surveyed the damage. 'I suppose we were lucky that the floorboards had been sanded and varnished,' said Julia. 'A damp cloth should get that out.'

'I would think so,' said Lulu. 'Shall we clean it up now?' They were looking down at a pool of dried blood a few feet from the fireplace. There were also flecks of blood across the floor. Spatter, it was called. Lulu knew that some people referred to it as splatter, but spatter was the term that SOCO used.

'No, the cleaners can do it.'

'Are you sure? If they're just regular cleaners they might get a bit squeamish. It is blood, after all. Not everyone is used to the sight of blood like we are.'

Conrad was standing looking at the dried blood, his nose twitching.

Julia nodded. 'Yes, of course, you're right. Silly me. You wait here, I'll go and get a cloth and a bucket of water.'

'Two cloths,' said Lulu.

'Two cloths it is,' said Julia.

'And a dustpan and brush; there's still broken glass by the window.'

'Will do,' said Julia, and she disappeared into the hallway.

Lulu looked around the room. Because the study had been created by knocking out the dividing wall between two rooms, there were large cast-iron fireplaces and chimney breasts at either end. The only structural difference was that there were French windows leading on to the terrace to the left and two large picture windows to the right.

The more modern side of the study was obviously Julia's domain, with modern furniture and feminine touches including a vase of flowers, framed family photographs and her collection of Victorian perfume bottles. There was a low grey sofa in front of a marble coffee table and a Bang & Olufsen stereo system linked to an Alexa speaker. To the side of her desk was a large printer and an industrial-sized shredder. There were half a dozen framed paintings on the wall behind her desk, along with her degrees and professional qualifications. There were three gaps on the wall, where pictures had obviously been removed.

Bernard's side of the study was much more masculine, with old, heavy furniture, an oak bookcase filled with art books, and an antique globe which Lulu instinctively knew was filled with bottles of spirits. There was an overstuffed red leather sofa by the windows and a matching winged armchair set around a battered old chest that was used as a coffee table. Whereas Julia had a state-of-the-art computer system, Bernard had a small MacBook.

The thieves had taken three pictures from Julia's side of the room, and five from Bernard's. Some of the pictures were quite small, judging from the gaps that had been left. The largest, from Bernard's end of the room, was about three feet square.

She walked to the fireplace at Bernard's end of the room. It was tall, almost reaching her shoulders, and there were logs in the grate. There was a set of brass irons hanging from a cast-iron rack, including a brush, tongs, a shovel and a poker. She took the poker and stared at it for several seconds. It would make a formidable weapon that could easily crush a man's skull. She smacked it against her hand and the sound echoed around the room.

Conrad looked up from the bloodstain. 'I suppose as a police officer you saw a lot of crime scenes,' he said.

'When I was a PC, yes, pretty much every shift. That's what the job was, really. Walking a beat and answering calls.' She put the poker back on its rack. 'But it would be unusual to come across a murder. Plenty of accidental deaths and people dying alone in their homes, but as a PC you'd be unlikely to stumble across a murder. But then, when I was an inspector, I worked for an Area Major Incident Pool, part of Scotland Yard's Serious Crime Group, and I'd visit a murder scene pretty much at the start of every investigation.' She walked back to Julia's side of the room. 'Then, about ten years before I retired, they set up the Homicide and Major Crime Command and I ran major investigation teams. By then I was a chief inspector and later a superintendent, so at that point the job was mainly admin. But yes, to answer your question, I have been to a lot of crime scenes over the years.'

'And Julia seems very calm about everything that has happened.'

'Well, she was a SOCO for almost ten years, so she'll have been to more crime scenes than me. In fact, that's how we first met, at a house in Stoke Newington where a young girl had been raped and murdered. I was part of a group doing an area search, like the officers searching the woods out there. I was in the garden and I found the body.' Lulu shuddered at the memory. 'It was terrible. I was so sick, I couldn't stop throwing up. Julia took care of me, talked me through it.'

'That sounds awful.'

Lulu shrugged. 'It goes with the job.'

They heard footsteps in the hall and then Julia returned with a brush and dustpan in one hand and a bucket of soapy water in the other. She was wearing bright yellow Marigold rubber gloves. She put the bucket down by the stain and gave the brush and pan to Lulu, along with another pair of Marigold gloves. 'Did I hear you talking?' Julia asked.

'I was chatting to Conrad.'

'Meow!' said Conrad.

'He is such a cute cat,' said Julia. She put her hands on her hips and looked down at the stain.

Lulu held up the poker. 'Is this similar to the one they used?' she asked.

'Identical,' said Julia. 'They were matching sets. So what's your professional opinion about what happened?'

Lulu sighed as she looked around. 'It's a pity we don't know whether the body was face up or face down, or how it was lying, but from the position of the stain it looks as if the killer was standing with his back to the fireplace. That was presumably when he took the poker. The first blow would have got blood on it, and there's spatter on the wall where he raised the poker for a second blow, and possibly a third. So he hit Billy Russell two or three times and Billy fell. Then the blood pooled around the body. There are no footprints in the blood so the killers were careful where they stepped.' She put the pan and brush on a coffee table and slipped on the rubber gloves.

Julia smiled. 'You've still got it, Lulu. You always knew how to read a crime scene.'

'Then the killer stood over the body for a while. You can see the circular drops where the blood fell vertically. More than a dozen, so he was in no hurry.' Lulu frowned and looked at Julia. 'Where was Bernard when he was hit?'

Julia pointed at the marble coffee table. 'He said they hit him and he fell against that. That's what gave him the black eye.'

Lulu peered at the marble but couldn't see any blood. 'And what about the poker? Where was that found?'

'I wasn't allowed in the crime scene; it was all taped off by the time I got here, but you can see where it was on the floor over here.' She pointed at the floor. There were two thin lines of dried blood, each about a foot long. And more spatter. 'I think that might be the spatter from where Bernard was hit,' she said.

'So who was hit first?' asked Lulu.

'Bernard says that he remembers seeing them hit Billy, so Billy must have been attacked first.'

'Okay. I suppose Bernard and Billy walked into the room and saw the men waiting there. So they stop and what, the men grabbed them?'

'That makes sense.'

'Well, it has to be that way because if they were in the study when the men broke in, they could have run and sounded the alarm.' Lulu walked across the study and out into the corridor. 'Okay, so presumably Bernard and Billy would have been talking and not paying attention. So they walk into the room and the men are hiding behind the door or against the wall. Then they stop as they realize there's someone there and they're grabbed. But that means the intruders would be here, by the door. Not by the fireplace. If they were standing by the fireplace, Bernard and Billy would have seen them right away.'

Julia frowned. 'I see what you're getting at. If the men grabbed them as soon as they walked into the room, then why get the poker and start hitting them?'

'Only Bernard can answer that question,' said Lulu.

'Maybe the men broke in and began stealing the pictures,' said Julia. 'They think they're alone but then they hear Bernard and Billy come back. So one of them grabs the poker and they both hide. Bernard and Billy come into the room and they're attacked.'

Lulu pointed at the large bloodstain. 'Except we know that Billy was over there when he was hit. And his attacker was between him and the fireplace. You know, it would be a big help if we could have a look at the crime scene photographs.'

'Well, I don't see that happening,' said Julia. 'I mean, Tracey is lovely, but at the end of the day we're civilians now.'

Lulu nodded. 'You're right, of course.' She frowned. 'But wait. Bernard said he and Billy were in the study and the men barged in, remember? He made it sound as if they were already in the room.'

'He's still confused.'

'He sounded definite enough. Minding their own business in the study, he said. If that was the case, then why didn't they see the men on the terrace?'

'We can ask him later,' said Julia. 'I think he's still in shock. You know that eyewitnesses are always the most unreliable form of evidence.'

Lulu sighed and picked up the brush and pan. 'You're right, of course. Okay, I'll get started on the glass.'

Julia knelt down and took a wet cloth from the bucket. She squeezed the water out of it and began to rub away at the large bloodstain.

Conrad jumped onto the sofa and sat and watched them work, occasionally grooming himself.

5

It took them just half an hour to clean up the blood, and by the time they had finished there was no way of telling that a murder had been committed in the study. There had been a small amount of spatter on one of the walls and Julia had taken great care to wash it off without damaging the wallpaper. 'It's one of your namesake's wallpapers, more than five hundred pounds a roll,' she said.

'My namesake?'

'Lulu Lytle, the woman who did Boris Johnson's interior design at Number 10. When Bernard heard that, he insisted we use her wallpaper in the study. We looked at the one that Boris had but it was pretty appalling, so we went for this one instead.'

'It's a lot of money to pay for a joke,' said Lulu.

'Well, I think Bernard saw it as a talking point rather than a joke.'

They took the bucket and the brush and pan to the kitchen and Lulu tipped the broken glass into a stainless-steel bin, the top of which obligingly popped open as her hand approached. 'Oh my goodness, now that is hi-tech,' she said.

'It's fun, isn't it? Another of Bernard's impulse buys.' Julia took off her Marigold gloves and washed her hands. Lulu followed her example. Conrad jumped up onto the island and used his paws to wash his face.

'Right, so how about I give you the full tour?' Julia said.

Lulu looked at her watch. 'I should be going,' she said. 'I'll be back tomorrow for the party.'

'Nonsense,' said Julia. 'You're staying the night. Conrad, too. That was always the plan. There's a lovely guest room waiting for you.'

'Julia, I'd love to, but after what's happened . . .'

'No buts,' said Julia, cutting her off with a wave of her hand. 'You and I are the same size and I have wardrobes full of clothes I've yet to wear. Of course you're staying.'

'Meow!' said Conrad from the sofa.

'See? Conrad wants to stay.'

'He does, doesn't he?' Lulu looked over at Conrad. 'Then we'll stay.'

'Excellent,' said Julia. 'I tell you what, let me print out the details of the paintings that were stolen.'

'Good idea,' said Lulu.

They went back to the study. Julia walked around her desk and sat down. She tapped on the computer and studied one of her screens. She pressed a button and the printer kicked into life, then she twisted around in her chair to look at the spaces on the wall where the missing pictures had been. She turned back to her keyboard and started typing again.

Lulu went over to the printer and took out the first sheet. It was a photograph of an oil painting, a view of a beach with a castle in the background. 'This is nice,' she said. 'Bamburgh Castle, isn't it? In Northumberland?'

'It was a gift from Bernard on our first wedding anniversary. He found it in a shop in Newcastle and bought it for me. He proposed to me on that beach. Actually went down on one knee. It cost just a few hundred pounds but there's no way to really value it because it has no clear signature. Not that I care about the money: its value is sentimental. He pretty much emptied his bank account to buy it.'

Lulu looked at the sheet. 'It's valued at two thousand pounds.'

'I know, the insurers insist on a value. To be honest, for me it's priceless. It's the one I'm most concerned about.'

The printer spewed out a second sheet. This one was a watercolour, valued at ten thousand pounds. 'This is nice, too,' said Lulu, holding it up so that Julia could see it.

'Ah yes, we bought that together when we were on holiday, must have been ten or eleven years ago. It was in a junk shop in Exeter. The old guy who owned the shop didn't appreciate what it was. It's by John Ruskin, who was a good friend of J. M. W. Turner and tended to paint like him. That's actually a seascape but it almost looks like an abstract. I'm embarrassed to say that we paid the grand sum of twenty-five pounds for it.'

The third sheet was an abstract painting, dots and splashes across a white canvas. It was valued at a hundred thousand pounds. Lulu raised her eyebrows. It wouldn't have looked out of place on a primary school wall. She turned it so Julia could see it. 'Seriously?'

'You either appreciate abstract art or you don't,' said Julia. 'That's an Ad Reinhardt. Bernard bought it for me last year.'

'A hundred thousand pounds?'

'Oh, they've been selling for more than that recently,' said Julia. 'That was another of Bernard's pre-IPO purchases. He said he bought it for my birthday but really I know he wanted it for himself. I have to say, I really like it.'

She got up from the desk and walked over to Bernard's

side of the study. 'I'm trying to remember what was hanging here,' she said, gesturing at the blank spaces. 'The problem is that most of these pieces Bernard bought on his own.'

'And you like the abstract pieces, too?' said Lulu, looking around.

'Oh, very much so. He almost never buys a picture that I don't like.' She pointed at a red, blue and black abstract canvas on the wall between the two windows at the far end of the room. 'That one is by a Nigerian American artist, Njideka Akunyili Crosby. Bernard bought it for two hundred thousand dollars after we got the pre-IPO money, and this year one of her pieces sold for three million dollars.'

'Oh my goodness me.'

'Exactly. Her prices just took off. That's the thing about the art world: beauty really is in the eye of the beholder. If an artist gets hot, the sky's the limit, and Bernard does seem able to pick winners. Last year he started buying paintings by Chinese artists: Zhou Chunya, Luo Zhongli, Liu Wei. Names I'd never heard of, but their works are all going up like crazy.'

She frowned as she looked at the blank spaces, then nodded and went back to her desk. Her fingers tapped on the keyboard and the printer began spewing pages again, this time with five abstract pictures valued at between twenty and forty thousand pounds.

Lulu studied the eight sheets. The total value of the stolen paintings was just shy of a quarter of a million pounds. She gave the sheets to Julia, who placed them on the desk. 'So they were all insured?' Lulu asked.

'I assume so, but I'll have to talk to Bernard. All the recent purchases should have been insured at the sale price, but I'm not sure about the older works. They might not have been valued for a long time.'

'If so, that would be unfortunate, the paintings being stolen before they were fully insured.'

'I'll talk to Bernard about it. I suppose we were lucky.'

'Lucky?'

'I'll show you.'

She went out through the door on the left. Lulu looked over at Conrad to see if he wanted to ride on her shoulders but he stood up, stretched, then jumped down off the sofa and padded across the floor. Lulu followed him. In the hallway there were two large canvases, each about six feet square. They were a mass of coloured shapes and swirls of colour; one was predominantly green and had the feel of a jungle, the other was mainly blues, which gave the impression of a swirling sea. 'These are both by Joan Mitchell, an American painter. She died in 1992 and her paintings are in galleries around the world. Bernard got them at Christie's. Just over a million pounds for the pair, plus all the commissions et cetera et cetera.'

'So the thieves could have got four times the money just by taking these two?'

'Exactly. Right, the tour begins.' Julia opened a door on the other side of the corridor. 'This is our private movie theatre,' she said. 'The screen is bigger than the Everyman we used to go to in London and the sound system is something special. German, state of the art. Bernard spent literally weeks working out the specs with a sound designer.'

There were eight beige La-Z-Boy chairs lined up in two rows of four, plus what looked like a double bed with massive pillows. The floor and walls were a dark red and the ceiling was black, dotted with LED lights that gave it the feel of a night sky.

'We can stream whatever we like, and Bernard has something like two hundred Blu-ray discs. We get a delivery from Amazon pretty much every day: he can't seem to stop buying them.'

She closed the door and took Lulu along the corridor. 'The theatre is very much Bernard's domain,' she said as she opened the next door. 'But this is where I spend a lot of time.' The room was a pine-panelled changing room with a terracotta tiled floor, pine lockers and two leather easy chairs. There was a water dispenser and a large glass-fronted fridge filled with soft drinks. There were two doors at the far end of the room and Julia opened the one on the right. Inside was a wood-lined sauna with benches at various levels stacked around a wooden box filled with smooth stones.

'Oh, that's lovely,' said Lulu.

'Well, wait until you see the pièce de résistance,' said Julia, closing the door. She opened the second door and Lulu's jaw dropped when she saw the swimming pool. It was huge, with blue and white tiles and a motif of two almost naked gladiators in the centre surrounded by tigers and lions. In the corners of the room were life-size marble statues of Greek warriors, who all appeared to be naked, and the roof had been hand-painted with dozens of naked angels and cupids around a stylized sun.

'Oh my goodness,' said Lulu.

'I know. Bernard wanted to rip it all out but I said leave it, it has a style all of its own. The previous owners used to have parties here.' There was a touchscreen on the wall and Julia ran her finger along it. The overhead lighting changed from white to yellow to blue to green and then to red. 'Isn't that fun?' she said. She set it back to white again. 'I try to swim here every morning,' she said. 'Either that or there's a gym.'

'You have a gym?'

'Darling, this house has everything,' laughed Julia.

To the left of the doors was a row of white wooden loungers, and beyond them there was a seating area with boxy sofas and armchairs around a glass coffee table. Conrad padded over to the loungers and began sniffing at one of them. At the end of the pool were two louvred doors. 'What's behind the doors?' asked Lulu.

'Oh nothing, just storage for the pool chemicals and the filter system that keeps the water clean.'

Conrad stopped sniffing at the lounger, looked over at Lulu, then began to sniff again, his tail up.

'Conrad, come on, we're going!' shouted Julia.

Conrad came back over to them and meowed.

The gym was in the next room, with more than a dozen hi-tech exercise machines, two large punch bags, several sets of weights and a full-size boxing ring. Lulu couldn't help but laugh. 'You and Bernard don't box, do you?'

Julia laughed. 'No, but the previous owners did. Thai boxing. They had a trainer come in every week.'

'They left all this equipment?'

'They wanted to start afresh in the Hamptons. They left pretty much everything and said we should just throw away what we didn't want, or give it to charity. They left every book in the library and there are thousands of them. To be honest, I think they bought them by the yard and never took them off the shelves.'

'More money than sense,' said Lulu.

'More money than God, is what Bernard says.'

She closed the door. Lulu bent down so that Conrad could jump onto her shoulders. Julia took them back to the main entrance hall and around to the other wing of the house. The library was impressive, as big as the study and lined with books, most of which were bound in leather. There was a movable wooden stairway on each side of the room, two large leather-topped circular tables and several captain's chairs and a leather chaise longue under one of the windows. On one wall was a collection of framed antique maps of the Oxford area, some of them clearly very old.

Next to the library was a billiards room with a full-size table and a bar against one wall; then there was a huge dining room with a table large enough to seat sixteen people. The walls were lined with abstract paintings. 'Oh, now these are nice,' said Lulu.

'Yes, they're Bernard's most recent purchases,' said Julia. 'You should have seen what used to be there. They were, let's say, interesting. Quite a bit of nudity of the male kind. Thankfully their artwork was the one thing they did take with them.'

Opposite the dining room was a set of double doors; Julia opened them to reveal a large high-ceilinged room with tall windows overlooking the gardens. In the middle of the room was a grand piano, under an ornate chandelier. 'Don't tell me they left this,' said Lulu. She walked over to it and her eyebrows shot up when she saw the maker's name – Steinway.

'No, I bought this,' said Julia. 'Bernard has his paintings, I have the piano.'

'It's beautiful. I didn't know you played.'

'Oh, I played a lot as a child. And I put myself through university playing background music in hotels.'

'I didn't know that,' said Lulu.

'Well, all the time you knew me we never had a place big enough for a piano. Now that we have, I thought I might as well go the whole hog.'

'My mother-in-law played. She had a Steinway, a baby grand.'

'Of course. Emily. She was a lovely lady. Alzheimer's is a terrible thing.'

'Yes, it is. Awful.'

'I think that's why Bernard and I went on this spending spree. Life is just too short. There's no point in dying with a fortune in the bank: you have to live life while you can.'

'I feel the same way,' said Lulu. 'You have to live every day as if it were your last.'

'Meow!' said Conrad.

'He agrees,' said Julia. 'Though cats have nine lives, don't they?'

'That's what they say,' said Lulu.

'Now, Bernard doesn't know this, but I've arranged for one of his favourite opera singers to perform at the party. She's driving up from London for a private performance at eight o'clock and we'll do it in this room. It's a complete surprise, so mum's the word.'

'You're pulling out all the stops.'

'Well, he's been working so hard over the past few years he deserves a treat. And I've hired one of his favourite orchestras to play in the garden, assuming the weather stays good.'

'Really? That's amazing.'

Julia nodded. 'Well, ensemble rather than orchestra, I suppose. The Vauxhall Band. They're a group of musicians who play eighteenth- and nineteenth-century music on period instruments. He loves them.'

'He's going to be so surprised.'

Julia pulled the doors closed and walked down the hallway to another set of double doors. 'This is our main sitting room,' she said. 'It's where we spend most of our downtime, really.'

The room was as large as the study but it had only one fireplace, around which were three comfortable-looking floral-print sofas and a thick rug. At the other end of the room was a huge television on the wall with another three sofas. There were large abstract paintings on all the walls, and on a circular oak table were several dozen small framed photographs of Julia and Bernard with family and friends. There was a little glass-fronted oak bookcase filled with books and an old seaman's chest that Lulu recognized from Julia's old London flat. 'Oh, this is lovely,' said Lulu.

'It feels so comfortable when we're here,' Julia said. 'It's as if it doesn't matter what's going on in the world. We close the doors and pour ourselves a drink and just chill.' She looked at her watch. 'Speaking of which, shall we treat ourselves to a glass of wine?'

'Perfect,' said Lulu.

They went back to the kitchen. 'Now, this I have to show you,' said Julia. She opened a white door and a light came on automatically, illuminating a flight of tiled stairs leading down. Lulu followed Julia down into a wood-panelled wine cellar that was almost as big as the kitchen. It was lined with wine racks and there were four large wine fridges against the far wall. Most of the racks were empty. 'I see they took their wine with them,' said Lulu.

'Oh yes,' said Julia, 'and it was one hell of a collection. A lot of it was clearly for investment, but they did enjoy their wine. I gather they hired a private jet just to ship it over to the States. A big jet.' She pointed at two bottle-filled racks. 'This is what we've bought so far but Bernard keeps promising to bring in a wine dealer and fill the place up.'

'It is amazing,' said Lulu as she looked around. 'But then the whole house is amazing.'

Julia opened one of the fridges and took out two bottles. She showed them to Lulu. 'Pinot Grigio?'

'Oh, yes.'

They went back upstairs, where Conrad was waiting for them. Julia put one of the bottles in the fridge and opened the other. She had just poured wine into two glasses when there was a buzzing sound from a small white box above the door. 'The doorbell,' Julia explained. 'There are a dozen of those things dotted around the house, or you'd never hear anyone at the door.' She put down her glass. 'I won't be a minute.'

As Julia hurried out of the kitchen, Conrad jumped up onto the island. He sat down in front of Lulu and tilted his head on one side. She stroked him along the back. 'What did you see, on the lounger by the pool?'

'Blood,' he said.

'Blood?'

'Blood. A few smears.'

'You're sure?'

'I'm a cat; of course I'm sure. Dogs get all the kudos for having a great sense of smell, but we cats are fourteen times better at picking up scents than humans.'

'Whose blood?'

Conrad blinked at her. 'I'm a cat, Lulu. Not a DNA analyser.'

'How could blood get on a lounger by the pool?'

'That's a very good question,' said Conrad. 'I suppose it could have been there for a while. Do you want to mention it to Julia?'

'How would I explain that I'd seen the blood from twenty yards away?'

'Eyes of a hawk?'

Lulu chuckled. 'Yes, I'm sure she'd believe that.' She sipped her wine. 'Okay, I'll find a reason to go back. Maybe I'll go for a swim. Then I could pretend to notice it.'

'You're quite the actress.'

'Well, the alternative is for you to talk to her, and I guess that's not an option.'

'You're the only one I talk to, Lulu. You know that.'

'Julia is a good friend. A very good friend. I would trust her with my life.'

'The world isn't ready for a talking cat,' said Conrad. 'And she's a scientist. She'd have questions and the next thing I'd know, I'd be being experimented on like a lab rat.' He shook his head. 'Only you.'

Lulu reached out and stroked his head and he purred. 'Okay, I'll work something out. It might be perfectly innocuous. Was there a lot of blood?'

'Just a couple of smears. As if something bloody had brushed against it.'

'For all we know it could have been there for weeks.'

'The house looks as if it's regularly cleaned,' said Conrad.

They heard footsteps in the hallway. Lulu took a step back from the island and sipped her wine.

'It's always the way: you think you have everything sorted and someone throws a spanner in the works,' said Julia. She strode over to the island and picked up her glass. 'The car valet people put the wrong date in their diary so they've arrived with the grass covers now. I told them to come back tomorrow but their trucks will be tied up elsewhere, so they're going to lay them down now.'

'What about the valets?'

'Oh they'll be fine. That's the crazy thing: the grass covers were booked for today but the valets were booked for tomorrow. You would have thought somebody would have noticed, wouldn't you? I sometimes get criticized for micro-managing, but it's true what they say: if you want something done properly then you have to do it yourself.'

Lulu chuckled. 'Does that mean you'll be parking the cars yourself?'

Julia laughed. 'Chance'd be a fine thing. Come on, let's see how Bernard is getting on and then I'll show you your room.'

6

Bernard was still propped up in bed with three pillows and was tapping on his smartphone when Julia and Lulu walked in. Conrad was sitting on Lulu's shoulders.

'How are you, darling?' asked Julia as she sat on the edge of the bed.

'I'm feeling much better,' said Bernard.

'And you'll be okay for the party tomorrow?'

'I'll be fine,' he said.

'No dizziness, no nausea, no throbbing pains?'

Bernard laughed. 'You're a PhD, darling, not a GP.'

'I just want to make sure you're okay. You were knocked unconscious.'

'Yes, I am all too well aware of that,' said Bernard. 'But really, I'm perfectly fine. Well, apart from the cut on my head and a black eye that makes it look as if I did five rounds with Mike Tyson.'

'Well, you do have a boxing ring in the gym,' said Lulu. She sat down on a Chinese-style sofa by the window. Conrad jumped off her shoulders and sat next to her. 'It is an amazing house. They clearly had a good eye, design-wise.' She stroked Conrad behind his ears and he purred.

'They did, no question. Miles and Stefan just had a strange taste in art. Taste-less, more like. But each to his own.'

'I love the wine cellar,' said Lulu.

'I know, they had that put in. Did Julia tell you about their wine collection? It was all big names, there were stacks of cases that they'd bought at auction and never opened. I have to say that when we finally got the keys, I stood in the kitchen and said a silent prayer before I went down and checked what, if anything, they'd left behind.' He grinned. 'There was just one bottle. Admittedly it was a Bollinger 1996 Vieilles Vignes Françaises which probably cost two thousand pounds, but I did have hopes we'd inherit the entire cellar.'

'The Bollinger was a lovely thought,' said Julia. 'And there was a note saying that they hoped we'd enjoy the house as much as they did.'

'They're a lovely couple,' said Bernard. 'So, did I hear someone pull up outside?'

'Yes, they're setting up the car parking stuff this afternoon,' said Julia. 'There was a mix-up over dates. And I've arranged for the glazier to come around to replace the broken glass in the study this afternoon. Everything else will be done tomorrow.'

'I'm really looking forward to it,' said Bernard.

'Me too,' said Julia.

Lulu twisted around and peered out of the window. Off to the left she could see men in overalls carrying large sheets of green plastic mesh over the lawn. In the distance were the woods. 'Bernard, why was the man from the insurance company here?' she asked.

'What?' said Bernard.

'Julia was showing me your paintings – you have an amazing collection now. Julia says you were about to increase your insurance coverage.'

'We're always reviewing our insurance, because we keep buying more paintings.'

'So that's why Mr Russell was here?'

'Sure.'

'And what about an alarm system? Did he make any recommendations?'

'We already have an alarm.'

'Yes, you do, but it's a relatively simple one.'

'I wouldn't say that. It's connected to a security company control room and they contact the police if they think there's been a break-in. I'm sure you know how it works.'

'But you're in the middle of nowhere. How long would it take for the police to get here?'

'I don't know, we've never used it. But if they treated it as an emergency and used their sirens and lights . . . what is it you call it? Blues and twos?'

'Okay, maybe. But from what I've seen you only have a perimeter system and I don't think that's enough, considering the value of the paintings you have.'

Bernard frowned. 'I don't know what that means. Perimeter system?'

'It means the alarm is activated if an outside door or window is opened. But what you really need are internal motion sensors and some sort of CCTV system. First of all, a professional burglar could actually get into the house without triggering the perimeter alarm. By removing the glass from a window, for instance. But more importantly, even if the alarm sounds, by the time the police turn up, the thieves will almost certainly be long gone. But if you have CCTV, the thieves know that everything they do will be recorded. You can imagine how useful it would have been if you had had CCTV in the study. Then there'd be no doubt about what happened.'

Bernard's frown deepened. 'What do you mean, doubt?'

'I mean that if there was CCTV footage, the police could see the men entering and assaulting you, then leaving with the paintings.'

'Yes, but they were wearing masks. CCTV wouldn't identify them.'

'Oh, you'd be surprised what they can glean from CCTV footage. Height, weight, body shape, clothing, even shoe size. They've got computer programs that can do all sorts of analysis.'

'Well, that's good to know.'

'Also you should think about having the most expensive paintings individually alarmed. That way, if they are removed from the wall, the alarms are triggered. And motion detectors in the downstairs rooms to detect anyone who breaches the perimeter, plus CCTV cameras covering the building inside and the approaches to it.'

'Lulu, seriously?' said Bernard. 'I wouldn't want CCTV cameras watching my every move. It would be like living in the Big Brother house.'

'No, you wouldn't be watched – that's not how it works. The video would stay on the hard drive or the cloud and no one would look at it unless there was an incident.'

'That's not the point, though. The point is that every single thing we did would be recorded. I wouldn't want to live like that.'

Lulu nodded. 'I understand. So this Mr Russell, he didn't recommend a CCTV system?'

'We barely had time for a conversation. I let him into the house, we walked to the study and bang! We were attacked.'

'Oh, so you hadn't been in the study, prior to the attack?'

'I just said, we were walking to the study.' He sighed. 'The doorbell rang. I went to answer it. We walked to the study, looking at several of the paintings, and when we got there we were attacked.'

'Ah, okay. I thought you were in the study first, then went into the corridor and when you got back they had broken in. I must have misunderstood.'

'Yes, you must have.'

Lulu frowned. 'It's just I remember you saying you were in the study and they barged in.'

'No, I was in the corridor.' He laughed and shook his head. 'Lulu, you were invited here for my birthday party, not to take part in some sort of murder mystery weekend.'

Lulu smiled ruefully. 'I know, I'm sorry. Once a detective, always a detective.'

'Well, I'm sure Inspector Calder knows what she's doing,' said Bernard. He lay back against his pillows.

'Are you okay?' asked Julia, patting him on the arm.

'Just tired,' he said.

'I was going to cook something, do you want to come downstairs and eat with us?'

Bernard chuckled. 'By cook you mean you're going to microwave something from M&S.'

'Well, you can come down and cook if you're up to it.'

'Maybe tomorrow,' he said. 'In fact, I'll do breakfast. Tonight maybe just bring me something on a tray.'

'Of course,' said Julia. 'I've got salmon with soy and ginger dressing, fish pie and lamb with redcurrant gravy and mash. What do you feel like?'

'Fish pie would be lovely, thank you.'

'And a glass of Pinot Grigio?'

'I don't think I'm supposed to have alcohol with the painkillers they've given me, so maybe just a small glass.'

Julia laughed. 'You are so naughty.'

'Just a small glass won't hurt.' He pouted and Julia laughed again.

'Okay, a small glass it is.' She stood up, leaned over, and kissed him on the forehead. 'You get some rest. I'll bring up your tray at about six.'

'You are such a good nurse.'

Conrad jumped up onto Lulu's shoulders and she stood up. 'We'll see you tomorrow,' she said.

'Definitely,' said Bernard.

They left the bedroom and Julia closed the door behind them. 'I hope he'll be okay for the party,' said Julia.

'He just needs to rest,' said Lulu. 'The painkillers are probably making him a little drowsy.'

Julia took Lulu down a corridor, then turned right. There was a line of doors, each with a small plaque on them with the name of a country. 'There are eight guest bedrooms,' said Julia. 'We haven't got around to changing them yet, and to be honest we might leave them as they are. The previous owners got a top hotel interior designer to do them and she did an amazing job. Each room is themed around a country, so there's a Russian room, a Chinese one, a French one. I remember you saying you always enjoyed Italy so I thought you might like the Italian room.' She opened a door and stood aside so that Lulu could walk in first. It was a stunning bedroom with a huge ornate white and gold bed in the middle, heavy rugs on a marble floor, and matching bedside tables with marble horses standing on them. There were two paintings on the walls: a cityscape of Rome and another of Naples. Conrad jumped down off Lulu's shoulders and plopped onto the bed.

The wardrobe was as ornate as the bed and Julia opened it to reveal dozens of dresses. 'Help yourself to anything you want,' she said. 'Most of them haven't been worn.'

'I can go back to *The Lark* to change,' said Lulu.

'Please, don't,' said Julia. 'I really don't want to be on my own at the moment.'

'Then I'll stay,' said Lulu. She looked around. There were heavy brocade curtains covering the window and two small chandeliers with fake candles at either end of the room. 'This room is so pretty, I love it.'

'Why don't you freshen up? There's a huge bath with loads of bath stuff, so take your time. Then, when you're ready, come down and I'll cook.' She grinned. 'Or as Bernard would have it, I'll microwave.' She walked over to Lulu and hugged her. 'I'm so glad you're here,' she said.

'Me too,' said Lulu. 'You don't think I annoyed Bernard, do you?'

'With all your questions, you mean? No, of course not. He knows you were a detective, and a bloody good one. It stands to reason that you're going to express an interest.'

'I really didn't mean to give him a hard time. I'm just curious.'

'He knows that. I think he's worried that you'll think he was stupid, that he could have handled it better. He's the head of the house – or at least he likes to think he is – and he was assaulted and robbed. That's got to hurt his confidence, right?'

'I really was simply trying to help.'

Julia patted her on the arm. 'I know you were, and I'm sure he does too.'

'I'll try not to ask so many questions.'

'Don't be silly. It shows you care about him. What do you think we want you to do, shrug and change the subject? Talk about the weather? No, don't you even think about it. You carry on exactly as you are.' She hugged Lulu and patted her on the back, then left the room and closed the door behind her.

Lulu sat down on the bed and stroked Conrad's fur. 'Do you think I was too hard on him?' she asked.

'You asked the same questions that I wanted answering,' said Conrad. 'And he did say that he was in the study when they broke in, the first time he talked about it. Then the second time he said he was in the hall and that when they went into the study the men were there.'

'I knew I was right,' she said. 'So he changed his story?'

'Well, he might have been confused the first time. He's been hit on the head and he's been taking painkillers. But he clearly doesn't want to discuss it, does he? As soon as you start asking questions, he changes the subject.'

'I suppose he might not want to be reminded of what happened,' said Lulu. She yawned and stretched. 'I'm so tired.'

'You've had a busy day. You should cat-nap.'

'Yes, I think I might.' She lay down and sighed. 'Oh, now this is a comfortable bed. It's like resting on a cloud.' Conrad walked along the bed and curled up next to her. Within seconds they were both asleep and snoring softly.

7

'Lulu, wake up,' said Conrad. Something patted Lulu on her cheek and she opened her eyes. Conrad was standing over her, butting his head against her neck. 'You've been asleep for almost two hours.'

Lulu rubbed her face with her hand. 'The bed is so darn comfortable.' She sighed. She rolled over and closed her eyes again. Conrad padded around her and butted her again. 'Come on, sleepyhead, Julia's waiting, remember?'

Lulu rolled onto her back, blinked, and then sat up. It was starting to get dark outside. 'I didn't realize how tired I was.' She looked at her watch. Conrad was right: she had slept for almost two hours. She climbed off the bed and hurried to the bathroom for a quick wash. She gasped when she saw how big it was – with a roll-top bath, a huge shower with multiple jets, and two massive washbasins with gold-plated swans as taps. The floor and walls were green-veined marble and there were fluffy white towels as big as bedsheets hanging on gold-plated rails. She would have loved a bath but she had already kept Julia waiting long enough, so she took a quick shower. She wrapped one of the super-sized towels around her and went back into the bedroom and opened the wardrobe. There were several dozen dresses and shirts on elegant white hangers and many of them still had price tags attached. There were two rows of drawers at the bottom of the wardrobe and Lulu opened them to find underwear and several pairs of trousers, all of them brand new. 'You know, I think I could get used to living here,' she said to Conrad.

He jumped off the bed and walked over to the wardrobe, putting his front paws on one of the drawers so that he could look inside. 'I think you would miss *The Lark*,' he said.

'Yes, I would.'

'And your freedom. You like being able to go wherever you want whenever you want. You don't like being tied down.'

'That is very true.' She chose a white short-sleeved calf-length dress with a large rose motif on the front, held it against herself and checked it out in an ornate gilded mirror.

'You have a lot of cat in you,' said Conrad.

'Why, thank you. That is possibly the nicest compliment I have ever had.'

Lulu finished dressing, then sat down on the bed so that Conrad could jump onto her shoulders. She started chuckling as she walked to the stairs and Conrad asked her what was so funny. 'I was just thinking about being on *The Lark* and wanting a drink in the middle of the night. It's half a dozen steps to the fridge. But here? It's crazy. You have to walk more than a hundred yards.'

'That's why houses this size usually have maids and butlers; you ring a bell and someone attends to your every need.'

'I know. I can understand why Julia and Bernard don't want live-in servants. But can you imagine getting into bed and then wondering if you'd left a window open downstairs? You'd have to go all the way there, switching lights on, and then all the way back switching them off. And what if you heard a noise somewhere? I mean, how long would it take to check every room?' She shuddered. 'I don't think I'd ever be comfortable.'

They reached the top of the sweeping staircase and went down. 'I do love this staircase, though. And the chandelier. It makes me feel as if I'm a princess in a palace.'

She went down the stairs and along the corridor to the kitchen. Julia was sitting at the island, a glass of white wine in front of her. 'Well, the sleeping beauty finally awakes,' she said. 'I did pop my head around the door an hour ago and you were both fast asleep. I thought about waking you up but you were so peaceful I just left you to it. Wine?'

'Wine would be lovely.' Conrad jumped off her shoulders and landed on the floor with a soft thud. He took a quick few steps and climbed up onto a wooden chair next to the door that led to the conservatory.

'There's an open bottle of Pinot Grigio in the fridge.' Julia pointed at one of the overhead cabinets. 'And glasses are in there. I've already taken Bernard up his fish pie. What can I get you?'

'Whatever you're having is fine,' said Lulu, as she took the bottle of wine out of the fridge.

'The salmon with soy and ginger dressing is lovely, and I can throw a salad together. And I have some amazing frozen wholemeal rolls that only need half an hour in the oven.'

'Sounds perfect,' said Lulu. She took a glass from the cupboard, sat at the island and poured herself some wine.

'It was all go while you were asleep,' said Julia. 'The glazier came and went, and the valet people finished laying the mesh stuff on the grass. Several of the caterers rang to check that the party was still going ahead. They'd read about the robbery in the paper and apparently it's been on the radio, too.'

'They probably don't get that many murders out here,' said Lulu. 'And if there have been similar robberies, people are going to be worried.' She sipped her wine. 'I didn't want to press Bernard, but you should get some sort of security system installed. These big houses really are sitting ducks, especially when you don't have staff in overnight.'

'I know what he means about CCTV, though. I wouldn't want to be walking around with cameras following my every move.'

'Well, you needn't have them everywhere. But at the very least you should have them on the building covering the approaches to the house. They are a really good deterrent. If thieves see CCTV cameras on a building, more often than not they'll move on and find one that's not so well protected. And maybe have a look at using a different security company. If all they do is inform the local police, chances are the call won't be taken seriously. For all the police know, it could be a false alarm. Some companies will send out their own people, and they'll definitely be quicker. I'm sure there are companies in Oxford you could use.'

'Okay, I'll look into it,' said Julia. 'Though, to be fair, that horse has well and truly bolted, hasn't it?'

Lulu smiled. 'Yes, I suppose you're right. But they only took eight paintings, there's a lot more still here.'

'You think they might come back for the rest?'

'They might. Or someone else might. If they get away scot-free, other burglars might decide to have a go.'

'I hope not,' said Julia.

'What I meant was, all the publicity about the robbery and the murder will probably only serve to highlight what a valuable collection of paintings you have, so you need to beef up security.'

'Yes, ma'am,' said Julia, and she threw Lulu a mock salute. She slipped off her stool and went to the fridge. 'Right, I'll get started on dinner. You can watch and appreciate my skill with the microwave.'

'I am here to learn,' said Lulu, raising her glass.

8

Once they had finished their meal, Julia put the plates and cutlery into a dishwasher, then they carried their glasses and the bottle into the conservatory and dropped down onto one of the sofas. There were fragrant Jo Malone candles dotted around and Julia asked Alexa to play some jazz. The salmon and salad had been delicious, eaten in a matter of minutes. Julia had even put some of the fish on a plate for Conrad, and he had polished it off in no time.

'This is idyllic,' said Lulu as she looked out over the grounds. There was a full moon overhead and they could see right across the lawn to the woods in the distance. Conrad had curled up on the chair next to Lulu and had closed his eyes, but she was fairly sure he wasn't sleeping. She reached over and stroked his back and he purred softly.

'I wish we had more time to enjoy it,' said Julia. 'But we are so busy at the moment. We've taken time off for this party, but then it's noses back to the grindstone.'

'Do you think you'll ever retire?'

'That's a good question. You know, I'm not sure that I want to. The work we're doing is so worthwhile, Lulu. We are literally saving lives. And the techniques we've patented – you really wouldn't believe the possibilities. We might well be on the way to finding cures for several cancers. Not therapies, actual cures.'

'That's fantastic.'

'It's an amazing opportunity, and I'm determined to grab it with both hands.'

'And what about Bernard? Is he involved in the company?'

'Sort of. He helps out with the admin and the marketing, but obviously the science is beyond him and he was never great at the business side of things.' She sipped her wine. 'You know all the problems we had with the shop in Portobello Road? Debt collectors banging on the doors at all hours. Bernard is a genius when it comes to art, but he really has no business sense. He'll talk about art and artists until the cows come home, but you could never get him to do his VAT returns. Remember that time he was having problems with the taxman and you and Simon came in and bought two paintings? I never said anything at the time, but that was a lifesaver.'

'I still have those paintings,' said Lulu. 'One was a water-colour of Fleet Street with St Paul's in the background. It was in our hallway for the longest time.'

'Well, the money you paid kept the taxman at bay for a few months.' Julia took another sip of wine. 'Of course it all fell apart eventually. As fast as the money came in, it went out.'

'What about the shop in Oxford? Is that doing well?'

'No, we lost that a few years ago. There was a fire and luckily we were fully insured so we got our money back. That was the time they were setting up the vaccine company and we decided to invest in that rather than starting another shop. Best decision we ever made.'

'Was Bernard okay with that?'

Julia laughed. 'I think he'd realized by then that he didn't have what it takes to run a successful business. I mean, he knows his art, and he has an eye for a bargain – there's no question of that. And he's able to spot artistic talent, better than almost anyone I know.' She leaned over and poured more wine into her glass. 'You know, we're making more money from the capital appreciation of the paintings we've bought over the last few years than we ever made from the shops. He's an amazing investor, but a lousy businessman. And I'm not being disloyal in saying that because he'd be the first to agree with me.'

'The good news is that now he can do whatever he wants,' said Lulu.

'Exactly. That's why I've been pushing him to start painting again. He used to be so good at it. I loved his work. But then he pretty much gave up, said that he'd never make any money at it. Now money isn't an issue and he can just paint for himself. And what about you, Lulu?'

'What about me?'

'What are you doing with your life?'

Lulu chuckled. 'Living it, I suppose. Day by day. I go where I want, my time is my own, there are no demands on me, no one telling me what to do.'

'And you're happy on the boat?'

'Oh my goodness, yes. I couldn't be happier. Every day is a joy. I can go somewhere, or I can use my mooring in Little Venice, which is a delight. There are always jobs to do on the boat, and Conrad is amazing company.'

'I always remember you being a dog person.'

'I think I was, until Conrad came into my life.'

'How did that come about?'

'I was on the boat one day and he came walking down the towpath. He jumped on board and introduced himself and I gave him some Evian water and that was that.'

'He didn't have an owner?'

'I don't think you can ever own a cat like Conrad. He's his own boss.'

'That's so sweet. It's as if he chose you.'

'Oh, he did. There's no question of that.'

Julia stifled a yawn. 'Sorry, it's been a tiring day. I'm going to go to bed. I'll take you to your room.'

'I can find my own way,' said Lulu. 'The house is big, but it's not that big, I won't get lost.'

'Nonsense, you're my guest,' said Julia, getting to her feet.

Lulu put her arm across the chair that Conrad was sitting on. He stood up, stretched, then walked carefully along Lulu's arm and settled around her shoulders.

'I love how he does that,' said Julia. 'Doesn't he ever fall off?'

'Meow!' said Conrad.

Julia laughed. 'I guess not.'

They went into the kitchen, and upstairs and along the corridor to Lulu's bedroom. 'So what do you want to do tomorrow?' Julia asked. 'I'll be dealing with the party people from early on, but let's have breakfast, say half eight?'

'Perfect,' said Lulu. She kissed Julia on both cheeks and gave her a hug. 'See you tomorrow.'

Julia stroked Conrad's head. 'And I'll see you tomorrow, too.'

As Julia headed to her own bedroom, Lulu opened the door to the Italian room and switched on the light. She closed the door and sat down on the bed. Conrad jumped down off her shoulders and bumped his head against her arm. 'Are you okay?' he asked.

'Yes, I'm fine.'

'You're worried about something, I can tell.'

'I'm sure you can read my mind sometimes,' she said.

'Not really, it's just that you're frowning and there's a faraway look in your eyes.'

Lulu chuckled. 'You know me so well.'

He butted her arm again. 'Yes, I do.'

'I keep thinking about what happened to Bernard and that poor man Billy. Going about their own business and suddenly, out of nowhere, they're attacked. Bernard was lucky that he wasn't killed, too. And for what? A few paintings.'

'You're worried about the poker, aren't you?'

Lulu nodded. 'Yes. But how could you possibly know that?'

'The way you were looking at the other poker in the study. I saw you frowning. But you didn't want to say anything to Julia.'

'Well, she has enough on her mind.'

Conrad jumped onto her lap. Lulu began to stroke him and he purred softly. 'The thing is, the men who stole the paintings came prepared. They had gloves and ski masks. They must have come in a vehicle and they parked that on the neighbouring farm. So up to that point, everything was planned and prepared.'

'So why didn't they bring a weapon with them?'

'Exactly. The poker was opportunistic, whereas everything else had been well thought out.'

'So if they had expected to use violence, they would have brought something with them,' said Conrad. 'A knife, or a gun.'

'Well, I'm assuming they were big guys and young, and they wouldn't need a gun or a knife to threaten someone like Bernard. You've seen him – a gust of wind would blow him over. Just the threat of violence would probably have been enough. But, yes, if the plan was to use violence, they would have brought a weapon with them.'

'We don't know what Mr Russell was like. He might have been big and strong. Maybe he attacked the men and they got angry. One of them grabbed the poker and lashed out, killing Billy and hurting Bernard.'

'But Bernard didn't say anything about that, did he?' Lulu sighed. 'Maybe he does have concussion. Temporary amnesia, perhaps. It just doesn't make sense that they were so violent. They clearly didn't come prepared for violence, which shows they were professionals.'

'Why do you say that?'

'Because if you break into a house and just steal, that's theft. Once you use violence it becomes burglary or robbery.'

'How does that work?' asked Conrad.

'Well, theft is when you take someone's property without using force. So if they stole and didn't use violence, then it's theft and the maximum they would get prison-wise is seven years; most thieves would get a lot less. Now, once you break into a house – which they apparently did – then it becomes burglary. Basically illegally entering a property in order to steal from it. Then there's robbery, which involves using violence to steal. Then you have armed robbery, which is the most serious offence, and that comes with a maximum sentence of life imprisonment. So if they were real pros and they didn't carry a weapon or attack their victims, they'd only face seven years in prison if they got caught, which under the UK system means they would be back out on the streets in three. There's a huge difference between three years and a life sentence.'

'So you think they broke in without any weapons, intending just to steal the paintings without hurting anybody?'

'That would make sense, yes,' said Lulu.

'Then, as I said, something must have happened to change that. They went in intending to steal, but ended up by killing Mr Russell and knocking out Bernard.'

'That's what I keep coming back to,' said Lulu. 'A simple theft turns into a terrible murder. That's the mark of amateurs, not professionals. And look at the paintings they stole. Okay, they were valuable, but they left the painting by that Nigerian American woman, the artist whose paintings sell for millions of dollars. And there were two paintings in the hallway together worth a million pounds. Would professionals have left behind paintings like that?'

'Maybe they panicked. They just grabbed what was nearest and ran?'

'That's possible, I suppose.'

'Or perhaps they grabbed the smaller paintings because they'd be easier to carry. Anyway, let's hope Bernard can shed some light on it tomorrow.'

'Yes,' said Lulu. 'Let's hope so.'

9

Lulu woke up at eight and frowned when she didn't see the wooden ceiling above her head. It took a few seconds before she remembered where she was. Conrad was nestled at her feet and he opened his eyes as she sat up. 'Good morning,' she said. 'Did you sleep well?'

'I cat-napped,' he said. 'As I do.'

'This bed is so comfortable, isn't it?'

'To be honest, I can sleep anywhere.'

'Of course you can. But this mattress is something special. I think it's one of those ones that moulds itself to the shape of your body.'

Conrad stood up and stretched, then jumped off the bed and onto the sofa. He curled up again as Lulu went into the bathroom.

One of the few things she missed about living on *The Lark* was the luxury of a bath, so she turned on the taps and ran a deep bath, complete with some Lush foam and a multi-coloured bomb.

As she lay in the soothing hot water, Conrad padded in. He stood up with his front paws on the bath and sniffed. 'That does smell good,' he said. 'Jasmine. And bakuchi, if I'm not mistaken.'

'Bakuchi?' repeated Lulu.

'They're kidney-shaped seeds that come from a plant that grows in India. The powder they extract from the seeds is anti-inflammatory and good for the skin. It's been used in traditional medicine for thousands of years.'

'Well it feels wonderful.'

Conrad dropped down on all fours. 'I'm not a big fan of baths.'

'Cats aren't, generally, I suppose.'

'We're self-cleaning.'

'Of course you are. But that just wouldn't work for me. Far too many inaccessible places.'

'That's true. Humans are very inflexible.'

'Physically, or generally?'

Conrad chuckled. 'That's a very good question.' He strolled out of the bathroom.

Lulu lay in the bath for twenty minutes, then put on one of Julia's Karen Millen dresses and went downstairs. Julia was in the kitchen, standing by her Nespresso machine. 'Wow, that looks great on you,' she said when she saw the dress.

'That's what I thought. It's lovely.'

'Keep it, I have so many Karen Millen dresses. I went through a Karen Millen phase and I haven't worn most of them. Coffee?'

'Coffee would be lovely, thank you. And thank you for all the bath stuff. It's been ages since I had a real bath.'

'There isn't one on the boat?'

'Just a shower. It's a good shower, but nothing compares with a lovely, hot bath.' Lulu walked over to the window. There were figures wearing high-vis jackets moving through the woods. 'What time did the police get here?'

'Just after eight. I think I saw Tracey out there but I haven't spoken to her yet. So, scrambled eggs and smoked salmon? How does that sound?'

'Sounds lovely.'

Julia handed her a mug of coffee. 'And what about Conrad? Does he eat breakfast?'

'I'm sure he'd love some smoked salmon.'

'Meow!' said Conrad, and Julia laughed.

'That's a definite yes,' she said. She opened the fridge and took out a box of eggs.

'So you don't have a cook?' said Lulu.

Julia laughed again. 'Why on earth would I have a cook?'

'I suppose I just assumed that with a house this large that you'd have staff.'

'Including a butler and a footman and a parlour maid or two?'

'Well, it is a very large house,' said Lulu.

'Yes, but it's not Downton Abbey,' said Julia. She sipped her coffee. 'Anyway, Bernard does the cooking usually. You know how good he is.'

'He is a very talented cook, I remember.'

'Don't let him hear you say that. He's a chef, nothing less. But I can hold my own in the breakfast department. Other than that, it's Marks & Spencer for me.'

'But what about the cleaning? You can't do all that yourself, surely? Even just hoovering the floors would take a full day.'

'Well, yes, we have cleaners, obviously, but they're not staff. We use a company in Oxford and they send people out three times a week. And there's the landscaping firm that takes care of the grounds. But we don't have any live-in staff, I couldn't abide that. You'd always be having to watch what you said and what you did, it'd be like living in a goldfish bowl.'

'What about the day of the robbery? Did you have cleaners in then?'

Julia nodded. 'We did, yes. Why?'

'I was wondering why no one saw the men crossing the lawn from the woods. They'd be very exposed.'

'Well, I'd hope that the cleaners would be busy cleaning and not staring out of the windows.'

'Who does the windows? Can't possibly be a man with a bucket and a ladder?'

'It's a team with a cherry-picker and a high-pressure hose. They come twice a month.'

'Not complaining about our sex life, are you, darling?' said Bernard from the doorway. He was wearing a dark blue silk dressing gown over his pyjamas.

'Darling, what are you doing up?' said Julia. 'I was going to bring you breakfast in bed.'

'I'm fine,' said Bernard, walking over to the stove.

'You really should take it easy,' said Lulu. 'Bangs on the head can be worse than they appear.'

'Really, Lulu, it's nothing to fuss about. And if I leave Julia to make the scrambled eggs, she'll only put milk in them and ruin them.'

'A splash of milk and a knob of butter, that's how my mother always made them,' said Julia.

'Your darling mother and I have always agreed to disagree on this,' said Bernard. 'A tablespoon of water and coat the pan with just olive oil, extra virgin, of course.'

'Of course,' said Lulu.

Bernard waved Julia away and she went to sit next to Lulu. He began breaking eggs into a bowl. 'Olive oil is the key: it makes the eggs scramble quicker, which traps in steam, which makes them fluffier. That's not a matter of opinion, that's a scientific fact.'

Julia sighed and rolled her eyes. 'Can you at least trust me to open the smoked salmon?'

'Of course, darling. Get the gin and tonic out, Lulu will love it.'

'Gin and tonic?' repeated Lulu, as Julia headed for the fridge.

'I always order our smoked salmon from H. Forman & Son in London: they're the oldest producer of smoked salmon in the world,' said Bernard. 'For years I always stuck with their London cure but then I discovered they do a gin-and-tonic smoked salmon.'

'To die for?'

'You took the words out of my mouth,' said Bernard as he began to whisk the eggs. 'They take grade one salmon from Scottish lochs and they smoke it within forty-eight hours of catching the fish. They add juniper berries and hand-grated lemon zest to the salmon and it just melts in your mouth.' He smacked his lips as he put a pan onto the stove and poured in some olive oil. 'The great Heston Blumenthal chose it for British Airways Club Class, but long after I'd started eating it.'

'Bernard is right about the salmon,' said Julia as she opened the fridge. 'It's delicious.' She took out a pack of smoked salmon and closed the door.

Bernard poured the eggs into the pan and began stirring them.

Julia opened the pack and put slices of smoked salmon onto three plates, then poured orange juice into three flutes. 'I can open a bottle of bubbly and go the Buck's Fizz route,' she said to Lulu.

'Orange juice and coffee is fine for me,' said Lulu.

'Meow!' said Conrad.

'Yes, Conrad, I'll get you your salmon now,' said Julia. 'I love the way he talks.' She put two slices of salmon on a plate, cut it up, and placed it on the floor. Conrad trotted over and began to nibble at it.

Bernard carried the pan over to the plates and spooned scrambled eggs next to the smoked salmon, then put the pan in the sink. 'Get it while it's hot,' he said.

They sat down at the island and tucked in. Lulu nodded her appreciation after the first bite. 'Oh, I see what you mean.'

'About the eggs or the salmon?' asked Bernard.

'Both. Delicious.'

'Told you,' said Bernard. He looked over at Julia. 'So what's the plan today, darling?'

'The cleaners will be here by ten and they can give the study a deep clean. I thought then you might put some paintings up to replace the ones that have been stolen.'

'Are we going to tell people about the robbery or not?' he asked.

'What do you think?'

Bernard shrugged. 'I suppose they'll find out soon enough. A man was killed; I'm surprised it's not been in the papers already. I think it's best we just let everyone know. Be up front with them.' He pointed at the bandage on his head. 'No one is going to believe that I banged my head on a kitchen cupboard, are they?'

'Well, I hope they don't think that I gave you the black eye,' said Julia. 'But yes, you're right, better we just tell everyone what happened.'

'What about bringing some paintings from upstairs to fill in the gaps where the stolen ones were?' asked Julia.

'I don't think we need to do that, do we?' said Bernard. 'Actually, it can be a talking point.'

'Next you'll be saying we should leave the crime scene tape up,' said Julia.

'And put a circle outline where the body was!' Bernard grinned but stopped when he saw the look on Lulu's face. 'I'm sorry, that was in bad taste. Very bad taste. I'm still in shock, I think.'

'People often use humour to try to deal with shocking situations,' said Lulu. 'You must have been terrified.'

Bernard shook his head. 'To be honest, it all happened so quickly that I barely remember it. Billy and I were in the hallway looking at some of the larger paintings and when we walked into the study, there they were.'

'How many of them were there?'

'Two,' said Bernard. 'Big buggers, dressed in black. Then I don't know what happened. They cracked me over the head and when I woke up Billy was on the floor, dead, and they'd gone.'

'And they took eight paintings with them?'

Bernard nodded.

'But not the most valuable ones?'

'Well, they were all valuable, but yes, some were more valuable than others. I suppose they must have panicked.'

'And you didn't hear them breaking the glass in the French window?'

'We were some way down the hall.'

Lulu put down her knife and fork, her food forgotten. 'Do you usually lock the windows?'

'Only when we go out,' said Julia. 'And at night, obviously.'

'So why did they break the glass? Couldn't they just have walked in?'

'They might have been locked, I can't remember,' said Bernard. He reached up to touch his bandage. 'I still get a bit woozy.'

'Do you want to go back to bed?' asked Julia.

'No, no, I'll be fine,' said Bernard. 'I just need to take it easy. And what about the caterers? They're all primed and ready to go?'

'They'll be here at three, which will give them two hours to get ready. They'll bring the tables and chairs with them. The weather forecast is sunny all day so we'll have everything on the terrace. In addition to the main catering company, I arranged a sushi bar, an oyster bar and a champagne bar, all with separate companies. That way, if one falls through we're still covered. The bars should be here at four.'

'Sounds like a lot of planning has gone into this,' said Lulu.

'You don't know the half of it,' said Bernard. 'But you only turn sixty once, so we want to make sure this is special.' Bernard carried the plates over to the sink. He glanced through the window. 'They're not going to be here all day, are they?'

'The police?' said Julia. 'No, I think they'll be finished by the end of the morning.'

'What do they expect to find?'

'You'd be surprised what people drop when they're rushing to get away,' said Lulu. 'It's standard practice to do a search of any crime scene and the surroundings. They'll probably work their way all the way to the farm.'

'Seems like a waste of time to me, but I suppose they know what they're doing.' He looked at his watch. 'I think I will go and lie down for a bit. Get my strength up for this afternoon.'

'Sounds like a good idea,' said Julia.

'And thanks for the breakfast,' said Lulu. 'It was delicious.'

Bernard flashed her a smile and disappeared into the hallway. As he left, a figure appeared at the conservatory window. It was Tracey, wearing a high-vis jacket over her suit. She waved and Julia and Lulu waved back. They went through to the conservatory and Julia opened the door. 'Come in,' said Julia. 'I'll make you a coffee.'

'No, that's all right, I'll only tread dirt all through your house.'

They looked down and saw that she was wearing dark green wellington boots.

'Anyway, I've heard back from our forensic people and the only fingerprints on the poker were yours and your husband's. But that was to be expected as the intruders wore gloves. Did you both use the poker?'

Julia nodded. 'On cold nights we like to have a real fire in there if we're working.'

'Your husband's blood is on it, and Mr Russell's. So there's no doubt it was the murder weapon.'

'And we're no closer to finding out who did it?' asked Julia.

'I'm afraid not. Our best hope is to track the paintings. Is your husband available for a quick chat?'

'He's in bed again. Let me go up and check.' Julia hurried out through the kitchen and into the hallway.

'Have you had time to take a look at the murder victim?' asked Lulu.

The inspector frowned. 'Billy Russell?'

'Yes, did you look into his background?'

'Well, I know who he is, obviously. Or rather, who he was. He was a loss adjuster who works for an insurance firm in Oxford. Divorced with two children and then married again.'

'Did you go to see the next of kin?'

'Yes, the evening of the killing. Well, I went to see the wife. The ex-wife and kids live in Exeter, so Devon and Cornwall cops handled that. His wife – widow – was obviously distraught.'

'Did you ask if he'd been having any problems with anyone?'

'Not specifically, no.'

'And what about the insurance company? Did you talk to them?'

Tracey's frown deepened. 'Why would I do that?'

'To see who – if anyone – knew that he was visiting the house.'

Tracey opened her mouth to reply but was interrupted by the return of Julia. 'I'm sorry, Bernard is fast asleep. I think he just needs a nap before his party.'

'That's not a problem,' said Tracey. 'I'll call him over the next day or two. He obviously needs his rest.'

'Do you think he'll be all right for this evening?' asked Lulu.

'Oh yes, I'm sure he will. He just needs to take it easy.' Julia grimaced at Tracey. 'Sorry.'

'It's fine, really. He should rest.' Tracey smiled. 'And good luck with the party tonight,' she said. 'I hope it all goes well.'

'Thank you,' said Julia.

Tracey looked at her watch. 'So, we'll be another hour or so here, then we'll be off your land. At that point I'll send people back to collect the vans and drive them to the farm. We'll be out of your hair long before the party starts.'

'Thank you so much, Tracey. If you'd like, why not come by later tonight.' Julia grinned. 'In your civvies.'

'I might take you up on that,' she said.

'And bring a plus one.'

'Thank you. Right, I'll be off.'

'Actually, Tracey, I could do with stretching my legs,' said Lulu. 'I'll walk with you.'

10

Tracey turned to look at Lulu. They were walking across the lawn towards the woods, where more than a dozen uniformed officers in high-vis jackets were working their way through the trees. Conrad was riding on Lulu's shoulders, his hair ruffling in the breeze. 'Does he go everywhere with you?'

'Everywhere he wants to,' said Lulu.

'What you said about Billy Russell . . . you're suggesting that the break-in was in some way connected to him being here?'

'It's a possibility. He was the only one killed, wasn't he? So it is possible that they came here to kill Russell and then made it look like a robbery.'

'That's a stretch, isn't it? They could have killed him somewhere a lot more private.'

Lulu nodded. 'I know. It's just that back in the day when I was on a murder investigation, I made it a point to cover every possibility.'

'And you think I should have spoken to his employer?'

Lulu held up her hands. 'I didn't mean to sound critical, I was just offering suggestions,' she said.

'Can I be honest with you, Lulu?' said Tracey. She looked around as if checking there was no one nearby to overhear what she was about to say. 'This is my first murder investigation as senior investigating officer.'

'Well, that's exciting,' said Lulu. 'You never forget your first.'

'Exciting is one way of describing it,' said the inspector. 'Scary is another.'

'I'm sure you'll be fine.'

'Don't get me wrong: I know what I'm doing. And I know the Murder Investigation Manual back to front. But DC Collier is even younger than I am, so it's not as if I have a safe pair of hands to fall back on, and I'm feeling very much exposed at the moment.'

'Tracey, you're doing fine. Everyone has a crisis of confidence at some point, especially when you're on your first case as SIO.'

'You too?'

'Very much so. But I was lucky: when I did my first homicide investigation as SIO I had a really experienced sergeant as my bag carrier. He kept me on the straight and narrow.'

'That's what I need right now, I think.' She put a hand on Lulu's arm. 'Can I ask you a favour?'

'Of course.'

'Can I use you as a sounding board? Bounce ideas off you? I can't really do that with DC Collier, but you have had all that experience, it would be a big help for me.'

'It would be my pleasure, Tracey. If you don't mind me asking, how old are you?'

'Twenty-eight. I know, that's young to be an inspector, never mind an SIO, but they have been going out of their way to fast-track women over the past few years. I truly would value your input, Lulu. As I told you yesterday, we really haven't got anything to go on at the moment, so I am very much open to any and all suggestions.' She smiled. 'But, hand on heart, if they did plan to kill Mr Russell, they'd hardly have used a poker, would they? And I don't see them going to all the trouble of breaking into the house to kill him. It would have been so much easier to attack him in his own house. Or in the street.'

'That's true. You're right. It's just that last night I lay in bed and all sorts of things were running through my mind.'

'Such as?'

Lulu shook her head. 'I don't want to muddy the waters. Your job is difficult enough as it is.'

'No, please, tell me.'

Lulu sighed. 'Okay. It just feels to me too much of a coincidence that at the very moment two robbers break into the house, there's an insurance assessor there.'

'Coincidences happen.'

'Yes, of course they do. But then I got to thinking, what if this Billy Russell was in league with the robbers? He could have told them about the layout of the house, and what paintings were there.'

'An inside man?'

'Exactly. But then something goes wrong and they hit him with the poker.'

'What could have gone wrong?'

'I know, even as I say it I can hear how ridiculous it sounds. But that was why I was asking if you'd spoken to his employer.' She ran a hand through her hair. 'I'm sorry, it's none of my business.'

'No, don't say that. Your friends were robbed – of course it's your business.' They reached the edge of the woods. The police search team had spread out so that they were two or three metres apart, and their heads were swivelling left and right as they slowly made their way through the trees. Tracey sighed. 'The poker worries me. If they were planning on using violence, they would have taken a weapon with them. A knife. Or a gun. The fact that they didn't suggests that violence was the last thing on their minds. So what happened to change their minds? Why did they go from simple burglary to beating one man and severely injuring another?'

'It's a good question.'

They stopped walking and turned to look at the house. 'That's a lot of lawn,' said Tracey.

'Yes, it is.'

'If you were planning an art theft, would you run across this much lawn in a ski mask? In full view of, how many windows?'

'Fifteen?' said Lulu. 'Sixteen?'

'That's a lot.'

'An awful lot.'

'Why take the risk? That's what I can't understand.'

'Maybe they didn't go this way.' Lulu pointed at the greenhouses close to the house. 'They could have worked their way through the trees to the greenhouses, then approached the house from there. Much less grass to cross.'

Tracey nodded. 'That makes sense.'

'Then, when it all went wrong, they grabbed what they could and ran.' Lulu shrugged. 'But that's so . . . unprofessional.'

The inspector nodded in agreement. 'It is, isn't it? The other burglaries have all been so well organized. No one saw them, no forensic evidence, and certainly no violence.'

'It's the violence that makes no sense to me,' said Lulu.

'They couldn't be identified because of the masks, so there's no way Bernard or Billy Russell could be a threat to them. Unless Billy was a tough guy and he started throwing punches.'

'No, he was no Jackie Chan. Quite short, overweight; he wouldn't have put up a fight.'

'Which brings us back to the same question – why suddenly get so violent? And, having used the poker, why just grab a few paintings and run for it? They had all the time in the world. They could have taken a lot more, including some really valuable ones.'

'They panicked?' said the inspector.

'Yes, that's what it looks like. But everything else was so professional. How come they panic at the last minute?' Lulu sighed. 'I keep coming back to the fact that something must have happened to change the way they were operating.'

Tracey nodded. 'I'll have to have another word with Bernard at some point. Is he okay, do you think?'

'He was up and about earlier. In fact he made breakfast. But he was a bit strange when I asked him about the broken glass. Changed the subject almost immediately.'

'You were asking him why they broke the glass if the French windows weren't locked?'

Lulu smiled. 'Yes, I was.'

'When I asked him that question, his head started to hurt and he said he needed to rest.' She shrugged. 'He did take a serious knock to the head.'

'But the question needs to be asked, why did they smash their way in when they could have just turned the handle?'

'They might have assumed it was locked.'

'Wouldn't they have tried it first?'

The inspector wrinkled her nose. 'Maybe they aren't as professional as we're assuming they are. Maybe it's not the same team that have carried out the other burglaries. Do you mind if I smoke?'

'No, of course not. Go ahead.'

Tracey took out a pack of Benson & Hedges and a disposable lighter. She lit a cigarette and offered the pack to Lulu.

Lulu shook her head. 'I gave up years ago.'

'I admire your willpower.'

'Smoking and the job sort of went together,' said Lulu. 'Once I left the police, I pretty much lost the urge to smoke. And my husband always hated me smoking.'

'Will he be at the party tonight?'

Lulu shook her head. 'He died.'

'Oh I'm sorry.'

'It's a long story.' She made a helpless gesture. 'I'm still not over it. I don't think I ever will be.'

The inspector blew smoke up at the sky as she looked over at the house and the grounds. 'I suppose if they came from the direction of the greenhouses, they wouldn't have seen the cars parked at the front of the house,' she said.

'True. But they must have assumed there were people inside, mustn't they? How often would a house this size be empty?'

'I know, I know. It just doesn't make sense. Night time would have been so much easier. The alarm they have is basic, just doors and windows. No motion sensors or CCTV.'

'Bernard didn't seem interested in upgrading his security system. I thought maybe that was why Billy Russell was here but I couldn't get a straight answer from Bernard. So you think it could be an inside job?'

'I'm just clutching at straws, to be honest,' said Tracey.

'My copper's instincts keep coming back to the victim,' said Lulu. 'If the aim was to kill Billy Russell, then everything else falls into place. It would have to have been during the daytime because that was when he was here. They could have smashed the glass to emphasize it was a robbery, then, once they'd killed him, grabbed a few paintings and left.'

'So Bernard was collateral damage?'

'It's just a hunch.'

'I see the logic in what you're saying,' said Tracey. 'I'll run some checks on Russell when I get back to the station.' She took a long pull on her cigarette and made a passable attempt at blowing a smoke ring.

'It's probably me just being irrational.'

Tracey shook her head. 'No, don't say that. I've been in the job long enough to respect a copper's instincts. It'll cost me nothing to check.' She looked up at the clouds and sighed. 'That's him, isn't it? Top-floor window, off to the right.'

Lulu glanced at the top floor of the house. There was a dark shadow at the side of the corner window. 'That's their bedroom, yes.'

'He's been watching us for the last few minutes.'

Lulu chuckled. 'He obviously doesn't want to talk to you,' she said. 'Whatever happened in the study, there's no faking that black eye and it must still hurt, so I can understand him wanting a little peace and quiet.'

'How long have you known him?' said Tracey, turning back to the woods.

'For as long as I've known Julia, going on thirty-five years. They were married when I met her.'

'Is he a scientist too?'

'No, he was an antiques dealer. Antiques and paintings. He used to run a shop in Portobello Road. I met him through Julia and ended up buying several paintings from him. But business wasn't great and the shop closed. It was pretty awful: they had debt collectors banging on their doors at all hours and they lost their house. Anyway, Bernard decided to start again in Oxford. He got a job teaching art at a college and eventually opened up another antiques shop. Julia left the Met and was planning to look for work as a SOCO in Thames Valley but she joined a small research company as a stopgap and really enjoyed it. She ended up running the company and started researching ways of producing vaccines and after a few years hit the jackpot. They've made a lot of money already and there's more to come once the company goes public.'

'So it won't have been an insurance job, a fake robbery so that they could claim off the insurance?'

'If that was the case, they would have taken the more valuable paintings, surely?' said Lulu. 'And if it was a set-up, why the violence?' She shook her head. 'And they have so much money coming in at the moment that it wouldn't make any sense. They were definitely short of money when they first moved to Oxford, but those days are long gone.'

'Like you said, you have to consider every possibility. But yes, the more I look at it, the more it looks like a simple burglary that went wrong. Badly wrong.' She gestured at the search team. 'Right, they're getting to the edge of the woods. I'll have the vans driven around to the farm.'

'Will you be coming to the party this evening?'

'I'll try to make it.' She smiled. 'If nothing else it will

give me the opportunity to speak with Mr Grenville.' She took a last drag on her cigarette, blew smoke and flicked what was left of it to the ground. 'Right, I'll love you and leave you.'

11

The first guests started arriving at five o'clock. There were four valets – two men, two women, wearing black trousers, white shirts and red waistcoats with ornate powdered wigs – who quickly and efficiently relieved the partygoers of their vehicles and parked them on a lawn at the side of the house.

Guests were greeted at the door by a strapping six-footer in a footman's uniform, also sporting an ornate wig, who took their invitation. Once inside, the guests were welcomed with champagne and nibbles, served by a team of young men and women wearing black trousers, white shirts, black waistcoats and wigs. Lulu had laughed when she had first seen the wigs. 'Was this your idea or Bernard's?' she'd asked.

'Mine,' Julia had said. 'I went to a party once where I asked a very nice young man in a suit if he would bring me a glass of champagne. Turns out he was a Silicon Valley billionaire venture capitalist. It was funny but at the same time I wished the ground would swallow me up. With the wigs, there's no confusion between a guest and a waiter.'

Chairs and tables with exquisite flower arrangements were dotted around the terrace. On the lawn, close to the terrace, were small tents serving sushi, oysters and Moët & Chandon champagne and beyond them a large marquee had been erected.

Julia had spent the afternoon in a blaze of activity, organizing the setting up of the tables and the tents, checking the food and dealing with guests on the phone, most of them requiring last-minute directions. The caterers had taken over the kitchen, with six chefs busying themselves over the food, shouting at each other – and the waiters – in French.

Bernard came down from his bedroom at just after four-thirty. He had changed into white trousers, a pink silk shirt and a dark blue blazer. He had replaced the bandage with a plaster, most of which was covered by his hair, but there was no mistaking the dark green bruise around his eye. Julia insisted on dabbing some concealer on it and actually did quite a good job, but it was still visible to anyone who came close.

He and Julia spent the first hour in the hall, greeting guests and chit-chatting. Lulu took Conrad out to sit on the terrace, grabbing a corner table which gave them a view of the French windows and the gardens. Conrad curled up on the chair next to her. A young man with a wig came over with a tray of champagne and she took a glass. 'I have to say, you do look good in that wig,' she said.

He grinned, showing perfect white teeth that wouldn't have been out of place in a toothpaste advert. 'Thank you,' he said. 'It's starting to grow on me. Not literally, though.' He winked at her. 'Give me a wave when you want a refill.'

'I will,' said Lulu.

The waiter winked again and then headed off. Conrad opened one eye. Lulu sipped her champagne and looked out over the garden. The ensemble was getting ready to play and several of the musicians began tuning up.

'What are you doing, hiding out here?' said Julia, walking across the terrace. 'You should be mingling.' She had changed into a lovely long purple and white dress and had a string of pearls around her neck.

'I will, I'm just enjoying the day.'

Julia grabbed a glass of champagne from a passing waiter and sat down. 'I'm so glad you came.'

'I'm so glad you invited me.'

Julia nodded. 'I'm sorry we seem to have drifted apart. Oxford is only ninety minutes from London, but once we made the move we rarely went back.'

'Takes a lot longer on a narrowboat,' said Lulu. 'But yes, I should have made the effort.'

'Well, now we have this house, there's always a room for you.' She smiled down at Conrad. 'And for you, obviously, Conrad.'

'Meow,' said Conrad.

'I'll definitely be a more frequent visitor, Julia, I promise.' Lulu held out her glass and Julia clinked hers against it.

As they drank, Bernard came over, holding his own glass. 'Let me in on that,' he said, clinking his glass against Julia's and then Lulu's.

'Happy birthday, Bernard,' said Lulu. 'And many more of them.'

He pulled up a seat and sat down. 'If I have to explain to one more person how I got the black eye, I'll scream.'

'Just tell them I punched you,' said Julia. 'There'll be an embarrassed silence and they'll leave you alone.'

Bernard settled back in his chair and waved his glass at the musicians. 'I am so looking forward to this,' he said. 'They have this amazing flautist, the girl over there with the long black hair in the red dress. She's awesome. We saw them a couple of times last year.'

'I'm looking forward to hearing them,' said Lulu. 'So how's the head?'

'Oh, it's fine. I even skipped the painkillers so that I can enjoy the champagne. And the eye looks worse than it is.'

'You were lucky,' said Lulu.

'Well, if I'd been lucky I wouldn't have been hit in the first place,' he said. He looked over at the French windows and frowned. 'What the hell is she doing here?'

Julia and Lulu turned to see what he was looking at. Tracey had just stepped onto the terrace and was looking around. She was wearing her work suit and her hair was loose around her shoulders. The inspector's face broke into a smile when she saw Lulu and she waved.

'I invited her. Please don't give her a hard time,' said Julia out of the side of her mouth. She stood up and gestured for the inspector to come over. 'Tracey, wonderful that you came,' she said.

Tracey walked over, her heels clicking on the flagstones. Bernard got to his feet. 'I need to visit the bathroom before the recital starts,' he said. He nodded at Tracey. 'Nice to see you again, inspector.' He gave a polite smile and headed for the study.

'Happy birthday!' said Tracey, but Bernard either didn't hear or he ignored her.

'This looks amazing,' said Tracey, looking out over the gardens.

'You've taken off your glasses,' said Lulu.

'Contacts,' said the inspector. 'I never wear them when I'm working, I had an unfortunate experience a few years ago. I lost one while I was chasing a suspect and I ended up running with one eye closed and I fell over a dog. It's a long story, but ever since I've worn glasses on the job.' She sat down and looked around. 'Oh, wow, an orchestra? You really have pulled out all the stops.'

'We have an opera singer coming later; it's a surprise for my husband so mum's the word.'

'Oh, I love opera.'

Julia raised her hand to attract the attention of a waitress, who came over and offered her tray. Tracey took a glass and thanked her. 'Why the wigs?' she asked Julia as the waitress walked away.

Julia laughed. 'I was just telling Lulu, I once confused a very wealthy guest with a waiter and I swore that no one would ever make the same mistake at one of my parties.'

'What a good idea,' said Tracey. 'I went through a phase about ten years ago that whenever I walked into a WH Smith people would assume I was a manager.' She sipped her champagne and smacked her lips. 'Oh that is nice.'

'Did your husband come with you?' asked Julia.

'No, we couldn't get a sitter at such short notice so he's looking after our son.'

'Lovely,' said Julia. 'What does your husband do?'

'He's a freelance programmer, mainly involved with cyber security. He started working from home during the Covid lockdowns and actually loved it, so he's always at home now. Which works out well, childcare-wise. He would have loved this.' She spotted the sushi station. 'And he adores sushi. He'll be so jealous.'

'You must take some home with you,' said Julia. 'The kitchen is full of it.'

'Brilliant, I will, thank you.'

'And I printed out the details of the paintings that were

stolen. They're in the study. I'll give them to you before I go.'

'Thank you so much.'

Julia finished her champagne and stood up. 'Right, I need to press some flesh. The party is for Bernard's birthday but there are lots of investors here and I need to keep them happy.'

'Busy, busy, busy,' said Lulu.

'And you need to mingle, too,' said Julia, wagging a finger at her.

'I will, I will.'

Julia walked down the steps to the lawn and headed over to a group of middle-aged men in sharp suits.

'She's a very smart lady,' said Tracey.

'She is,' agreed Lulu. 'And a hard worker. It's great that she's finally reaping the rewards.'

'How is Bernard today? I get the feeling that he couldn't get away from me fast enough. It looked as if he didn't want to talk to me.'

Lulu wrinkled her nose. 'It's his birthday. And you're a reminder of what happened. I guess he's trying to put it behind him.'

'I understand, but I still have some questions for him. He can't avoid me for ever.' She sipped her champagne and sighed. 'Oh this is really lovely. I'm starting to regret bringing my car.'

'You can always Uber it back home.'

Tracey laughed. 'That might well happen,' she said.

'And you have a son?'

'Yes, Archie. He's six. I had him between leaving university and joining the police.'

'You haven't made it easier for yourself, have you?'

Tracey chuckled. 'Archie wasn't planned. The idea was

to get started on my career and then have kids, but what is it they say? God laughs when we make plans? Anyway, I wouldn't have it any other way. And my husband is a huge help.'

'Even so, SIO on a murder case is twenty-four-seven.'

'Tell me about it.' She paused for a few seconds. 'So, I ran a check on Billy Russell. Nothing to report. A few speeding tickets over the years, but that's it. An upstanding citizen. His wife, too. Widow, I should say.'

'Did Mrs Russell know if her husband had any enemies?' asked Lulu.

'She didn't mention anyone,' said Tracey. 'You still think they broke into the house to kill Mr Russell?'

Lulu sighed. 'I don't know, maybe I'm overthinking it. But when you see the list of paintings that were stolen, you'll see that they weren't particularly valuable. I mean, they had value, but there were some very expensive paintings in the hallway that were left behind. And at least one painting in the study that was left behind was worth six figures.'

'Like we said before, maybe they panicked.'

'Yes. Maybe. But they took a painting worth a few thousand pounds and left behind one that cost two hundred thousand dollars and has probably gone up a lot in value since. It seems to me as if they weren't that knowledgeable about the art market. And if they weren't professional art thieves, what were they doing breaking in?'

Tracey nodded thoughtfully. 'You talk a lot of sense.'

'I just think that it might be worthwhile talking to Mrs Russell. This might not have been the first attack on her husband, or he might have been threatened in the past.' She flashed the inspector a tight smile. 'I'm sorry, I sound like

I'm second-guessing you and I always hated it when people did that to me.'

'No, I value your input. To be honest, I'm still not making any progress. We found dozens of tyre prints over at Featherdown Farm, but they have a sideline selling sacks of potatoes to the public, so there are people coming and going all day.'

'But you said the farmer lives alone. How does he sell potatoes if he's out in the fields every day?'

'He runs an honesty-box system. You take what you want and leave the money in the box. The end result is that vehicles are in and out all day, so I doubt the tyre tracks will help.'

The ensemble began to play. The flautist had taken centre stage, her long black hair swaying as she played. Julia and the men in suits had turned to listen, and other guests were gathering in front of the marquee. A group came through the French windows and hurried across the terrace and down to the lawn.

'Do you want to get a closer look?' asked Lulu.

'Frankly, I'm happy to be sitting down,' said Tracey. 'I've been on my feet all day.'

Bernard appeared in the French windows. He was holding a glass of champagne but there was a faraway look in his eyes, as if he wasn't sure what he was doing. He shuffled forward and stopped, swaying softly. Lulu frowned. He didn't look well. Tracey sensed that something was wrong and she twisted around in her seat. 'Is he still annoyed that I'm here?' she said.

'No, he looks ill.'

Bernard took another two shuffling steps onto the

terrace, then the glass fell from his hand and smashed on the flagstones.

Conrad leaped up in his chair and turned to see where the noise had come from. Lulu got to her feet. 'Something's wrong.'

A bloody froth appeared from between Bernard's lips, dribbling down his pink shirt, then his legs folded underneath him and he stumbled backwards through the French windows. Several guests on the terrace screamed as Bernard fell back into the study and hit the floor.

Tracey jumped up and ran towards him. Lulu followed.

The ensemble continued to play as Lulu and Tracey reached Bernard. His mouth was moving and there was a look of panic in his eyes. 'What's wrong with him?' asked one of the waiters.

'Can everyone please stand well back!' Tracey shouted. 'Give him some air.'

Bernard's chest was in spasm and he was breathing in short, sharp gasps. Pink foam sprayed from his mouth with each breath.

Lulu knelt down, grabbed Bernard's hand and held it tightly. 'Bernard, can you hear me?'

There was no answer but he looked pleadingly at her.

Tracey looked around. 'Can someone please call 999 and ask for an ambulance?' she said. A dozen shocked faces stared down at her. 'Now!' she shouted. Several of the guests took out their phones.

'Now can everyone please move back!' Tracey shouted. 'Unless you're a doctor.'

'I'm a doctor,' said a grey-haired man with gold-rimmed spectacles. He pushed through the crowd.

'So am I,' said an Asian woman in a black dress carrying a Chanel handbag.

They stood facing each other and the man nodded. 'Paediatrics,' he said.

'I'm Bernard's GP, but I did five years in A&E,' said the woman. The man waved for her to go ahead. 'Can you look after this?' she said, passing him her handbag. As he took it, Tracey moved out of the way and the woman knelt down beside Bernard. She put her hand to his throat, feeling for a pulse. The woman put her face closer to Bernard's. 'Bernard, it's Sita. Can you hear me?'

Lulu let go of Bernard's hand and stood up. Some of the guests had moved away, but there were still a dozen or so people crowded around, trying to see what was happening. One of the waitresses had taken out her phone and was videoing what was happening. 'Put that phone away now!' said Lulu, her eyes hardening. The waitress did as she was told and backed away.

Lulu moved through the crowd, heading towards the steps. Down on the lawn, the chefs had stopped serving sushi and oysters and the two servers at the champagne bar were staring open-mouthed towards the terrace.

Lulu reached the top of the steps. The ensemble was still playing but most of the audience were looking up at the house, obviously wondering what had caused the disturbance. One of the suited men said something to Julia and she nodded and smiled, but then she locked eyes with Lulu and the smile froze. Lulu was biting down on her lower lip, close to tears. All she could do was to wave for Julia to join her. Julia swallowed, and put her hand up to her mouth, then hurried over the grass towards the steps. She rushed up to the terrace and grabbed Lulu's arm. 'What's happened?' she said. 'Tell me.'

'It's Bernard. The doctor's with him now. He's had some sort of attack.'

Julia turned and then saw the crowd of guests around the French windows. 'Oh no,' she said. She let go of Lulu's arm and ran towards the crowd. Lulu followed her.

'Let me through, let me through,' gasped Julia. She moaned when she saw Bernard lying on the floor, his chin covered with bloody saliva. 'Darling, no!'

She knelt down by his side and took his hand. 'What's wrong with him, Sita?' she asked.

The doctor shook her head. 'I don't know. We've called 999 and there's an ambulance on the way. His pulse is weak and slowing, and he's having trouble breathing. It's as if he's having some sort of seizure, but that wouldn't explain the blood in his mouth.' She put her face close to Bernard's. 'Bernard, can you hear me?' Bernard didn't react. She looked up at the other doctor, who was clutching her bag to his chest. 'Am I missing something?' she asked.

'Ruptured ulcer was my first thought,' he said. 'Or ebola, but he didn't mention having been to Africa. Maybe a lung problem?' He raised his hands helplessly. 'I'm sorry, I've never seen anything like this.'

'You have to do something!' Julia shouted.

Lulu's heart was pounding. Bernard's eyes were open but Lulu could see that they were blank and almost lifeless. Something cold gripped her heart and she gasped.

A pool of blood emerged from Bernard's right side. Julia noticed it first and she screamed. The doctor looked over and frowned when she saw the blood. 'Help me turn him on his side,' she said to Julia and together they moved him. The blazer made a sucking sound as it pulled away from the wooden floor. It was soaked in blood and so were the wooden floorboards.

'He's bleeding!' shouted Julia. 'Why's he bleeding?'

'Get me something – a towel or a cushion,' said Sita. She looked up at the guests standing over her. 'Give me something. Quickly.'

Julia was staring at Bernard, clasping his hand with both of hers, oblivious to what the doctor was saying.

The doctor looked up at the guests. 'I need something to stop the bleeding. Please. He's been stabbed.'

'Stabbed?' said Julia. 'What do you mean, stabbed? How can he have been stabbed?'

A middle-aged woman pulled off her cardigan and gave it to the doctor. 'Will this do?'

The doctor grabbed it without replying, rolled it up and pressed it against Bernard's back.

Lulu backed away, blinking away tears. There was nothing she could do and she didn't want to stand and watch.

Conrad was standing on the table on the terrace, his ears pricked up and his tail vertical, staring off into the distance. Lulu sat down and he turned and rubbed his head against her shoulder. 'I heard a motorcycle, driving away,' he whispered.

The ensemble had stopped playing now and most of the guests were walking towards the terrace. Tracey walked to the top of the stairs and held up her warrant card. 'Ladies and gentlemen, I am Inspector Tracey Calder of Thames Valley Police. There has been a medical emergency and the doctor is dealing with it. Could you all please stay on the lawn for the time being.'

The guests began talking among themselves. A young woman with a long blonde ponytail raised her hand. 'I'm an A&E nurse, can I help?'

'Please,' said Tracey, waving her up the stairs.

The nurse hurried towards the crowd, though Lulu doubted that there was much she could do. From the look of the blood on the floor, there wasn't much anybody could do. Lulu gently stroked Conrad's fur. 'This is terrible,' she whispered.

'I know,' said Conrad.

12

The ambulance arrived less than thirty minutes after the first 999 call but Bernard was already dead. The paramedics placed the body on a wheeled stretcher and took it away. Tracey had immediately imposed her authority and asked everyone on the terrace to move onto the grass and to stay there. She had asked for Lulu to make sure that no one tried to enter the study while she went inside to talk to the people in the house. The first police vehicle arrived a few minutes after the ambulance and Tracey stationed the two officers at the front door to ensure that no one left the house.

The doctor had taken Julia over to one of the tables on the terrace and sat down with her. Lulu stayed at her table with Conrad, not wanting to intrude.

Eventually a Mercedes Sprinter van with seven uniformed officers arrived and Tracey had them carry out a search of the house while everyone else was herded into the room with the piano. Then four detectives arrived in two Ford Mondeos. Tracey assigned two of them to collect names and contact details of everyone on the lawn, at which point they were told they were free to go. The other two began interviewing the people in the house.

Once most of the guests on the lawn had left, Lulu went to sit down next to Julia. The musicians had packed up their instruments and gone, and the tents offering sushi and oysters had shut up shop. There were still a dozen or so people standing in small groups on the lawn as if they weren't sure what to do.

Sita looked at her watch. 'I have to call my husband,' she said to Lulu. 'Can you stay with Julia?'

'Of course,' said Lulu.

Julia reached over and held Lulu's hand. 'Thank you,' she whispered.

Sita walked away, taking her phone from her handbag.

'Can I get you anything?' Lulu asked Julia. 'Water? Wine? Something stronger?'

Julia shook her head. 'You know what's crazy? I haven't smoked for more than twenty years and I want a cigarette.'

'Do you want me to get you one?'

Julia forced a smile. 'No. It's just . . .' She shook her head. 'I'm just so confused. It doesn't feel real. It's as if I'm in this horrible dream and at any moment I'm going to wake up.'

'You're in shock.'

'That's an understatement, if ever I heard one.' She lifted up Lulu's hand and gently kissed it. 'Thank you for being here. You're such a good friend. I'm so sorry we lost touch.'

'We didn't lose touch. Not really.'

Tears welled up in Julia's eyes. 'What am I going to do, Lulu?'

Lulu bit down on her lower lip. It wasn't a question she could answer.

Tracey stepped out of the study. She came over to the table and sat down opposite Julia. 'How are you?' asked the inspector.

'Not good,' said Julia.

'I'm so sorry for your loss, Julia. We're going to catch whoever did it, I promise you.'

'Where have they taken Bernard?' Julia asked.

'The mortuary. There'll have to be a post mortem, obviously.'

'I don't understand, how could he possibly have been stabbed?'

Tracey shifted uncomfortably in her chair. 'I'm sure you don't want the details,' she said quietly.

Julia leaned towards her. 'I was a SOCO, remember? I've seen more than my fair share of dead bodies. Giving me the details isn't going to change the way I feel. I'm his wife, I have the right to know.'

'Yes, yes, I know, I'm sorry. Of course.' Tracey took a deep breath. 'There were three or four stab wounds to the back. All quite small, so a very narrow knife was used. Probably three or four blows in quick succession; it would have been done in a matter of seconds. At least one of the blows punctured a lung, which is why he was having trouble breathing. Because the wounds were small, he would have bled out internally.' She looked pained. 'I'm so sorry.'

'So that's why he could walk from the study to the terrace,' said Lulu.

Tracey nodded. 'Depending on the internal damage, he could have been bleeding slowly. He had been to use the bathroom, so the attack could have happened anywhere between the bathroom and the terrace.'

'But wouldn't he have cried out?' said Lulu.

'Not necessarily. If the knife was sharp it might have just felt like he was pushed in the back. Then he'd be in shock. The blood would have drained from his head so he would have felt a bit woozy.' She grimaced. 'I'm sorry, Julia, you really don't want to hear this.'

'Oh, but I do,' said Julia earnestly. 'So he had the strength to walk to the terrace but then it all got too much for him and he collapsed. Once he was lying down the blood would flow out through the wounds.'

'There really wasn't anything that anybody could have done,' Tracey said. 'He'd lost too much blood.'

Lulu reached over and squeezed Julia's hand. Julia squeezed back.

'So the killer must have been in the house, there's no question of that,' said Tracey. 'We're keeping everyone who was in the house or at the front of the house for questioning. Obviously the people who were on the terrace or in the garden aren't suspects, so we've taken their names and addresses and they are free to go. I have our people going through all the rooms to make sure that there is no one hiding. There are a lot of rooms.'

'So you think the killer is still here?'

'I'm assuming so,' said Tracey. 'There are about forty people inside. There are the chefs in the kitchen, plus waiting staff, plus the valet parking people and about twenty guests. I'll have a full list shortly. We'll question everybody and examine their hands and clothing.'

'And there's no sign of the murder weapon?' asked Lulu.

'No. There are a lot of knives in the kitchen, obviously, and we've bagged them. Really, it's now a matter of questioning everybody and seeing who vouches for who. There are four detectives here already and two more are on the way. We're stopping everyone in the house from leaving, but to be honest so far everyone seems more than happy to help.'

'We heard a motorcycle,' said Lulu. 'Driving away while the doctor was working on Bernard.'

Tracey frowned. 'We?'

'Conrad and I. Well, his ears stood up so I assumed he heard something. It was a motorbike driving away.'

'No one mentioned it. I'll check on that.'

'So what do we do?' asked Julia.

'What would you like to do?' asked Tracey. 'We'll be here for a while yet, a couple of hours at least.'

'I don't know,' said Julia. She put her head in her hands. 'I just don't know.'

Lulu stood up and put her arm around her. 'Do you want to stay here tonight, or do you want to sleep somewhere else? You're welcome to stay on *The Lark* with me.'

'No, no, I can stay here.' She looked up at Lulu, her eyes wet with tears. 'Will you stay with me?'

'Of course I will. Conrad will, too. We'll stay as long as you want.' Lulu nodded at the French windows. That part of the terrace had been cordoned off with police tape. 'So we're back to it being a crime scene again?' she said to Tracey.

Tracey nodded. 'I'm afraid so. SOCO are backed up today so it'll be an hour or so before they're here. We're trying to keep everyone at the far side of the house, away from where we think it happened.' She leaned towards Julia. 'Julia, I know the last thing you want right now is to answer questions, but there are some things I have to ask – I'm sure you realize that.'

Julia nodded. 'I know. And no, Bernard didn't have any enemies, certainly not anyone who would want to kill him.'

'He didn't mention having problems with anyone? Had anyone threatened him?'

'No. Nothing like that.'

'No problems with the neighbours? Boundary disputes? Local tradesmen?'

'We've had problems with decorators and builders, but I handled most of that and they weren't disputes, just the normal snagging you get on any project.'

'No threats of legal action, no one suing you? Or are you suing anyone?'

'No.'

'And at work? Obviously the IPO involves a lot of money; is anybody losing out?'

'Everyone is making money. And even if they weren't, we're drug manufacturers, not drug dealers. We don't go about killing our competition.'

'And Bernard wasn't worried about anything? Anything at all?'

'He was fine. We both were. We were excited about the party, and excited about the way things are going with the business. A couple of years of hard work and then we were going to sit back and enjoy life.' Tears ran down her cheeks and she wiped them away with her hands. Tracey took a pack of tissues from her bag and gave one to Julia. She took it and dabbed at her tears.

Tracey nodded sympathetically. 'The thing is, this obviously wasn't random. Or if it was, it's an amazing coincidence that it was his birthday and it happened just two days after he was robbed. But I really don't believe in coincidences, not in cases like this. So whoever killed your husband knew him and had a reason. A motive. It was planned.'

Julia sniffed. 'I guess so.'

'So there's every possibility that whoever killed him was on the guest list. Do you have a copy?'

'It's on my computer.' She gestured at the French windows with her tissue. 'In the study.'

'Okay, I'd prefer to wait until SOCO have been through, just in case. Can you think of anyone on the guest list, anyone at all, who might have wanted to hurt Bernard?'

'No, of course not.' She dabbed her eyes again. 'Why would I invite somebody who wished him harm? The party was for friends and investors. We knew every single person.'

'Isn't it more likely that it was one of the waiters or cooks?' asked Lulu. 'Someone from the outside?'

'Possibly, yes. But then it comes down to motive, doesn't it? To go to all that trouble, it has to have been planned, which can only mean that whoever it was must really have hated Bernard. How could that happen without Julia or Bernard being aware of it?'

Julia shook her head and sniffed. 'I don't know. I just don't know.' She dabbed at her eyes again. 'I'm going to go to my bedroom. I need to lie down.'

'Do you want me to get the doctor to prescribe something to help you sleep?' asked Lulu.

'I don't want to sleep,' said Julia. 'If I sleep and I wake up then I'll have to go through it all again, realizing he's dead. I don't want that.'

Lulu patted her on the shoulder. 'I'll come up with you.'

'It's okay. You stay with the inspector.' Julia got to her feet but then she seemed to lose her balance and swayed precariously.

Lulu reached out and held her. 'I'll take you upstairs,' she said sternly.

'Okay, thank you,' said Julia. She looked at Tracey and tried to smile. 'I'm sorry about this.'

'You have nothing to apologize for,' said the inspector, getting to her feet. 'We can talk more whenever you're ready.'

Julia nodded and turned towards the French windows, but Lulu held her back. 'We can't go that way, it's a crime scene, remember?'

'I'm sorry,' said Julia.

'And stop saying sorry – as Tracey said, you haven't done anything to apologize for,' said Lulu. She linked her arm through Julia's and walked her towards the steps. Conrad jumped off his chair and followed them, his tail sticking up like an antenna.

They went down the steps and walked across the lawn. Two of the men in suits who had been watching the ensemble with Julia came over, their faces serious. 'We're so sorry, Julia,' said the older of the two. He had steel-grey hair and a sharp Hugo Boss suit. 'We're going to head back to London, but if you need anything, absolutely anything, don't hesitate to call.'

'Thank you, Giles.'

The younger man, with swept-back black hair, wearing a pale blue suit with white trainers, reached out and gently touched her arm. 'We're here for you, Julia. We'll talk soon.'

Julia smiled and nodded and Lulu walked with her around the side of the house. Conrad trotted along behind them. 'They seem nice,' said Lulu.

'They're just protecting their investment,' said Julia. 'They have a large stake in the company and if anything damages the IPO they'll lose money.'

'They sounded genuine.'

'You can never tell with the money men.' She sighed. 'I'm sure they meant it. But at the end of the day, it's just words, isn't it?'

A uniformed constable in a high-vis vest held up his hand

as they approached the front door. 'I'm sorry, no one is allowed in at the moment,' he said.

'This is Mrs Grenville, it was her husband who was killed,' said Lulu. 'Inspector Calder said it was okay for her to go to her bedroom.'

'Okay, that's fine.' As he stepped to the side, he noticed Conrad. 'Oh, is he with you?'

'Yes, he is,' said Lulu. They crossed the threshold. There were two more uniformed constables standing under the chandelier, deep in conversation. Lulu took Julia up the staircase on the left and Conrad followed.

As they reached the top of the stairs, two more uniformed constables came down the hall on the left. One of them opened his mouth to speak but Lulu beat him to it. 'Inspector Calder said Mrs Grenville could use her bedroom.' The two constables moved to the side to let them by.

Lulu and Julia walked arm in arm to the bedroom. Lulu opened the door and took Julia over to the bed. Julia rolled onto the covers and took the top pillow. She held it to her chest and buried her face in it.

Conrad jumped onto the bed and curled up at Julia's feet. Lulu sat down on the edge of the bed and stroked Julia's shoulder. 'Are you sure you don't want something to drink?'

'No, I'm fine,' said Julia. She rolled onto her back, still clutching the pillow to her chest. 'Do you think they'll catch whoever did it?' she said.

'Almost certainly. It's just a matter of time.'

'I hope so.'

'More often than not a victim knows their killer. I think the figure is close to eighty per cent, and the majority of killers are related to the victims. Only one in five murders is a stranger on stranger killing. That's why the inspector was asking so many questions.'

'She doesn't think it was me, surely?'

'Of course not. You were listening to the ensemble when Bernard was attacked. Lots of people saw you there. But there's a very good chance that you know who the killer is.'

Julia shook her head. 'I don't believe that, Lulu. I really don't.' She turned onto her side, holding the pillow tightly. 'I hurt so much, inside.'

'Just take it minute by minute, Julia. Minute by minute, hour by hour.'

'I don't think I can,' she whispered. 'I'm not strong enough.'

'You have to be strong, for Bernard,' said Lulu quietly. 'That's what he'd want. He wouldn't want this to wreck your life.'

'But that's what's happened. My life is wrecked. The life I had, the life I thought I had, it's gone.'

'You still have your memories. He'll always be in your heart, that's never going to go.'

Julia began to cry softly and Lulu rubbed her arm. She knew there was nothing she could say that would make her friend feel any better. She had to deal with it herself. Lulu could show that she cared, that she empathized, but at the end of the day you had to deal with the death of a loved one yourself, no one could bear the pain for you. Lulu had lost both her parents and her husband, so she knew how hard it was to deal with grief. In fact, she hadn't been able to deal with it; she had simply allowed it to run its course.

Lulu sat with Julia until the sobbing gradually stopped and was replaced with slow, even breathing.

'You want to talk to the inspector, don't you?' said Conrad.

'I don't think Julia should be alone at the moment.'

'She's not alone. I'm here.'

Lulu smiled. 'Yes, you are.'

'She needs to sleep. I'll watch over her. You go and talk to the inspector.'

'You are one very smart cat.'

'It has been said.'

13

As Lulu walked down the stairs she saw Tracey talking to a bearded man in a leather jacket. By the time Lulu reached the bottom of the stairs the man had gone out of the front door. Tracey smiled at Lulu.

'Is Julia okay?'

'She's asleep.'

'Probably best for her, but I would like that guest list this evening. Is there any way you can get it for me?'

'It's on her computer and I'm pretty sure it'll be password protected. But I can check.'

'SOCO are in there at the moment, so let's wait until they've finished.'

'How's the investigation going?'

'Slowly but surely. And you were right about the motorbike. The chap I was just talking to was in charge of the car valets. He remembers a motorcycle leaving at about the time Bernard was killed. He says he thinks it was a man driving but isn't sure. He thinks it was a Triumph, an old bike anyway. And whoever was driving was wearing a full-face helmet.'

'I would have thought the valets would remember a bike arriving.'

'They remember some. But unlike the cars, the bikers parked themselves. Also some of the waiting staff arrived on bikes and they got here before the valets.'

'Well, I suppose that's good news. If we know the killer rode away on his – or her – bike, then everyone still here isn't a suspect. A simple process of elimination.'

'I hope so,' said the inspector. 'Providing we have an up-to-date guest list and a list of everyone who was working here, we can work out who left. But we don't know for sure it was the killer. It could just have been someone heading off early. What we're doing at the moment is interviewing everyone with a view to ascertaining who was where and who they were with at the time. Once we've interviewed everybody we should be able to spot someone who doesn't have an alibi.'

'Any idea how long it will take?'

'A few more hours. Most of the interviews are fairly straightforward because most people were in groups and so can vouch for each other.' She looked at her watch. 'I'm going to have to call Tim to let him know I'll be late.'

'Your husband?'

She nodded. 'Strictly speaking this wouldn't have been my call, but as I was here my governor has said I should run with it. Plus there's probably a connection with the robbery.'

'About that,' said Lulu. 'Can I show you something in the swimming pool? Well, not in the pool, but in the pool room.' She frowned. 'That sounds wrong, doesn't it? What do you call a room with a swimming pool in it?'

Tracey grinned. 'An extravagance, is what I'd call it. Sure. Lead the way.'

Lulu took Tracey down the corridor to the swimming pool. 'It is something, isn't it?' said Tracey. 'I had a look around earlier and this did make my jaw drop.'

'Julia quite likes the statues,' said Lulu.

'Maybe it's an acquired taste. I do like the ceiling. It's the sort of thing Michelangelo might have done if he'd painted swimming pools, back in the day.'

Lulu walked along the side of the pool to the loungers. 'It isn't the statues I wanted to show you, it's this.' She pointed at the stains on the lounger she was standing next to.

Tracey walked over and bent down to get a better look. 'Is that blood?'

'I don't know. I thought you could get SOCO to check.'

Tracey frowned as she straightened up. 'When did you spot this?'

'Yesterday, when Julia was showing me around.'

'But you didn't think to mention it?'

Lulu shrugged. 'I wasn't sure that it was relevant. The burglars were in the study, they didn't come here, did they? They broke in and then ran across the lawn.'

'Did you say anything to Julia?'

'I didn't. She was chattering on about something and I noticed the stains but then she asked me something and I forgot about it.'

'You forgot about it?'

'It really didn't seem important. In fact it's probably nothing, right? There's no way of knowing how long it's been there.'

'I'll get SOCO to look at it,' said Tracey. 'Did you see blood anywhere else?'

'I didn't notice any,' said Lulu. That was the truth. She hadn't seen any bloodstains at all; it had been Conrad who spotted them.

Tracey walked along the line of loungers. She stopped at the last one. 'There's another spot here.' Lulu joined her and looked at where she was pointing. There was a small spot, half the size of a penny, on the side of the lounger, a smear rather than a drop.

Tracey looked down at the floor and walked slowly along the side of the pool. She reached the boxy sofas and armchairs around the glass coffee table and inspected them all carefully. 'I don't see anything else,' she said eventually. She went over to the double louvred doors and pulled one of the handles. The doors were locked. 'Any idea what's behind here?'

'Julia said it was the pool cleaning system. Chemicals and stuff.'

Tracey looked around the pool and couldn't stop herself from grinning at the naked statues. 'Plenty of witnesses, anyway,' she said.

'If only they could talk,' said Lulu.

They both chuckled as they walked back along the pool and out into the hallway. 'I need to keep an eye on the interviews,' said Tracey as they headed for the main hall. 'But I really could do with that guest list before I leave tonight.'

'What time will that be?'

'I'm hoping to be done by ten,' said the inspector. 'Eleven at the latest. I don't want to be keeping people here past midnight.'

'I'll go up and stay with her,' said Lulu. 'I'll make sure we get the list for you, one way or another.'

14

Julia slept fitfully, but always clutching the pillow. From time to time she muttered in her sleep but neither Lulu nor Conrad could work out what she was saying. Lulu lay down on the far side of the bed and Conrad remained curled up at Julia's feet.

'Do you think she'll be okay?' asked Conrad.

'She's strong. But she and Bernard were together a long time.'

'They never had children?'

'I think they loved each other so much they didn't feel they needed children. Plus they were always short of money when they were younger.'

'Julia had a good job. She worked as a SOCO, you said.'

'Yes, but Bernard was never lucky with money. The shop in London never really made a lot of money, in fact sometimes Julia had to use her salary to keep it going. Then they moved to Oxford and again his business wasn't great. So it was a combination of the two things, I think.' She sat up and looked at him. 'You're thinking that she and I were similar in that way, were you? Neither of us having children.'

'I guess that might be one reason why you were such good friends. Friendships sometimes end when children arrive.'

'That's certainly true. And we've both lost our husbands.'

'That's why I was asking if you think she'll be okay. I know what you went through.'

'And you helped me, Conrad. I'll always be grateful for that.'

'Julia's going to need your help.'

Lulu nodded. 'I know.' She smiled. 'You don't have a feline friend who could step in, do you?'

'I'm sorry, I'm one of a kind.'

Lulu smiled. 'Yes, you are.'

'Bernard?' Julia mumbled, holding her pillow tighter. 'Bernard?' she repeated, louder this time, then she opened her eyes and rolled over. Her face fell when she saw Lulu. 'Oh,' she said quietly.

'Sorry, did I wake you?'

'No, I was just . . .' She smiled regretfully. 'I was dreaming about Bernard.'

'That'll happen a lot,' said Lulu.

'Part of me wants to follow him, Lulu. That's what scares me. Part of me wants to be with him.'

'You've got too much to do here, so you need to stop thinking like that,' said Lulu. 'Do you want some water?'

'You know what I'd really like? A cup of tea.'

'That sounds like an excellent idea,' said Lulu. 'Why don't you come downstairs with me? Maybe get a snack.'

'Just tea, I think,' said Julia.

'And Tracey would like the guest list for the party,' said Lulu. 'I'm assuming your computer is password protected?'

Julia nodded. 'I'll get it for her.' She sat up and rubbed her eyes, then smiled when she saw Conrad. 'Conrad was in my dream, too. He was following me, purring.'

'He does get everywhere,' said Lulu. She rolled off the bed and helped Julia to her feet. 'Do you want to change into something more comfortable?' she asked.

'That's a good idea. Come and help me choose something.'

She walked over to a set of double doors and pushed them open. Lulu laughed out loud when she saw the size of the dressing room. It was a good ten metres long with sliding door wardrobes to the right and floor-to-ceiling cupboards, shoe racks and display cases on the left. There were two dozen designer handbags on show, and twice as many pairs of shoes. At the far end was an open door leading on to a bathroom, and Lulu could see green-veined white marble and brass – or possibly gold – fittings. 'Oh, I love this,' said Lulu. She slid open one of the wardrobe doors. It was full of dresses and shirts. 'Where does Bernard keep his clothes?' She winced at the use of the present tense, but Julia didn't seem to notice.

'His dressing room is on the other side of the bedroom, and he has his own bathroom. No more arguments over who left the toilet seat up.' She smiled but Lulu could see the tears welling in her eyes. 'All those years we spent with tiny bathrooms and no wardrobe space; we promised ourselves that we were going to treat ourselves to the biggest dressing rooms and bathrooms we could find.'

'Well, you certainly kept that promise,' said Lulu.

Julia slid open another section of wardrobe and took out a pair of Versace jeans and a pale blue silk shirt. 'What about you, why don't you change?' Julia asked Lulu. 'I mean, you look lovely in that dress but the party's over. Grab yourself something more comfortable.'

While Julia slipped off her dress and put on the jeans and shirt, Lulu looked through the wardrobes. Most of the dresses clearly hadn't been worn. She found a knee-length wrap-around dress with a pretty floral print and changed into it.

Lulu bent down so that Conrad could jump onto her shoulders and then they all headed downstairs and went along the corridor to the study. Tracey was at the entrance, talking to a female SOCO. Julia and Lulu waited until the SOCO had walked away before approaching the inspector. 'How are you?' Tracey asked Julia.

Julia forced a smile. 'I slept a little,' she said.

'I'm really sorry about this, but it would be a big help if I could have a guest list tonight.'

'That's perfectly okay. I wanted to make some tea anyway.'

'Well SOCO have finished in the study, if you'd like to do me a printout, that would be great.' Tracey stepped to the side and gestured for them to go through.

Julia went in first and Lulu followed with Conrad on her shoulders. Julia looked over at the French windows and shuddered at the large bloodstain. Lulu put a hand on her shoulder and gave her a gentle squeeze. Julia looked as if she was about to cry, then she took a deep breath and steadied herself. 'Oh, these are the stolen paintings,' she said, picking up the list she had printed the day before.

Tracey flicked through the sheets as Julia sat down at her desk and switched on her computer.

'I never really understand this modern art stuff,' said Tracey. 'Just splashes of colour on canvas.'

'Abstract, they call it,' said Lulu. 'Sometimes they go for crazy prices, literally millions of pounds.'

'Now this I like,' said Tracey. She held up the painting of Bamburgh Castle. 'You can see right away what it is.'

'That was an anniversary present. Bernard bought it for Julia.'

Tracey read through the details. 'Two thousand pounds? Wow.'

'That's cheap compared with some of the paintings they have.'

Tracey flicked through to the next one. It was an abstract canvas, two feet square, and valued at twelve thousand pounds. 'I see what you mean,' she said. 'That's a lot of money for something my six-year-old could have painted.'

The printer kicked into life and Julia stood up.

'Thank you for these,' said Tracey, holding up the printouts of the paintings. 'It's just what we need. We'll run off copies and show them around.'

The printer stopped and Julia pulled out the sheets and checked that they were all there before taking them over to Tracey. The inspector was looking at the Bamburgh Castle painting again. 'Of all the paintings that were taken, that's the one I really want back,' said Julia. 'They're all insured, but that one is special.'

'Lulu said it was an anniversary present?'

Julia nodded. 'Bernard bought it back when we barely had two pennies to rub together.'

'It's very distinctive.' She smiled. 'It's easy to describe, whereas the others . . .' She held up one of the abstract paintings. 'I mean, what would you say? Red and green blobs with yellow streaks?'

Julia smiled. 'I see what you mean. But the experts know. If you show them that printout, they'd be able to say if they'd seen it before.' She gave the inspector the guest list. 'I hope this helps.'

'Oh, it will,' said Tracey. 'We can immediately rule out everyone who was in the garden or on the terrace at the time Bernard was attacked. Then we can cross off those who were seen by others in the house, alibiing each other. If we're lucky, that will leave us with the suspect.'

'Assuming he is on the list,' said Lulu. 'Or she, of course.

They could have come in passing themselves off as one of the waiting staff.'

'Yes, that had occurred to us,' said Tracey. 'We're taking photographs of all the staff who were officially here and we'll show them to the guests, see if we can get a description of anyone else, someone they saw who shouldn't have been there.' She tried a hopeful smile. 'It's a long shot, but we'll give it a go. It would be so much easier if there was CCTV.'

'I was going to make some tea,' said Julia. 'Would you like some?'

'I would love some, but I've got to talk to my detectives. Can I join you in the kitchen in about half an hour?'

'What time do you finish?' asked Julia.

'Oh, I won't be off duty for a while,' said Tracey. 'This is me with my nose to the grindstone for the next week or so. We will catch whoever killed your husband, I promise.'

Lulu's heart lurched. It was never a good idea to make promises to victims. Tracey would do her absolute best, Lulu was sure of that, but sometimes even an officer's best wasn't enough and some crimes, even murders, went unsolved.

15

Julia opened the fridge door. 'Is wine a mistake?' she asked. 'What do you think?' She turned around to look at Lulu.

'I don't think wine is ever a mistake,' said Lulu. She was sitting at the island. Conrad was lying on the stool next to her.

'It's late, caffeine might not be good for me.'

'Wine is fine,' said Lulu. She smiled. 'I'm a poet, who knew?'

'I don't know what I'm supposed to be doing, Lulu. I'm supposed to be grieving but I'm just . . . I don't know . . . numb.'

'You're in shock,' said Lulu. 'Maybe tea would be better. Hot, sweet tea is good for shock.'

Julia closed the fridge door. 'Tea it is, then.'

Lulu slid off her stool. 'I'll make it,' she said. 'Why don't you sit in the conservatory?'

Julia nodded. 'Okay,' she said. She walked through to the conservatory. Conrad stood, stretched, jumped off the stool and followed her.

Lulu made two cups of tea. When she carried them into the conservatory, Conrad was lying in Julia's lap and she was stroking him. 'He's lovely, isn't he?' said Julia as Lulu put the cups on the coffee table and sat down next to her.

'He is,' said Lulu.

'It's as if he knows that I'm not happy and he's trying to comfort me.'

'Oh, I'm sure he does and he is. You should maybe eat something.'

'Perhaps later. I'm really not hungry at the moment.' She sipped her tea. 'Thanks for being here for me, Lulu. I really couldn't face being alone at the moment.'

'No problem. I'm more than happy to keep you company. But I'll have to move *The Lark* tomorrow.'

Julia frowned. 'I have no idea what that means.'

'My boat. I can only stay in one spot for forty-eight hours. So I'll have to move tomorrow. It won't take long – she only has to be moved a couple of hundred yards – and then I'll come back. Or you could come with me.'

'Maybe,' said Julia. She drank her tea. 'That might be fun.' She sighed. 'Oh Lulu, what am I going to do?'

'Like I said, just take it one day at a time.'

'A day feels like a lifetime.'

'Then you take it minute by minute. And you keep a tight hold on everything you have. Your memories. He's still there, in your mind. You can relive all the wonderful times you had.'

'They just make me miss him all the more. Knowing that there'll be no more new times. That it's all come to a crashing halt.' Tears were welling up in her eyes and she blinked them away. 'Why would anyone want to kill Bernard? Why?'

'I don't know, Julia.'

'He didn't have an enemy in the world. Everybody liked him. He'd help anybody, even more so after we got the money. All sorts of people came out of the woodwork asking for handouts and I don't think he ever said no. I was the one who would say that they were trying it on. Especially his relatives. There was a cousin he'd never seen before who phoned from Cambodia asking for money to pay for medical treatment. It was an obvious scam, and I told Bernard as much, but he still sent the money. That's the sort of man he was, you know? Generous to a fault.'

'Could it be someone he turned down?'

'Lulu, he didn't turn anyone down. He would always give them something. Maybe not all they wanted, but he would never turn anyone down flat.' She shook her head. 'And he didn't have any enemies. Not one.'

'What about the business? Could he have made any enemies there?'

'The company? No. He wasn't involved in the major decisions. I mean, we talked about everything, of course, but we had bankers advising us on the money side and he wasn't involved with the science side. He was more marketing and PR, pressing the flesh and keeping everyone happy.'

'What about before? When he had the galleries? Did he ever cross anybody?'

Julia chuckled. 'If he had done, maybe we wouldn't have lost so much money.' She shook her head. 'No, Bernard was as honest as the day was long. He never ripped anyone off. He always said that if you treat people right, they will treat you the same way. And you know how that worked out. And even if there was an argument over money, how would killing him help? No one profits from his death.' She saw the look that flashed across Lulu's face and she held up a hand. 'Yes, well, obviously I do, financially. Everything is in joint names so now it's all mine.'

'Julia, no one thinks that you had anything to do with Bernard's death.'

'Most murder victims know their killers, don't they? That's a fact.'

'Yes, it's a fact. But you were in the audience listening to the music when it happened. And even if you weren't, nobody in their right mind would think that you would want to harm Bernard.'

'I could have paid someone to do it.'

'Did you?'

'Of course not.'

'That's what I thought.'

Julia nodded tearfully. 'Maybe it was a mistake. Maybe whoever it was wanted to kill someone else and they killed Bernard by mistake.'

'That's possible,' said Lulu.

'Really?'

Lulu nodded. 'It's possible, Julia. Anything is possible. But it's not likely. Bernard is quite distinctive; I don't see that it could have been a case of mistaken identity. I suppose it might have been a totally random attack, but you would have to ask why someone would suddenly decide to kill somebody at a birthday party.'

'So it wasn't a mistake? Somebody came here to kill Bernard?'

'That's the most likely scenario, yes. But then you would have to ask why anyone would choose to kill him at his birthday party? Why not wait until he was on his own somewhere?'

'But if someone sought him out to kill him, they must have had a reason.'

'Yes, exactly. Most murders have a motive, very few are random. There's almost always a reason, though that reason might well be a twisted logic that wouldn't make sense to most people.'

'Psychopaths, you mean? You think a psychopath killed Bernard?'

'Psychotic or not, whoever killed Bernard had to have a reason. And the fact they used a knife means there was almost certainly a close connection. A knife is a very personal way of killing someone. You have to be right next to them.'

Julia shook her head. 'No one hated Bernard enough to hurt him like that.'

'Somebody must have,' said Lulu quietly.

'Meow!' said Conrad.

'He agrees with you,' said Julia.

'He's a very smart cat,' said Lulu. 'The thing is, somebody must have had a reason for wanting Bernard dead. A motive.'

'I suppose you studied motives when you were a detective?'

'Not so much studied, but I learned. I was a bag carrier for a homicide detective by the name of Adrian Tanner. Inspector Adrian Tanner. They called him Lemon.'

'Lemon?' Julia frowned.

Lulu grinned. 'Adrian to Ade, for short. Then Lemonade. Then Lemon. Cops like nicknames.'

'What about you?'

Lulu's grin widened. 'Most people assumed that Lulu was a nickname.'

'And what did you mean, bag carrier? What's a bag carrier?'

'Did you never come across the phrase when you worked forensics? You know that every murder investigation has an SIO, a senior investigating officer. Well, everything the SIO does, everywhere he goes and every decision he makes has to be recorded in what they call the Book 194. Well, I say he, these days it's just as likely that the SIO will be a she. Like Tracey. She's obviously the SIO. Somewhere there'll be a bag carrier, whose job it is to fill in the 194 every day. The SIO and the bag carrier sign and date every page. The 194 is also called the key decision log, and bag carriers are sometimes referred to as scribes. Lemon used to call me Tonto.'

'And he was the Lone Ranger?'

'Exactly. Some SIOs keep their bag carriers on a long leash, but Lemon always wanted me close by. Partly to bounce his ideas off, partly to make sure he always had a cigarette when he wanted one. I was his bag carrier for almost a year and I learned a lot. One of the things he taught me was the top ten of murder motives, and I've never forgotten it.'

Conrad curled up next to Julia and kept his eyes open.

'So number one in his chart was sex. Or love. Lemon regarded them as interchangeable. Husband kills wife, lover kills husband, wife kills lover, any combination of the eternal triangle. Probably a third of all murders are down to sex, and the perpetrators almost always get caught within hours.'

'I know I wasn't having an affair,' said Julia. 'And I'm damn sure Bernard wasn't. We were together all the time. Well, not all the time, obviously, but we weren't apart long enough for him to have an affair.'

'Number two was greed. Money. Killing for material gain. From a robber killing a passer-by for his wallet to someone killing their business partner.'

'The only person who benefits financially from Bernard's death is me,' said Julia. 'I told you that. Everything we have is in joint names.'

'And no one at the company is better off because Bernard is dead? No one gets a bigger share?'

'No, everything stays the same except that I'll get Bernard's shares and dividends.'

'Then at number three we have revenge. The killer kills to get back at someone who did something wrong to them. Sometimes even a perceived slight is enough to set someone off.'

'Bernard never hurt anyone,' said Julia. 'He could be sarcastic, sure, but in a funny way. And he'd never hurt anyone physically. What's number four?'

'To hide a secret,' said Lulu. 'The victim knows something damaging about the killer, or maybe has been blackmailing him. The killer knows that the secret dies along with the victim.'

Julia shook her head. 'Bernard couldn't keep a secret,' she said. 'He told me everything. And vice versa. Really, we had no secrets from each other.'

'Well, if it was a big enough secret, maybe he wouldn't tell you.'

'But why would he blackmail anyone? We have more than enough money already, with more coming.'

'That's true,' said Lulu.

'If he did know someone had done something illegal, he'd go straight to the police. And for sure he would have told me.'

'Well, those are the top four,' said Lulu. 'The rest are much less common.'

'Top four what?' asked Tracey. The inspector was standing in the kitchen, holding her notebook.

'Lulu was just telling me the top ten reasons for killing somebody,' said Julia.

'Oh well, this I must hear,' said Tracey. She walked into the conservatory and sat down in an armchair.

'Would you like a cup of tea?' Julia asked.

'No, I'm good,' said Tracey. 'But I'd love a water.'

'I'll get it,' said Lulu. She went into the kitchen and took two bottles of Evian from the fridge, and collected a glass and a bowl. She gave the glass and one of the bottles to the inspector and poured water into the bowl for Conrad. He jumped off the sofa and began to lap quietly.

'So, how far along the top ten are we?' Tracey asked as Lulu sat down.

'Four,' said Lulu. 'Sex, greed, revenge and to keep a secret.'

'My goodness, yes, I can't argue with that,' said the inspector. 'They would probably account for as many as three-quarters of all murders. So number five?'

'Hatred,' said Lulu. 'Racist killings, homophobic killings, where someone kills because they hate the type of person, rather than the individual. It's often hard to catch a killer like that because there's no connection between them and the victim.'

'I don't think Bernard was killed because he was a middle-aged white male,' said Tracey.

'Agreed,' said Lulu. 'At number six we have a crime of passion. An argument develops, someone loses their temper and lashes out and someone dies.'

The inspector nodded. 'That does happen,' she said. 'People see fights on the TV and in films and they think you can punch someone in the face without consequences. They don't realize that you can quite easily kill someone with one punch, especially if they hit their head on the ground. They'll probably get manslaughter rather than murder, but a killing is a killing.'

'Well, we know that no one lost their temper with Bernard,' said Lulu. 'And he was stabbed in the back. Crimes of passion tend to be face to face.'

'And number seven?'

'To protect someone you love,' said Lulu. 'Killing someone you think might hurt your family. So you get your defence in first. Usually you know right away who the killer is but it can sometimes be difficult to prove. But we know that Bernard wasn't threatening to hurt anyone, he isn't the type.' She grimaced at the use of the present tense again, but didn't correct herself.

'Number eight is also about family, but in this case it's out of a sense of trying to help. Husbands killing their wives because they have an incurable illness, wives killing their husbands because they figure that a pillow over the face is better than months dying of dementia. Often they turn out to be murder suicides – they go together. They're always very sad cases and it's hard to blame them, it really is. My mother-in-law had dementia and I never, ever, thought of ending her life, but I could see how someone could think that it might in some way be the kind thing to do.'

'And nine?' said Tracey.

'Number nine is status. Someone kills a colleague so they can get his job, or kills someone who has a title they want. They think that by killing the person, they move up in the world. We had a case where an old man killed a chap who worked on a neighbouring allotment and whose vegetables were always bigger. Hit him over the head with a spade. Mind you, he was probably a number ten as well.'

'Which is?' said Julia.

'Number ten. Nutters. All killings are bad but these are often the worst. There's often no reason for the killings, other than the voices told them to do it.'

'To be fair, nutters are usually the easiest to catch,' said Tracey. 'There's usually no planning and they tend to just stand by the body waiting for someone to tell them what to do.' She sipped her water. 'One thing I'm sure of: whoever killed poor Bernard wasn't a nutter. It was well planned and they covered their tracks well.'

'How's the investigation going?' asked Lulu.

'We're still in the process of taking photographs of all the valet parking staff and the waiting staff, then we'll show those pictures to all the guests and see if they remember seeing anyone who isn't in the pictures.' She saw the look that passed across Lulu's face and she held up a hand. 'I know, I know, it's a long shot.'

'People rarely look at the person who's handing them a drink,' said Lulu. 'Unless he or she is exceptionally pretty. But yes, I vividly remember the young man who gave me champagne, so I'd know if his picture was there or not.'

'We've also done a lot of cross-referencing among the guests,' said Tracey. 'Most of them in the house and outside were in groups of three or more, which means anyone in a group has an alibi. So far we have three who were alone and don't have anyone to vouch for them.' She took out her notebook and flicked through it. 'There's a Faith Hooper – she says she was upstairs at the time Bernard was killed.'

'Upstairs?' said Julia. 'What was she doing upstairs?'

'Well, at first she said she was looking for a bathroom, but of course it was pointed out to her that there are five bathrooms on the ground floor. Then she changed her story and said she was just snooping around.'

'Snooping?' repeated Lulu.

'She said she wanted to look around. She said it was a beautiful house and she was just seeing what it looked like upstairs. The thing is, no one remembers seeing her go up. And no one remembers seeing her come down.' She looked at Julia. 'How well do you know her?'

'Oh, very well. She's been a friend for years. She used to run a market stall in Portobello Road close to where Bernard had his shop. We haven't seen so much of her since we moved to Oxford, but we're still close.' Her jaw dropped. 'Oh, you think Faith might have killed Bernard? Impossible. Out of the question.'

'Why are you so sure?'

'Faith's a vegan, she wouldn't hurt a fly. And where was her husband?'

'He was in the room with the piano. Half a dozen guests can vouch for him.'

'Faith is the sort of person who likes to snoop around,' said Julia. 'It's her character. She doesn't mean any harm. I can easily see her popping upstairs to check out the bathrooms.'

Tracey consulted her notebook. 'What about Mark Tomlinson?'

'Mark? He's one of our accountants,' said Julia. 'His partner is in Miami on business so he came on his own.'

'He claims to have been in the library. The door was open but no one remembers seeing him there.'

'Mark is a bibliophile. He collects first editions. I said he could have look around to see if there was anything that took his fancy. The books came with the house and I have no idea what there is.'

'And would he have any reason to want to hurt your husband?'

Julia shrugged. 'I can't think of anything. Mark's a lovely guy. I've never seen him lose his temper or even raise his voice.'

'As your accountant he'd have access to all the company's financial records. Is it possible there are some irregularities that he might have found or wanted to conceal?'

Julia grimaced. 'I'd say that was highly unlikely,' she said. 'The bankers have been through our books with a fine-tooth comb, several times. They'd have spotted anything untoward. And Mark is a junior member of the team.'

'But he would have known Bernard?'

'Oh yes, of course. There was certainly never any bad feeling between them.'

Tracey nodded and looked at her notebook again. 'And then we have Andrew Kingsley. He's a problem as he doesn't seem to know where he was at the time your husband was stabbed.'

'Ah, yes,' said Julia. 'Andrew is what we would call "on the spectrum".'

'Autistic?'

'Not full-blown autistic, but he has issues.'

'He works for you?'

'Yes, he's a fantastic technician. He's a real asset to the lab. He has an unfailing eye for detail that never flags. Say we are having a clinical trial and we need a thousand samples running. He'll do the thousand, and he'll do every run exactly the same. He's like an Energizer bunny. He just keeps on going. But that attention to detail tends to make him clumsy in social situations. He'll shake your hand but hold onto it for slightly too long. He'll make eye contact but then it'll turn into a stare. And conversations can quickly turn into interrogations. But he's a sweetheart, really.'

'He wasn't able to say with any certainty where he was.'

'That's typical of Andrew.'

'He says he remembers seeing half a dozen people, all of whom he named, but they don't recall seeing him.'

Julia smiled. 'People tend not to notice him. Unless they interact with him, that is. He doesn't have much of a presence unless he's in your face and then he's full on.'

'Could he be dangerous?' asked Tracey.

'Oh good Lord, no. He can be a bit intense, but that's because when he is focused on something or someone, that's all he thinks about. But he's as gentle as a lamb.'

Tracey closed her notebook. 'That's all we have so far. Though of course we don't know for sure that the killer is on the guest list.' She put the notebook into her pocket. 'So, we're getting ready to call it a night. I'm going to leave two officers here when we go.'

'There's no need for that, really,' said Julia. 'I don't need protection.'

'It's not just about protecting you,' said Tracey. 'It's about protecting the crime scene. We haven't found the murder weapon, which means that the killer might have hidden it somewhere in the house. We'll come back tomorrow and carry out a proper search.'

Julia nodded. 'Okay, I understand.'

'I'll stay with Julia tonight,' said Lulu.

Tracey nodded. 'Excellent.' She stood up. 'Okay, so we'll see ourselves out and there'll be a man at the front of the house and one at the rear.'

'Tell them they can use the bathrooms on the ground floor and to feel free to use the kitchen if they want to make themselves tea or coffee,' said Julia.

'I will,' said Tracey. 'That's very kind of you. I shall see you bright and early in the morning.' She smiled at Conrad. 'And I'll see you tomorrow, Conrad.'

'Meow,' he said.

16

Julia rolled over, hugged her pillow, and mumbled in her sleep. Lulu and Conrad were sitting on the sofa by the window. There was a full moon and Lulu was watching two rabbits playing on the lawn. 'Do you think she'll be okay?' asked Lulu as she turned to look at Julia.

'Her aura is strong,' said Conrad. 'There's some black, which is the grief, but it's only on the edges. Most of her aura is deep red: that means she has a strong warrior spirit. Deep red shows that a person is well grounded, they can overcome any obstacles thrown at them.'

'That's Julia, in a nutshell,' said Lulu. 'But didn't you once tell me that deep red was a sign of anger?'

'Dark red is a sign of anger. And blood red. But deep red is different. It's hard to explain.'

'No, I understand. Deep red, I suppose, is a vibrant red but dark red is blacker, I imagine.'

Conrad nodded. 'Yes, that's it. Exactly. You do understand. And there's silver in her aura, too, a sign of wealth coming her way. I saw silver in Bernard's aura, too.'

'What did you think of Bernard?'

'Of Bernard? Or his aura?'

'Well, both, I suppose.'

'She was the stronger of the two in the marriage,' said Conrad. 'He seemed a nice man, and they were obviously a good team. Bernard's aura was mainly green. Green can mean one of two things. It can mean that they have a kind and loving heart. Or it can mean that they are in love with someone who completes them.'

'Oh, well, that is definitely Bernard. They were the perfect couple and he really appreciated her, I know that. As for this house, that's really down to her.' Lulu sighed. 'I don't see how she can possibly continue to live here, do you?'

'It is a very big house.'

'It's huge. It was huge for two people, but for someone on her own?' Lulu frowned. 'But it's not just the size, is it? It's the memories. This was going to be their forever home and now that Bernard isn't here . . .' She left the sentence unfinished.

Conrad gently butted his head against her hip. 'That's why you moved onto *The Lark*. You didn't want to stay in your house after Simon passed away.'

Lulu gently stroked his soft fur. 'I know. I mean, the memories you have are all well and good, but everything you see and do in the house reminds you of what you've lost. I couldn't bear it. On *The Lark* I still have the memories but I don't keep expecting to see Simon.' She smiled. 'I guess everyone handles it differently. Me, I preferred a new start.'

'With me?'

Lulu laughed. 'Yes. With you.'

'Lulu? Who are you talking to?'

Julia had turned over and opened her eyes, still clutching the pillow. Lulu smiled at her. 'I was just talking to Conrad.' She stood up. 'I do that all the time.' She walked over to the bed and sat down on the edge.

'I heard voices.'

'It was just me,' said Lulu. 'And the occasional meow from Conrad.'

'You're lucky to have him: you always have company.'

'I am very lucky,' said Lulu.

Conrad jumped off the sofa, padded across the floor and onto the bed. He walked over the duvet to Julia and licked Julia's arm. 'Oh my God, he's kissing me,' said Julia.

'He likes you,' said Lulu.

Julia stroked Conrad behind the ears and he purred and pushed his head against her hand. 'He is adorable.' She moved to the side so that there was enough room for Lulu to lie down. 'Thank you so much for being here,' said Julia. 'Both of you.'

'Meow,' said Conrad.

'You're welcome,' said Lulu. 'But there's nowhere I'd rather be.' She lay down and put her arm around Julia.

Julia sighed. 'How did you know I wanted a hug?' she said, closing her eyes.

'I just knew,' whispered Lulu.

17

Lulu hadn't drawn the curtains so she woke at dawn as the first rays of the sun lit up the room. Julia was still asleep, hugging her pillow, and Conrad's eyes were closed. She walked through the dressing room into Julia's bathroom and ran the taps to fill the roll-top bath. She added Lush bath foam and another bomb, this one red and white and smelling of roses.

She spent half an hour in the bath, enjoying every second, then she dried herself and chose a pair of Diesel jeans and a blue linen shirt from Julia's extensive wardrobe. When she went back into the bedroom, Julia was sitting up, propped up with three pillows, checking her phone. Conrad was curled up next to her, apparently still asleep.

'Before social media, what did we do when someone died?' Julia sighed.

'We wrote letters, usually,' said Lulu, sitting on the bed. Conrad opened his eyes and stretched. 'Or rang the doorbell.'

'Now it's sad emojis and hearts. Or public tweets, mostly from people I don't know.'

'I suppose it's easy,' said Lulu. 'Easier than sending flowers or writing a letter.'

'I wonder if they're doing it for me or doing it for themselves,' said Julia.

'Either way, it shows that they care.'

'I suppose so.' She smiled. 'Oh, I do like those jeans on you.'

Lulu stood up and gave her a twirl.

'You have to keep them,' said Julia. 'And the shirt. That's what I picture a bargee wearing.'

'A bargee?' Lulu laughed. 'I never thought of myself as a bargee, but I suppose if the cap fits . . .'

'Well the jeans certainly fit.' Julia tossed the phone onto the bed. 'Right, I'll hit the shower. I suppose the inspector will be here soon.'

'I'll get started on breakfast.'

'I'm not hungry.' Julia shook her head. 'Really, I couldn't eat anything.'

'I know that's how you feel, but you need to eat something. Just to keep your blood sugar up.'

'Now you sound like my doctor,' said Julia.

'I'll do some eggs and that wonderful smoked salmon that . . .' She grimaced as she realized she was going to mention Bernard. 'Sorry.'

'No, don't say sorry,' said Julia. 'I'll never be able to eat smoked salmon again without thinking about him.' She sighed and shook her head. 'Croissants,' she said.

'Croissants?'

'They're in the freezer. Fourteen minutes in the oven and they're good to go. I could probably manage a croissant.'

'Croissants it is,' said Lulu. She bent down so that Conrad could jump onto her shoulders, and headed for the kitchen. Once she got there he jumped onto the island to watch her work. She pre-heated the oven and took a pack of three frozen croissants from the freezer, then made a pot of tea. She was just putting the croissants into the oven when she heard the front doorbell ringing. She closed the oven door and hurried along the corridor to the main hall and opened the front door. It was Tracey, wearing a beige trench coat over a blue suit. Standing next to her was a good-looking man in his twenties, also wearing a blue suit. He had jet-black hair and wire-framed glasses. 'Good morning, Lulu. I said I'd be bright and early,' said Tracey. 'This is DC Collier.'

'Your bag carrier?'

'Indeed.'

'Pleasure to meet you, DC Collier.'

'Before you take offence, Dave, you should know that Lulu here was a detective superintendent with the Met for many years,' said Tracey.

'Good to meet you, ma'am,' said Collier.

Behind them were two Mercedes Sprinter vans disgorging young men and women wearing white forensic suits and blue shoe covers.

'So, we have eighteen cadets under the supervision of three experienced search officers,' said Tracey. 'They'll start in the study and work out from there, eventually covering every inch of the house. It should take the best part of four hours, so with any luck we'll be gone by lunchtime. Is Julia around?'

'She's taking a shower but she should be down in a few minutes. I'm just making tea. Do you want some?'

'Tea sounds good,' said Tracey.

'And I can offer you a croissant.'

Tracey grinned. 'This gets better and better.' She nodded at Collier. 'Keep an eye on them, Dave. Make sure they don't get lost.'

'No problem,' said the DC. He walked over to the vans.

'Is it me or are the policemen getting younger these days?' asked Lulu as she walked through the hall with Tracey.

'He's twenty-two, just out of university,' said Tracey. 'He has a degree in English and Philosophy.'

'Well, I suppose he can discuss the whys and wherefores of sixteenth-century poets as he's putting crims behind bars.'

Tracey laughed. 'I wish it was a joke, but he'll probably be a chief super by the time he's thirty.'

They reached the kitchen and Tracey sat at the island while Lulu finished making the tea. As she took the croissants out of the oven, Julia appeared in the doorway, wearing a baggy blue pullover over black leggings. 'Those smell good,' she said. 'Hi Tracey.'

'You said you weren't hungry,' said Lulu, using an oven glove to pop the steaming hot croissants on plates.

'I wasn't, but they do smell good.' Julia opened a cupboard and took out pots of strawberry jam, marmalade and honey, and put them on the island. 'So I saw your team heading for the study,' she said as she sat on a stool next to Tracey.

'Yes, I'm sorry about the inconvenience but they've been told to be careful and to keep the noise down.'

'No, it's fine,' said Julia. 'I just hope they find something.'

Tracey and Lulu tucked into their croissants but Julia only toyed with hers, though she did take a sip of tea. Conrad sat by the door, looking into the conservatory.

'So, that blood we found on the lounger in the pool room, it's Russell's,' said Tracey, between bites.

Julia frowned. 'What blood?'

'There were spots of blood on a lounger by the pool. Well, two loungers, as it happens.' The inspector looked over at Lulu. 'I'm sorry, I thought you'd told Julia.'

'Sorry, my bad, no.' Lulu smiled at Julia. 'I noticed a drop of blood on one of the loungers. Well, a smear rather than a drop. I didn't mention it at the time because I didn't really think anything of it, but when I was in the pool room with Tracey I pointed it out and she had it tested.'

Julia's frown deepened. 'How on earth did you see anything on the loungers? We didn't go near them.'

Lulu's mind went into overdrive. There was no way she could tell them that it had been Conrad who noticed the blood. She smiled. She hated having to lie but she really didn't have any choice. 'It was when you changed the lighting, I just noticed something. When I was back there with Tracey, I got a better look.' She looked across at the inspector. 'So the blood was Billy Russell's.'

Tracey nodded. 'Yes. There's no doubt.'

'But that doesn't make any sense, does it?'

'Not really, no.'

'Wait a minute,' said Julia. 'You're saying Russell's blood was on a lounger by the pool? That's just impossible. He didn't go anywhere near the pool.'

'I'm just telling you what the lab is saying,' said Tracey.

'Well, the lab is wrong. Labs make mistakes. I know they do; I've made mistakes in the past. We all have.'

'Well, this is DNA and the DNA says the odds of it not being his are six billion to one.'

'But it's impossible,' repeated Julia. 'Bernard saw him killed in the study. They've probably mixed up their samples. Russell's blood was all over the study.'

'I know, I know,' said Tracey. 'I'm getting more tests done. But the search team have been told to keep an eye out for any more blood spots or smears.' She finished her croissant and sipped her tea. 'That was delicious,' she said.

'So look, I'm going to head back to Oxford to review the interviews we did yesterday. I'll be back as the search team are finishing up.'

'Could you possibly give me a lift?' asked Lulu.

'Oh Lulu, you're not leaving me?' said Julia.

'I have to move *The Lark*,' said Lulu. 'She can only stay where she is for forty-eight hours.'

'So you'll get a parking ticket. So what?'

Lulu laughed. 'You don't want to get on the bad side of the Canal & River Trust.' She patted Julia's hand. 'I'll be a couple of hours and then I'll get an Uber straight back.' She nodded at the barely touched croissant. 'And finish that. Every crumb. Okay?'

Julia smiled and nodded. 'Yes ma'am.'

'I can drop you,' said Tracey. 'Where is your boat parked?'

'Jericho.'

'That's on the way to the station. Perfect.' She slid off the stool. 'Thanks, Julia, that was just what I needed. I rarely get the chance for breakfast.'

Lulu got off her stool and went over to Conrad. She knelt down and Conrad jumped effortlessly onto her shoulders.

'That is one neat trick,' said Tracey. 'Did it take long to learn?'

'I picked it up in a day or two,' said Lulu. 'Conrad is a very good teacher.'

Julia gave them a little wave but it was clear from the look on her face that she wasn't happy at being left alone.

'I won't be long, really,' said Lulu.

Julia nodded. 'Okay.'

Tracey and Lulu walked to the main hall and headed outside. Tracey unlocked the blue Ford Mondeo and climbed into the driver's seat. Lulu sat in the front passenger seat and Conrad slid down onto her lap.

'Do you think the searchers will find the weapon?' asked Lulu as they drove to the main gates.

'Hand on heart, probably not,' said the inspector. 'My gut feeling is that the killer got away, probably on that motor- cycle that you heard. And if he – or she – got away, then they probably took their knife with them.'

'Have they done the post mortem yet?'

'They're doing it this morning. We'll have a better idea of what sort of knife it was then. But we have to do a search anyway. Tick all the boxes.'

They drove through the gates and headed towards Oxford. 'Speaking of box ticking, did you ever talk to Billy Russell's bosses?'

Tracey wrinkled her nose. 'I didn't. Do you think I should?'

'If it was me, I'd like to know exactly why Billy Russell was at the house and who else knew he was there.'

'You still think the robbery is connected to Bernard's murder?'

Lulu stroked Conrad's fur. 'I do. I really do.' She sighed. 'What if the attackers thought they had killed Bernard and Billy Russell? Bernard was badly hurt, they might have thought that he was dead. Then when they discovered that in fact he was very much alive, maybe they went back to finish the job.'

'So the day of the robbery, they were there to kill Bernard and Billy?'

Lulu grimaced. 'It sounds crazy, doesn't it? I'm sorry.'

'Maybe it was meant to be a burglary but something went wrong and Bernard and Billy saw something that would identify them?'

'But Bernard said he didn't know who they were,' said Lulu. 'He was quite definite about that.'

'He was. But he was also pretty confused about the whole thing. And he was concussed, remember? So maybe he had seen or heard something but didn't know it. So the intruders decided to come back and kill him in case he did remember at some point in the future.' Tracey nodded. 'You're right. We need to go to talk to Billy Russell's boss. Do you want to come?'

Lulu smiled. 'I'd love to. Does that make me your bag carrier?'

Tracey smiled back. 'I guess it does.'

18

The company that Billy Russell worked for was based in a nondescript three-storey brick building on an industrial estate on the outskirts of Oxford. The only differences between the buildings were the signs above the doors and the type of vehicles parked outside. The building that Tracey parked in front of had a sign that said OXFORD INSURANCE SERVICES LTD and most of the cars were gleaming BMWs and Jaguars.

Tracey showed her warrant card to a red-headed receptionist wearing a headset and asked to speak to whoever was in charge. The receptionist smiled brightly and said that the managing director was Andrew Drummond but that he never saw people without an appointment. Tracey held the warrant card closer to the woman's face and asked her to give Mr Drummond a call and to tell him that a detective wanted to speak to him about the murder of one of his employees.

'Please take a seat,' said the receptionist, gesturing at a low sofa by the window.

'I'll stand,' said Tracey.

The receptionist looked at Lulu and her mouth opened in surprise when she saw Conrad on her shoulders. 'Oh, look at the cat. Oh, wow, he's lovely.'

'He is,' said Lulu.

'I'd be grateful if you would call Mr Drummond, now,' said Tracey.

'Right, yes, sorry,' said the receptionist. She tapped on her phone console, spoke to Drummond's secretary, then flashed Tracey a smile. 'Mr Drummond will see you,' she said. 'You can take the lifts or the stairs, it's only two floors up. His secretary will be waiting for you.'

'Thank you so much,' said Tracey. 'The stairs will be fine, I was never a great one for lifts.'

'If you could give me your names I'll prepare your visitor's badges.'

'That's okay,' said Tracey, waving her warrant card. 'I'm sure this will be fine.'

Lulu chuckled as they walked towards the stairs. 'You know, for one awful moment I thought you were going to say that we don't need no stinking badges.'

Tracey smiled and held up her right hand, her thumb and first finger almost touching. 'I was this close,' she said.

They laughed as they walked up the stairs. A young man in a grey suit was waiting for them. 'You're the detectives?' he asked. He was tall and had long, blond hair.

'I am,' said Tracey, producing her warrant card. 'Detective Inspector Tracey Calder, Thames Valley CID.'

'Please, follow me,' said the man.

He turned and walked gracefully down a grey-carpeted corridor. Tracey and Lulu followed. Lulu was grateful that the man hadn't asked her to produce any identification. She wasn't actually passing herself off as a police officer, but he had obviously assumed that Lulu was there in an official capacity, which made everything much easier.

Drummond's office was at the corner, giving him views of other buildings and their car parks from two sides. He was a big man, overweight with receding hair and a forehead beaded with sweat. His suit jacket was hanging on the back of an executive chair and he had his shirt sleeves rolled up. A pair of reading glasses was hanging from a chain around his neck. He didn't get up, just waved for them to sit on two chairs facing his desk.

The secretary left, closing the door behind him.

'So, I've a bone to pick with you people,' growled Drummond. 'Which of you is the boss?'

'That would be me,' said Tracey. 'Detective Inspector Tracey Calder.'

'Well, Detective Inspector Tracey Calder, you put me in a very difficult position. A very embarrassing position.'

'How so?' said Tracey.

Conrad jumped down from Lulu's shoulders and landed almost noiselessly on the floor. Drummond looked at Conrad and frowned. 'You brought a cat with you? Why would you bring a cat with you?'

'We're taking him to the RSPCA,' said Lulu. 'It's on our way.' Lulu had taken an instant dislike to Mr Drummond so had no qualms at all about lying to him.

Conrad sat down and looked at Drummond, his ears up and his tail twitching.

'I'm not sure I like the way he's looking at me,' said Drummond, folding his arms defensively.

'Oh, Conrad is fine,' said Lulu. 'He never has a bad word to say about anyone.'

'What?' said Drummond.

'Mr Drummond, you said you were in an embarrassing position?' said Tracey.

Drummond stared at Conrad for a couple of seconds, then he looked over at Tracey. He shook his head as if trying to clear his thoughts. 'I phoned Billy Russell when he didn't turn up for work. He didn't answer his mobile so I called his home and his wife answered. I asked her where Billy was and she burst into tears and told me what had happened. Can you imagine how stupid I felt? I didn't know that he'd died and she's crying her eyes out. I don't understand why your people didn't call me to tell me that he'd been killed.'

'Procedure is to inform next of kin,' said Tracey. 'And obviously that was done.'

'That might well be, but it caused me all sorts of problems. You need to talk to your bosses and get that fixed. I was put into a very embarrassing position; I didn't know what to say.'

'I'm very sorry to hear that,' said Tracey, but Lulu could tell from her tone that she wasn't in the least bit sorry. 'The thing is, we have a few questions to ask you about Mr Russell. If you don't mind.'

Drummond sat back in his chair. 'Go ahead.'

'Mr Russell had gone to see Mr Grenville about increasing his insurance coverage, is that correct?'

Drummond frowned. 'I hardly think so. It was his day off. Well, it was a sick day.'

'I'm sorry, what?'

Drummond sighed. 'He took the day off. He called in to say that he had a cold. Aren't you people supposed to know things like that?'

'Is it possible that Mr Russell was doing some extra work on his day off?' asked Tracey. 'Drumming up new business, perhaps?'

Mr Drummond wrinkled his nose. 'Not really. He does the absolute minimum.'

'He's lazy?'

'Not lazy as such, more that he does what he has to do. So he's never in before nine. Ever. He'll either be on time or a few minutes late, but he's never early. And he leaves at five on the dot, no matter what he's doing. He takes one hour for lunch, no matter the workload, and he takes his full number of sick days every year. Personally, I would have preferred to have let him go but these days you can't sack a person just because they've run out of steam.' He forced a smile. 'I should be using the past tense, shouldn't I? I still can't get used to the fact that he's dead.'

'So why do you think he went to see Mr Grenville?'

'I have absolutely no idea.'

'We were told that it was because Mr Grenville was looking to increase his insurance. He'd recently acquired some valuable paintings to add to his collection.'

Drummond held up a hand to silence her, put his glasses on, then leaned towards his computer and tapped on the keyboard. He peered at the screen. 'As I said, he called in sick that morning. There were six meetings and phone calls in his diary and all were cancelled or postponed. There's no meeting with a Mr Grenville.'

'So can anyone see the diary?' asked Tracey.

'Only managers, and myself. It allows us to keep track of where our people are.'

'And did Mr Russell call in sick or was it his wife?'

'He did. He said he thought he would be off for just one day. He did that quite a lot, but what can you do? You're not allowed to sack people just because they call in sick. Anyway, when he didn't turn up for work the following day, I phoned his wife.' He sat back in his chair and took off his glasses. 'You do realize that Mr Grenville wasn't a client, right?'

'No, I didn't know that,' said Tracey. 'It doesn't make sense, does it?'

'No, it doesn't. When we found out what had happened we assumed that Billy had been there on a social visit.'

'No, he was there to talk about insurance. At least, that's what we thought.'

'Well, as I said, Mr Grenville isn't a client.'

'Was he ever a client?' asked Lulu.

'Ah, now that I don't know, I've only been here three years,' said Mr Drummond. He turned towards his computer and tapped on his keyboard again. He put his glasses on and peered at the screen. 'Yes, he was. Actually we were his brokers for almost ten years. We insured his antiques shop.' He wagged his finger at the screen. 'Oh, I remember this now. I was working at a different company at the time but it was in all the papers.'

'What happened?' asked Tracey.

'There was a fire in the shop and a woman died. She was living in the flat above the shop.' He looked over the top of his glasses at Tracey. 'I'm sure the police would have been involved.'

'I don't remember it,' said Tracey. 'Was it arson?'

'No, it was an accident, as I recall. Let me see if the details are here.' He peered at the screen again. 'Yes, there was a workshop at the back of the retail area and they left a heater on all night. It caught fire and the shop was gutted. There was a woman sleeping in the flat above and she died from smoke inhalation. But the fire brigade investigators confirmed it was an accident and the company paid out in full. Just over a million pounds.'

'That's a lot of money,' said Lulu.

'The shop was pretty much destroyed and all the stock was reduced to ashes. We had a full inventory and there had been a full valuation a few months earlier so it was a very straightforward settlement. Mr Grenville had a cheque within the month.'

'Mr Drummond, who at your company handled the paperwork?' asked Lulu.

Mr Drummond wrinkled his nose and scrolled through the spreadsheet on his screen. Eventually he smiled. 'Well, well, well. The claims adjuster was William Russell,' he said. 'Billy. What are the odds of that?'

19

'What do you think that means, William Russell being the claims adjuster for the fire that destroyed Bernard's shop?' asked Lulu. They were in Tracey's Mondeo, heading for Thames Valley Police Headquarters. It was in Kidlington, four miles north of where Lulu had parked *The Lark*, but Lulu really wanted to see what the police officer who had investigated the fire had to say, and Tracey had agreed to take her and Conrad, who was sitting in Lulu's lap.

'Well, clearly they knew each other, which Bernard didn't mention.'

'To be fair, I didn't hear you ask the question.'

'Why would I? He definitely led us to believe that Russell was there to discuss his insurance requirements, and that was clearly a lie.'

'Not necessarily,' said Lulu.

'How can you say that? You heard what Drummond said. Russell called in sick so that he could go and see Bernard. It clearly wasn't a business visit.'

'Well, yes, but maybe Bernard didn't know that. He might well have believed that Russell was there to talk about insurance.'

Tracey nodded. 'Okay, yes, I'll buy that.' She accelerated past a petrol tanker at well above the speed limit. 'So what was Russell up to?'

'I suppose he might have been trying to do a deal on

his own. Maybe sell a policy outside the company? Trying to make some money on the side.' She sighed. 'Except Drummond was very clear that Russell was lazy and did the absolute minimum.' She frowned. 'I suppose he might have been planning to sell Bernard a fake policy and pocket the cash himself. No, that wouldn't make sense. I'm starting to overthink it.' She grimaced. 'I'm getting a very bad feeling about this,' she said.

'In what way?' asked Tracey.

'I'm starting to think that Bernard might have been lying. But why? Why wouldn't he tell us the real reason that Russell was in the house?'

'Maybe Russell was in on the robbery? He calls Bernard to arrange a meeting about insurance, but he turns up with two masked men.'

'But why do they kill him?' said Lulu.

'That might have been the plan from the start. With Russell dead, there's no way he could identify his co-conspirators.'

'That's so cold-blooded, though. And if the plan was to kill Russell from the start, how come they used the poker? They would have taken a weapon with them.'

Tracey nodded. 'I can see the flaws in the logic, yes.'

'Plus, at the end of the day they only took paintings valued at a few thousand pounds. It doesn't seem worth taking a life for that little money. If the haul had been worth millions, then maybe.' She shook her head. 'I don't understand it, I really don't.'

'Sometimes murders don't make sense,' said Tracey. 'Someone gets angry and logic flies out of the window. In fact, most murderers wouldn't go through with it if they considered the ramifications of what they're doing.'

She indicated that she was turning and drove the Mondeo into the police car park. The Thames Valley HQ was a three-storey building, brick at the bottom and the top two storeys consisting of white concrete and blue panels. It had the look of an IKEA outlet, Lulu decided. Tracey parked and took Lulu inside.

'I know that strictly speaking I shouldn't be doing this,' said Tracey. 'But it would be ridiculous to leave you in the car. And you were in the job.'

'I wouldn't want to get you into trouble, Tracey,' said Lulu.

'Frankly, I could do with your input,' said the inspector.

Tracey's office was on the second floor and they went there first so that she could check her computer for messages. Lulu and Conrad sat and waited. 'Ah, the post mortem results are here,' said Tracey eventually. 'Four wounds, all deep and all very narrow. The weapon was long and thin and very sharp.'

'Like an ice pick?'

'No, more like a knife but with a very narrow blade. Have a look for yourself.'

Lulu stood up and walked around the desk. Tracey had four colour photographs on her screen, each showing a wound. Bernard's pale white skin had been cleaned so that the cuts were clearly visible. 'According to the pathologist the blade was two centimetres across, not serrated, and was at least twenty centimetres long.'

'So a stiletto, perhaps?'

'Probably not a stiletto, the pathologist said the knife was slightly curved. The wounds don't match any of the knives in the kitchen. All four blows went in deep. One punctured his spleen, two went into his left kidney and the final blow went into his left lung. The attack could have been carried out in just a few seconds. The wounds, and the damage to his clothing, suggest that the knife was very, very sharp. Because the wounds were relatively small, most of the blood stayed in his body cavity as he bled out. The pathologist says it would be at least a minute before he bled out, possibly two or three.'

'Which is why he was able to walk through the study and out onto the terrace.' Lulu shuddered at the memory, then went back to sit down next to Conrad.

Tracey picked up her phone. 'I'll just check if Alistair Reese is ready for us,' she said. 'He was a uniform on the neighbourhood policing team at the time of the fire. He's a sergeant now and office based.' She tapped out a number, had a short conversation, then replaced the receiver and stood up. 'Okay, let's go.'

'Is it okay if Conrad comes with us?' asked Lulu.

'Of course. Though I am fairly sure that Alistair is a dog person.'

Lulu bent down so that Conrad could ride on her shoulders, then they walked along the corridor and down a flight of stairs to an open-plan office with a dozen or so workstations. Alistair Reese was sitting at two desks angled together, each with a computer screen. He grinned when he saw Tracey, and waved a greeting. He was in his thirties, tall and gangly with a neatly trimmed moustache. 'Long time no see, boss,' he said.

'Only because you never get to a crime scene these days,' she said.

'The wife likes the regular hours, and the fact that my phone doesn't ring all night.' He looked over at Lulu and frowned when he saw Conrad on her shoulders. 'Wow, that's not something you see every day,' he said.

'This is Lulu Lewis,' said Tracey. 'She was a detective superintendent in the Met and is – was – a friend of Bernard Grenville.'

Alistair nodded at her. 'Sorry for your loss,' he said. He smiled. 'I'm sorry, I can't help looking at your cat. I've never seen a cat sitting on a person like that before.'

'His name's Conrad,' said Lulu.

'He goes everywhere with you?'

'Pretty much, yes.'

'That's amazing. You can't do it with a dog, right?'

'I think cats have a better sense of balance,' said Lulu.

'I have seen dogs riding on motorbikes, but I guess that's a whole different skill set.' He realized that Tracey was looking at him expectantly and he raised his hands. 'Sorry, bit of a tangent, right?'

'Bit of,' said Tracey.

'My bad,' said Alistair. 'So, you were asking about the fire at Bernard Grenville's antiques shop. I actually remember it well: it was my first body. You never forget your first, right? Anyway, I attended because there was a body but it was obvious from the start that it was an accident. The fire had started in a back room, spread to the main shop, and the smoke killed a lady who was sleeping upstairs.'

'Anything suspicious about the fire?'

Alistair shook his head. 'Nothing at all. But there was a claims adjuster on the case who kept insisting it was arson. He was on the phone every day, asking if we had a suspect yet. He became a right pain in the arse.'

'Do you remember the claims adjuster's name?' asked Tracey.

'Willy, or Billy. I could check my notebook.'

'Would you?' said Tracey.

'Sure.'

Alistair stood up and went over to a metal filing cabinet. There were four drawers and he knelt down and opened the bottom one. He took out a stack of notebooks bound together with a thick rubber band, flicked through them and pulled one out. He sat down and turned the pages, then smiled and nodded. 'William Russell. That's right, I remember him now. He turned up at the station half a dozen times, acting as if it was his own money he was going to be handing over.'

'Why was he so convinced that it was arson?'

'That was the thing. He had no evidence at all. He just said he had a bad feeling about it. But the fire investigators were sure that it was an accident. All the fire damage was downstairs, but the upstairs was full of smoke. By the time I got there they'd opened all the windows and the smoke had gone. The woman was lying on the bed as if she was asleep. But she was dead.' He turned a page of his notebook. 'That's right, her name was Victoria McBride. She lived there with her husband and their son.'

'Were they killed as well?' asked Tracey.

'No, they had a lucky escape. They were all due to stay over at his parents', it was their wedding anniversary and there was a party planned. Victoria got a bad cold and couldn't go but she insisted that her husband and son went. She stayed in bed.'

'That's awful,' said Lulu.

'Yes, well it was, but it was also her fault, as it turned out,' said Alistair. 'Victoria worked in the shop under the flat. Well, actually in a workshop behind the shop. She repaired furniture and restored paintings. It was winter and it was cold and she'd left an electric fire on so that everything would dry out. According to the fire investigators there was flammable material close to the fire and it ignited. Obviously there was lots of wood and varnish and stuff so it burned quickly. The fire brigade were there almost immediately but it had taken hold and by the time they put it out Victoria had been killed by the smoke.'

'And definitely no foul play? It was the smoke that killed her?'

'Not a mark on her. and the pathologist said her lungs were full of smoke.'

'But Mr Russell was convinced it was arson?'

Alistair shrugged. 'He was convinced that the fire had been deliberately set, that someone had put flammable material near the fire. But what he said never made sense. Like I said, I think he just didn't want to pay out. You know what insurance companies are like. A few years ago I lost a few roof slates in a storm. The insurance paid for the repair, but when I got the renewal the following year it excluded storm damage to the roof. You can't win.'

'And the fire itself was definitely accidental?' asked Lulu.

'The investigators were thorough and I had to go by what they said. They're the experts, right? And there was nothing to suggest that it might have been an insurance scam. The policy had been in place for several years and the business was doing okay. I mean, it was ticking over, there were no massive debts or anything. And Mr Grenville was clearly shaken up by what had happened. It was just one of those things.' He closed the notebook and sat back in his chair. 'So if you don't mind me asking, what's your interest in the fire?'

'Mr Grenville was killed yesterday, at his birthday party.'

Alistair's jaw dropped. 'Oh my God.'

'He was stabbed, by person or persons unknown. We don't have any witnesses but we do have a guest list so we have our fingers crossed. But where it gets really interesting is that William Russell was killed two days earlier, at Grenville's house. By masked intruders who stole some paintings.'

Alistair's jaw dropped even further. 'So what do you think happened? They went back to finish what they started?'

'At the moment we have no idea if it's the same killers or not.'

'Well, if it isn't, it's one hell of a coincidence, no?'

'We don't have a workable theory at the moment,' said Tracey. 'We're still gathering evidence.'

'But Mr Grenville was there when Mr Russell was killed?'

Tracey nodded. 'Yes, absolutely.'

'So he probably saw or heard something and when they realized he was still alive, they went back.'

'That did occur to us, but if they had wanted to kill him they had all the time in the world the first time.'

'They had guns?'

Tracey shook her head. 'They used a poker.'

'So it was opportunistic?' Alistair scratched his chin. 'And the second time?'

'A knife. We're searching the house for it as we speak, though of course the killer might have taken it with them.'

'That's one hell of a case, Tracey. I'd love to know how it works out.'

'You and me both, Alistair.'

20

Tracey apologized for not having the time to run Lulu and Conrad back to *The Lark*, she simply had too much work to do. She showed them out of the building and waited for their Uber to arrive, before heading back inside.

The Uber dropped them a short walk from where *The Lark* was moored. Lulu unlocked the doors, then started the engine to charge up the batteries while she made herself a cup of tea.

She was taking her first sip when she heard a woman calling from the rear deck. 'Hello? Hello there?'

Lulu went up the steps and out onto the deck, still holding her mug. Conrad followed. A grey-haired woman in a baggy Shetland pullover with a floppy camouflage-pattern hat was standing on the towpath. 'I'm sorry to bother you, but are you leaving?' she said. She had a West Country accent, Lulu realized, Bristol maybe.

'I'm about to, yes.'

'Could you do me a huge favour and let us have your spot? My husband is with our boat about fifteen minutes away. He sent me ahead to find a mooring and you can see it's chock-a-block at the moment.'

Lulu looked around. There were no free moorings and several boats were moving slowly, clearly looking for some-where to tie up. 'I don't see why not,' she said. She looked at her watch. 'Fifteen minutes, you say?'

'At the most. So it's okay?'

'Yes, go ahead. I'll finish my tea – just give me a shout when he's here.'

'Thank you so much,' said the woman, taking her mobile phone from her pocket. 'You're an angel.'

Lulu went back into the boat and Conrad followed. 'Would you like some water?' Lulu asked Conrad.

'I'm okay,' said Conrad. He jumped onto the sofa and looked at her, his head tilted to the side. 'This is all very strange, isn't it?'

'The robbery and the murder? Very strange.'

'They have to be connected, don't they?'

Lulu sat down next to him. 'I think they have to be. I know coincidences happen, but for Bernard to be attacked twice . . .' She shook her head. 'And what a horrible way to die.'

'Billy Russell, too. Beaten to death with a poker. That has to be personal, right? It takes a lot of anger to smash in someone's skull.'

Lulu nodded. 'Anger or hatred, yes. It takes a lot to stab someone four times or to keep hitting them with a poker.'

'But it can't be the same person, can it?'

Lulu frowned. 'Why do you say that?'

'Because the attacks are so different. When Billy Russell was killed, whoever did it grabbed a poker and hit him with it, then they dropped it, grabbed the paintings, and ran.'

'After hitting Bernard, too.'

'Yes. Exactly. With the same poker. It's like Alistair said, it was opportunistic. But whoever killed Bernard, had to have planned it because they brought the knife with them. That's a big difference.'

'It is, isn't it? But that doesn't mean that it's a different killer. It could be the same person but under different circumstances. They committed both murders but the first time it was opportunistic and then they went back with a plan.'

'But then if it was the same killer, why didn't they kill Bernard the first time?'

Lulu took a drink of her tea. 'Maybe they thought he was dead. There was a lot of blood, and he was out cold. If they didn't check for a pulse they might have assumed they'd killed him.'

Conrad nodded thoughtfully. 'So I guess the question is, was Bernard the intended target all the time? Maybe they turned up at the house, expecting to find Bernard on his own. They could have waited outside the gate until Julia left, then come in through the terrace. But instead of finding Bernard on his own, Billy Russell is there. They grab the poker, kill Billy Russell, then beat Bernard. They assume that Bernard is dead, they grab the paintings and run.'

'Why grab the paintings?'

'To make it seem like a robbery,' said Conrad. 'But it was never about a robbery, it was about killing Bernard. So when they realized that Bernard was still alive, they came back and stabbed him.'

'But according to Julia, Bernard didn't have any enemies.'

'Maybe he didn't tell her he was having a problem with someone.'

'I'm fairly sure that they had no secrets from each other.'

'Maybe he didn't want to worry her?'

'That's a good point,' said Lulu. She sipped her tea. 'So you think they used the poker the first time because they wanted to make it look as if it was a robbery?'

'That would make sense, wouldn't it? They wanted it to look opportunistic.'

Lulu nodded thoughtfully. 'That's interesting. I hadn't thought of that. Tracey hasn't either.'

'Sometimes cats have a different way of looking at things.'

'They certainly do, Conrad.' She took another sip of her tea. 'But that doesn't explain how William Russell's blood got onto the loungers in the pool room.'

'Julia said it must have been a mistake.'

'Mistakes do happen, that's true. But that's a serious mistake to make – to mix up samples like that. It's unlikely in the extreme. So if the blood is indeed Billy Russell's, how did it get there?'

'Hello! It's me again!' It was the West Country lady, back on the towpath.

Lulu went up onto the rear deck with her tea. 'Is everything okay?' she asked.

'My husband is five minutes away, if that's all right with you.'

Lulu looked at her watch. 'No problem, I'll be ready to go when he gets here.'

'Thank you so much.' She looked *The Lark* up and down. 'This is a lovely boat. Are you a liveaboard?'

'Yes, I am.'

'Just you?'

'Me and Conrad.'

'Your husband?'

Conrad ran up the steps and jumped up onto the back deck. 'This is Conrad,' said Lulu.

'Oh he's lovely. A real charmer.'

'Meow!' said Conrad.

'He says thank you.'

The woman laughed. 'I got that. Okay, so I'll walk down the towpath and bring my husband in. Five minutes?'

'I'll be ready,' said Lulu.

21

This time their Uber driver was called Ahmad and he had worked as a translator with the British Army in Afghanistan, escaping by the skin of his teeth with his wife and three children just before the Taliban closed Kabul airport. Ahmad was as amazed as Mohammed had been to discover that Hepworth House was a home and not a hotel and was equally appreciative of the white Bentley that was parked outside. 'How can I get as rich as this?' he asked as he brought his Prius to a stop.

'Buy lottery tickets,' said Lulu.

'I am a Muslim and cannot gamble,' said Ahmad. He sighed. 'Sometimes life is not fair.'

'That is certainly true,' said Lulu. She opened the door and held Conrad to her chest as she climbed out.

The car drove off and Lulu helped Conrad up onto her shoulders. The two Mercedes Sprinter vans were still there, but there was no sign of Tracey's Mondeo. Lulu rang the doorbell then stood back. 'I'm never sure how many times I should ring,' she said. 'I want to be sure that they hear me, but I don't want to sound pushy.'

'Twice is fine,' said Conrad. 'Three is too many and four is definitely rude.'

'Two it is,' said Lulu. She stepped back up to the door and pressed the bell again.

A full minute passed before the door opened. It was Julia

and her face broke into a broad smile when she saw Lulu. 'Thank goodness you're here,' she said. 'It's turned into a ridiculous game of hide and seek. They're opening every cupboard and pulling up the carpets.'

'They have to be thorough,' said Lulu. 'There's no point in half looking.'

'Well, at least they're done with the kitchen so we can have a cup of tea. Did you have lunch?'

'No, we moved *The Lark* and then came straight here.' That was the truth, strictly speaking, they had come straight from *The Lark*. But prior to that she had spoken to Mr Drummond and Alistair, and Lulu wasn't ready to discuss that with Julia. It was a lot to process.

Julia ushered them inside and closed the door. 'I had an M&S delivery while you were out,' she said as they walked to the kitchen. 'There's some really luscious cold cuts and some amazing cheeses. And a tiger bloomer that's to die for. It's Bernard's favourite . . .' She sighed. 'I have to stop doing that,' she said.

'No you don't,' said Lulu. 'It doesn't stop being his favourite just because he's not here. You need to remember the things he liked. Embrace them. I'll never be able to eat that gin-and-tonic smoked salmon without thinking of him. That's how it should be.'

Julia tried to smile. 'I suppose so.'

Lulu put an arm around her shoulder. 'Tiger bloomer sounds great.'

When they reached the kitchen, Conrad jumped down onto one of the stools around the island and Julia opened the fridge. She took out a pack of cold cuts, a pack of assorted cheeses and a bag of salad. 'Is it too early for wine?' she asked.

Lulu laughed. 'It's never too early for wine.'

'That's so true. I'll get a bottle. Or two.' She opened the white door and went down into the cellar.

'Do you think she's okay?' asked Conrad.

'As well as can be expected,' whispered Lulu.

'There's a lot of tension in her aura,' said Conrad.

'Well, you can understand why.'

'Meow,' said Conrad.

'Meow? That's all you've got to say? Meow?'

'Excuse me,' said a voice at the door. It was DC Collier, wearing a white forensic suit and blue shoe covers.

Lulu flashed him a smile, wondering how much he had heard. 'Sorry, Dave, I was talking to my cat, wasn't I?'

He grinned. 'That's okay, my mother does the same. She has two cats – Whisky and Soda – and they sit either side of her on the sofa, chatting away. It's as if they understand every word she says.'

'Meow!' said Conrad.

'Just like that!'

'I think they do understand,' said Lulu. 'Cats are very intelligent.'

'Meow!' said Conrad, and the detective laughed.

'Well he certainly agrees with you,' he said. He looked around the kitchen. 'I was actually looking for Mrs Grenville.'

'I'm here,' said Julia, emerging from the wine cellar with a bottle of wine in either hand. She showed the bottles to him. 'Would you like a glass?'

'I would love a glass, but I'm very much on duty,' he said. 'There are louvred doors in the swimming pool room and they're locked. Do you have the key?'

'Oh, there's nothing in there,' said Julia, putting one of

the bottles on the island. 'It's the filter for the pool and the chemicals that the pool guys use. It's always locked unless the pool guys are here and it's been a month since they were last here.'

'I understand,' said the detective, 'but my boss is a stickler for detail and when she says search everywhere she means everywhere.'

Julia put the second bottle of wine into the fridge, then opened one of the cabinets. On the back of the door were more than two dozen labelled keys hanging on hooks. She ran a hand across them, then pulled one out. 'Here you go,' she said, giving it to the detective.

'Thank you,' he said. 'I'll bring it right back.'

As he left the kitchen, Julia reached for a corkscrew and began opening the bottle. 'Can you get the glasses?' she asked.

Lulu took out two glasses and Julia was just about to start pouring when the doorbell rang.

'I'll get it,' said Lulu. She hurried out and along the hallway. She couldn't help but smile at what Conrad had said about the under butler having to fetch the butler to answer the door. It really was a huge house, and while she wasn't exactly out of breath by the time she reached the front door, it was certainly a fair walk. It was Tracey; Lulu took her through to the kitchen, where Julia was putting cold cuts onto a platter.

'Please tell me you're off duty and can have some Pinot Grigio,' said Julia.

'I wish that I could,' said Tracey. 'But no, I'm working.'

'Can I make you some tea or coffee?'

'Tea would be lovely,' said Tracey. 'I'm just here to check if the searchers have found anything.'

Julia switched on the kettle and picked up the teapot from the draining board. Tracey slid onto a stool and took a manila envelope from her handbag. 'I also wanted to run these by you,' she said. She opened the envelope and slid out a stack of cards, each about six inches by four. She laid them out on the island. There were eighteen in all and she placed four of them in a line at the top and two rows of seven underneath.

Julia walked over with the empty teapot and looked over Lulu's shoulder. 'These are the car valet people and the waiting staff,' said Tracey. She ran her finger along the four at the top, young men and women wearing red waistcoats and red bow ties. 'These are the ones who were parking the cars. They all vouch for each other, as does their boss. But that doesn't mean that our murderer couldn't have slipped into the house wearing a red waistcoat and bow tie and one of those wigs.'

'I was in the hall so I caught the odd glimpse of them but I wouldn't say I recognize any of them. And I certainly wouldn't remember anyone else passing themselves off as a valet.'

'Same with me,' said Lulu. 'I didn't go out front and when I was in the house, I didn't see a valet. And the wigs made it very difficult to tell them apart.'

'I think it's unlikely the killer tried to pass himself off as a valet, because anyone who saw them would wonder why they were inside the house,' said Tracey. 'What about the waiting staff?'

Lulu tapped one of the photographs, a young man with blond hair and a wide smile. 'He was on the terrace, I remember him,' she said. 'But of course it's not about who we recognize from the pictures, is it? We have to remember someone who isn't included here, right? And that's much harder.'

'Exactly,' said Tracey. 'What about you, Julia?'

Julia nodded. 'I remember seeing most of them, yes. But it's a lot harder to think of someone whose picture isn't there.' She frowned. 'The problem is, generally you don't look at the face of the person who's handing you a drink.' She pulled a face. 'Oh, that sounds awful, doesn't it? I mean, yes you smile and say thank you, but usually you don't actually look at them.'

'I know exactly what you mean,' said Tracey. 'I'm hoping that one of the guests might have seen someone acting strangely just before your husband died and that they might recall that he – or she – was dressed as a waiter and that their picture isn't here.' She grimaced. 'Even as I say that, I realize it's going to be unlikely in the extreme.' She gathered up the photographs and slid them back into the envelope. 'But we have to try.'

The kettle finished boiling and switched itself off. Julia went over and spooned tea into the pot. She was just pouring in the hot water when DC Collier appeared in the doorway. 'Ah, boss, you're here,' he said to Tracey. 'There's something you need to see.'

Tracey put the envelope into her handbag and slid off her stool. 'What have you got, Dave?'

'Best I show you, boss,' he said. 'And probably best if Mrs Grenville comes with us.'

'I'm intrigued,' said Tracey. DC Collier led the way, followed by Tracey and Julia. Lulu bent down so that Conrad could jump onto her shoulders and then she followed them down the hall.

DC Collier took them along to the pool. The door was open and half a dozen men and women in forensic suits were gathered inside. They fell silent when they saw Tracey and moved to the side.

DC Collier reached into his pocket and took out two packs of blue shoe covers. 'If you ladies wouldn't mind,' he said. He reached into his other pocket and pulled out a pack for Tracey.

The three women slipped on their shoe covers and then the detective constable took them along the side of the pool to the equipment room. The louvred doors were wide open to reveal a metal shelving unit filled with large plastic bottles and a square metal box with thick tubes running from it. There were four more policemen in forensic suits standing looking in, while a middle-aged man also wearing a forensic suit was taking photographs of the interior.

The policemen moved away as Tracey and DC Collier walked towards them. 'All right, Robbie, let the dog see the rabbit,' said DC Collier.

'Aye, no problem,' said the photographer in a broad Glaswegian accent. He nodded at Tracey. 'Inspector.'

Tracey returned the nod. 'Robbie,' she said. 'You know you've still got your lens cap on?'

She grinned as the man lifted up his camera to check. 'Made you look.'

Robbie chuckled as he moved to the side.

'So, this is what we found,' said DC Collier, moving inside the room and pointing at the rear of the metal box. 'We haven't touched them yet.'

Tracey craned her neck to see what he was pointing at. 'Oh my goodness me,' she said. 'That is not what I expected.'

'What?' said Julia, peering around the inspector. 'What is it?'

Tracey moved to let Julia get a better look. There were eight paintings lodged between the metal box and the concrete wall. 'That's impossible,' said Julia. She looked at Lulu, her face creased into a frown. 'That doesn't make any sense.'

DC Collier reached down and picked up one of the smaller paintings. Lulu recognized it immediately. It was the painting of Bamburgh Castle, the one that had been hanging behind Julia's desk. There were splashes of dried blood across one corner and smears across the gilt frame. DC Collier held it up so that Julia could get a better look. 'Mrs Grenville, could you confirm that this is one of the stolen paintings?'

Julia nodded. 'Yes,' she gasped.

DC Collier carefully leaned the painting against the wall and pulled out a second one. This one was bigger, almost three feet square, an abstract painting with blues and yellows. 'And this?'

Julia nodded again. 'Yes.'

Tracey blew air through pursed lips. 'Well, this is a turn-up for the books,' she said.

22

Julia sipped her wine, but the sip swiftly became a gulp. She was sitting in the conservatory on one of the sofas; Lulu was on the other sofa with Conrad on her lap, her glass of Pinot Grigio on the table in front of her. 'It doesn't make any sense,' she said.

'No, it doesn't,' said Tracey. She was standing looking out of the window at the lawn, holding a mug of tea.

'Do you think they panicked and decided to hide the paintings before leaving?' asked Julia.

Tracey shook her head. 'The doors were locked, you said. Always locked.'

'That's true. We only opened the doors when the pool men were here.'

Tracey turned around. DC Collier was standing at the kitchen door, still wearing his forensic suit.

'So how did the thieves get the paintings into the filter room?' said Tracey. 'They would have needed the key, right?'

Julia frowned. 'So they must have run to the kitchen and got the key.'

'You think so?' said Tracey. 'They get the key, hide the paintings, relock the doors and put the key back in the kitchen before running away?'

'That must have been what they did,' said Julia. 'They must have been planning to come back later.'

Lulu stroked Conrad. She could see how the conversation was going to go and she didn't want to make it even more difficult for Julia.

'But why would they do that, Mrs Grenville?' asked Tracey. She wasn't Julia any more. Now she was Mrs Grenville. And DC Collier was standing at the doorway for a reason. He wasn't taking notes but he was remembering everything that was being said.

'I suppose they didn't want to be seen running across the lawn with stolen paintings,' said Julia.

Tracey shook her head. 'Paintings or no paintings, they'd still be seen. But nobody did see them, and we've no evidence that they had a vehicle parked at the farm.'

'What are you suggesting?' said Julia. 'Do you think they were already in the house? Could they have come in with the cleaners?'

'The cleaning team were all women,' said Tracey. 'We've accounted for them all. And Bernard said the attackers were men, remember?'

'So tell me what you think happened?' Julia took another gulp of wine. Lulu saw that her hand was shaking.

'You know what I think happened,' said Tracey quietly. 'Only someone who knew where the key was kept could have hidden the paintings.'

'You mean me?'

Tracey shook her head. 'I mean Bernard.'

Julia laughed and it was the sound of an animal in pain. 'Now you're being ridiculous. They knocked Bernard out, remember? He was unconscious on the floor.'

'That's what he said, yes.'

'You think he lied?'

Tracey sipped her tea. 'You know we found blood on the loungers by the pool?'

'Yes, you said. Billy Russell's blood.' She frowned. 'So now you're suggesting that Billy Russell took the paintings to the filter room? That's even more stupid because Billy Russell was dead.'

'That's not what I'm suggesting.' She stared at Julia for several seconds. 'We had your husband's clothing checked. There was blood on his shirt and on his trousers.'

'Of course there was. He was hit on the head with a poker. He was covered in blood.'

Tracey shook her head. 'Some of it was his blood, yes. But a lot of it was Billy Russell's. There was Billy Russell's blood all over his clothing.'

Julia stood up. Her eyes were wide and staring. 'That's impossible!'

'No. Everything was checked and rechecked. Full DNA analysis. There's no doubt. Billy Russell's blood is all over your husband's clothing, and it was probably transferred to the loungers when he took the paintings to the pool room to hide them.'

Julia's breath was coming in short, sharp gasps and she was swaying on her feet. Her glass tumbled from her fingers and smashed onto the tiled floor, then her legs gave way and she fell sideways, crashing into the coffee table.

23

Tracey and Lulu watched from the doorway as the doctor sat on Julia's bed and gave her an injection in her arm. Conrad was sitting on the sofa by the window, watching as intently as they were. Lulu had phoned the doctor and she had arrived within twenty minutes, during which time Lulu and the inspector had managed to get Julia up the stairs and into her bedroom. Julia had only passed out for a few minutes, but when she woke up she was incoherent and clearly having trouble focusing. They had given her a drink of water, got her to her feet, and taken an arm each as they took her upstairs. Conrad had followed, giving them meows of encouragement. It had taken almost ten minutes to get Julia up the stairs and into bed. She had kept apologizing but was clearly struggling.

The doctor had introduced herself as Sita Patel. She was their local GP and a family friend. Sita had brought a large medical bag from her car and had checked Julia's blood pressure, breathing, and pricked her finger to get a blood sugar level. Julia was awake but clearly exhausted and answered Sita's questions in a whisper.

Once she had finished the injection, Sita put the used syringe in her bag, patted Julia on the shoulder and came over to Tracey and Lulu. 'She'll be fine,' she said. 'It's stress-related, obviously. Seeing Bernard beaten and then killed. Post-traumatic stress syndrome, plus I don't think she's eaten much.'

'I made breakfast, but she barely touched it,' said Lulu. 'And she collapsed before she had the chance to eat lunch.'

'Well, I've given her something to calm her down, and a vitamin shot, but she needs to eat. I could smell alcohol on her breath. Had she been drinking?'

'Just some wine,' said Lulu.

The doctor nodded. 'I know that at times like this a drink seems like a good idea, but really it isn't. Please discourage her from drinking.'

'I'll do my best,' said Lulu. 'But Julia has always enjoyed her wine.'

'I know,' said Sita. 'But alcohol won't react well to the medication I've given her, so she should abstain for a day or two at least.'

Julia began to snore softly.

'She'll sleep for a few hours, maybe the rest of the day. When she wakes up, make sure she eats something. Protein rather than carbs. As I said, no alcohol, and she should steer clear of caffeine.' She gave a Lulu a blister pack of tablets. 'I'm not a big fan of using anti-depressants to cope with grief, but in view of what's happened, give her one of these every twelve hours for a couple of days. And a multivitamin tablet or two wouldn't hurt.'

Lulu bent down so that Conrad could jump onto her shoulders, then she and Tracey took the doctor down the stairs. Lulu opened the front door. 'I'm sure she'll be fine, but if anything does happen, call me straight away,' said Sita. She smiled at Conrad, who was sitting comfortably on Lulu's shoulders. 'And it has been a pleasure making your acquaintance, Conrad.'

'Meow,' said Conrad.

'I love the way he does that,' said Sita. She went over to her Audi and climbed in. Tracey and Lulu stayed at the door to wave her off.

'Can we go and look at the study?' said Tracey.

Lulu nodded. 'Of course.' She closed the door and they walked along to the study, where Conrad immediately jumped down onto a sofa.

Bernard's blood was still on the floor; it had dried into two dinner-plate-sized circles, forming a figure of eight.

'I just want to talk this through with you,' said Tracey. 'So that I get it clear in my mind.'

Lulu nodded. 'Yes, it's getting confusing, isn't it?'

'So, the way Bernard told it, he was in the hallway with Billy Russell, looking at the paintings there.' She walked back into the corridor and Lulu followed her. Tracey went over to one of the larger abstract canvases and studied it. 'I still can't work out why these are so valuable,' she said. 'My kid could do better than this.' She smiled. 'Anyway, they go into the study. Bernard didn't say anything about hearing breaking glass, but when they enter the study they find two intruders standing there.' Lulu opened her mouth to speak but Tracey held up her hand to stop her. 'I know what you're going to say, but at this stage let's suspend our disbelief and take everything Bernard said as gospel. So they're in the study, facing two masked intruders. One of them picks up the poker, walks over to Russell and hits him, hard. Several times. Russell falls down, dead. Then they hit Bernard. Just once, and he falls down and hits his head on the coffee table. Now, we know he wasn't running away because he was hit on the front of his head.'

'Bernard wasn't in great shape,' said Lulu. 'He wouldn't have been able to run.'

'Plus he was in shock: he'd just seen a man killed in front of him. So he stands looking at them in horror, then bang, he's hit and he goes down. He's unconscious, so from that point on he has no way of knowing what happens. He told us that the men ran across the lawn, but of course that was an assumption: he couldn't have seen them leave. So now we put ourselves in the position of the intruders. They've killed two men – at least they think they have – but no one has seen or heard them and there's no CCTV in the house. They've got time to cover their tracks. That's when they decide to make it look like a robbery. That explains why the paintings they took weren't the most valuable. It was never about the money.'

She went to the French windows, taking care not to step on the dried blood. 'So they could have taken the paintings and run to their car, wherever that was. But instead they decide to hide the paintings in the pool room. But the door to the filter room was locked, so they needed the key.'

'The key was kept in a cupboard in the kitchen,' said Lulu.

'Right,' said Tracey. She walked out of the study. Lulu and Conrad hurried after her. 'Julia was out and the cleaners were upstairs, so no one saw them as they went to the kitchen,' said Tracey as they walked. 'One of them could have gone and the other one could have kept watch.' They reached the kitchen and Lulu opened the cupboard to reveal the keys. She took out the key labelled FILTER ROOM and gave it to Tracey. 'Okay, so they took the key and went back to the study to collect the paintings,' said the inspector.

'They could have brought the paintings with them.'

Tracey nodded. 'That makes sense. So they brought the paintings here, collected the key and went to the pool room. Let's go.'

She walked quickly to the pool room, with Lulu and Conrad following. Tracey checked her watch, and checked it again when she reached the door to the pool room. 'Just under three minutes,' she said. She opened the door and walked in, then headed over to the filter room, her heels clicking on the poolside tiles. She unlocked the louvred doors and opened them wide. 'They got here, hid the paintings behind the filter unit, relocked the doors, then left.' She looked at her watch again. 'So, three and a half minutes. They could well have left before Bernard regained consciousness.'

'If I'm suspending my disbelief, I suppose I can't ask why they hid the paintings rather than taking them with them?'

'I think the bigger question is how they knew to hide the paintings in the filter room, and how they knew where to find the key. Assuming that Bernard told the truth, they already knew the layout of the house and where the keys were kept. So who would have had that knowledge?'

'Bernard and Julia, obviously. And presumably the people who work for the pool maintenance company.'

'Exactly,' said Tracey. 'So the way to prove that Bernard's story is true is to talk to the pool maintenance company, find out who there knew about the key and what they were doing at the time that Bernard was attacked.'

'And if we draw a blank, we know that he was lying?'

Tracey nodded. 'Then we can stop suspending our disbelief. And we can start looking at the possibility that it was Bernard who brought the paintings here.'

'But how do we find out which company maintained the pool?'

Tracey grinned and picked up one of the large bottles and pointed at the label. Printed across the bottom was the name and address of a local firm.

Lulu smiled. 'Well, you are definitely a detective,' she said.

24

The pool maintenance company was based in a barn conversion on the outskirts of a small village some five miles south-east of Oxford. There was a large sign proclaiming 'PERFECT POOLS' at the entrance to the driveway and there were three small pools to the right and two large hot tubs. Tracey parked her Mondeo between a white Porsche and a black Range Rover and headed to the main entrance with Lulu. Conrad was on Lulu's shoulders, purring softly.

Tracey pressed a bell and a few moments later a bearded man in jeans and a denim shirt opened the door. He smiled, showing unnaturally white teeth. 'Hello there, how can I help you?'

Tracey flashed her warrant card and the smile hardened a little. 'I hope this isn't about that job in Fritford.'

'Fritford?' repeated Tracey.

'Gerry Taylor, I put in an indoor pool that he's not happy with and he keeps telling me he plays golf with the chief constable.'

'I can assure you the chief constable wouldn't get involved in a commercial dispute,' said Tracey. 'It's a bit more complicated than that. Are you the owner of Perfect Pools?'

'I am. Johnny Connolly. Managing director, head of sales, marketing manager and occasional pool digger.'

'Can we come in, Mr Connolly? We need some help with an ongoing investigation.'

'Okay, yes, sure.' He spotted Conrad sitting on Lulu's shoulders and frowned. 'That's a cat.'

'Yes it is,' said Tracey.

'No, I mean, there's a cat on your shoulder,' he said to Lulu. 'How? Why?'

'His name's Conrad,' said Lulu.

'I'm confused,' said Connolly. 'That's not a police cat, is it?'

'We don't have police cats,' said Tracey. 'Police dogs, obviously. But Conrad is just along for the ride.'

Connolly shook his head in bewilderment. 'Suit yourself,' he said. He stepped to the side and pointed to his office at the far side of the hall. They walked in and he closed the door. There was a large desk with two computer screens on it, and the walls were filled with framed photographs of swimming pools of various sizes and styles. There were French windows overlooking a large garden with a white gazebo, and at the far end of the room were two grey sofas angled around a low coffee table. Connolly waved for them to sit down. Tracey and Lulu sat on one and he took the other. There was a stack of brochures on the table and several glossy magazines. 'So how can I help you?' asked Connolly. He pointedly looked at his wristwatch, a gold Rolex, as if letting them know how valuable his time was.

'Did you hear about the two murders at Hepworth House?' Tracey asked.

Conrad eased himself down from Lulu's shoulders onto her lap, where he stared at Connolly with unblinking green eyes.

'Yes, I did. Terrible, terrible, what is the world coming to? You expect that sort of thing in London, I mean that's one of the reasons my wife and I moved here. The quality of life is so much better, isn't it? No gangs of marauding thugs waving machetes. No drug dealers on every corner. And then this happens. Do you have anyone in custody yet?'

'Not yet,' said Tracey. 'Enquiries are ongoing.'

'Well, you need to catch whoever did it, obviously,' said Connolly. 'It's a very worrying time for everybody.'

'I'm sure it is,' said Tracey. 'Anyway, the reason I'm here is to ask for a list of your employees, highlighting all those who have visited Hepworth House over, say, the last two years.'

Connolly's eyes narrowed. 'Wait just a minute now,' he said. 'Are you suggesting that someone who works for me might have been involved?'

Tracey held up a hand and flashed him a reassuring smile. 'We're just covering all the bases, Mr Connolly. We're compiling a list of everyone who has been at the house, we're not singling out your employees. It's more a case of eliminating people from our enquiries – the more people we can eliminate, the easier it will be to find the perpetrator.'

'I was told that Mr Grenville was killed at his birthday party,' said Connolly. 'No one from the company was invited, I can tell you that right now.'

'It's a robbery two days prior to the birthday party that we're looking at,' said Tracey.

'So that would be Monday?'

'Yes, and we'd like a list of where your employees were all day Monday.'

Connolly frowned. 'Tell me again why you've singled me out for this?'

'No, really, we haven't,' said Tracey. 'We're looking at all those businesses that have connections to the house. You maintain the pool for them, right?'

'Actually, we installed it, for the previous owners. Miles and Stefan. The odd couple, as we called them. Did you see those statues?'

Tracey smiled. 'Yes we did. You can't miss them.'

Connolly held up his hands. 'Nothing to do with me. We did the pool and the filtration system; the lighting and the decoration were all their idea.'

'Can you get a list for me?' said Tracey. 'It would be a great help.'

'Let me get my wife in here, she handles the rotas.' Connolly stood up, went over to the door and shouted down the hallway. 'Katy, babe, can you come down here, please?'

'What's wrong?'

'I just need you for a few minutes.'

'I'm doing my yoga.'

'I'm sorry, babe. It's important.' He went over to the desk and sat down. After a minute or so they heard footsteps on the stairs and a tall woman wearing a dark blue tracksuit appeared in the doorway. She had tied her dyed blonde hair back with a scrunchie and her face was bathed with sweat. 'I'm in the middle of my session, baby,' she said. 'What's so important?'

Connolly gestured at Lulu and Tracey. 'They're detectives investigating the killings at the Grenville place. They want to know which of our staff have been out to the house over the last two years. And they want to know where they were on Monday.'

Mrs Connolly turned to look at Lulu and Tracey and put her hands on her hips. 'Is there a problem?'

Tracey stood up and smiled. 'No, not at all. As I told your husband, it's really all about eliminating people from our enquiries.'

'And what happened on Monday?'

'There was a robbery,' said Connolly. 'It was in the paper. A man was killed.'

'You know I never read the paper, babe,' said Mrs Connolly. 'I heard that Bernard Grenville was killed, but I didn't know there'd been a robbery. So, you think one of our people was involved?'

'We're asking for lists from all the companies that did work at the house, just so we can get an idea of who was coming and going.'

'Yes, we can do that,' said Mrs Connolly. She went over to the desk and gestured at her husband. 'Come on, let me do it. You'll take forever.'

Connolly got out of his chair and his wife took his place. 'Would you ladies like a cup of tea or coffee?' asked Mrs Connolly.

Lulu was about to decline but Tracey got in first. 'Coffee would be lovely. White with one sugar.'

'White, no sugar, for me,' said Lulu. She assumed that Tracey wanted the husband out of the way for a while.

Mrs Connolly looked expectantly at her husband.

'Right, I'll get that sorted, babe,' he said.

She blew him a kiss and started tapping on the keyboard as he left the room.

'You weren't invited to Bernard Grenville's birthday party?' asked Tracey.

'We barely know them,' said Mrs Connolly. 'To be honest, our contract with them is really by default. I've never met them,

Johnny saw them soon after they moved in to draw up a contract and that was it. They have a state-of-the-art system that monitors the pH and purity itself, so we just send a team out once every other month to check and to make sure there are enough chemicals and whatnot.'

She peered at the screen. 'Yes, we had a team out three weeks ago and we're due back there next month.'

'When you say team, how many people would go?'

'It's really just one guy and a driver. And the driver doesn't stay, he just drops the technician off and picks him up.'

'Same guy every time?'

Mrs Connolly looked at the screen again. 'Same driver every time. To be honest, we only have the one. Though Johnny will drive if necessary. We're actually quite a small operation, manpower-wise. Johnny does the design and costings, I do the accounts and rotas, we both chip in on sales and marketing, then we have Sam, the driver, and four full-time technicians. One of the technicians – Jack – is our main installer. The other three help him with installations and do the servicing, and they handle the cleaning and so on. Everyone else is hired on a freelance basis. If we need a hole dug, we call in a guy, if we have a tiled pool we bring in freelance tilers, and so on.'

'And so far as the Grenville house goes, which members of staff would have gone out to work there?'

'All of them at some point,' said Mrs Connolly. 'It's one of the easier jobs. The Grenvilles' system is fully automatic. The system they have has all the reagents in IV-style bags and each is good for five hundred tests, so they last for six to eight months. All the technician has to do is check that the calibrations are good and that the system is fully stocked. To be honest, a monkey could do it.'

'If you could give me pictures of the staff, it would be great,' said Tracey.

'Okay, no problem,' said Mrs Connolly. She tapped on her keyboard and a printer kicked into life and began spewing out sheets of paper. She stood up and went over to the printer and waited for it to finish, then picked up the sheets and sat down next to Tracey on the sofa. 'So, this is Sam,' she said, handing one of the sheets to Tracey. Sam was a large West Indian man with a cheerful smile. 'Sam's a darling. A real sweetheart. He runs our people out to jobs, delivers chemicals, does whatever we ask him to do, really.'

'And where would he have been on Monday?'

'Ah, yes, Monday. Let me get you the schedule.' She went back to the desk, sat down, and began tapping on her keyboard.

Tracey and Lulu looked through the photographs. Other than Sam, they were all under thirty and wearing dark blue overalls with the name of the company emblazoned across the chest. Lulu didn't recognize any of the faces, and when Tracey looked across at her she shook her head.

The printer started to buzz just as Connolly returned with four mugs of coffee. He put the tray down on the coffee table, then handed mugs to Tracey and Lulu. Mrs Connolly took a sheet of paper from the printer and joined her husband. She looked at the tray, sighed, and shook her head. 'Biscuits, babe,' she said.

'I'm sorry,' he said. 'I'll go and get them.'

'Chocolate, mind.'

'Okay, sweetheart.'

'It's fine, really,' said Tracey.

'No, I love a chocolate biscuit with my coffee,' said Mrs Connolly. She sat down as her husband left the room.

'Right, this is the spreadsheet that shows where all our staff were on the Monday. The six members of staff are in the column on the left. Sam, Jack, Luke, Daisy, Don and Henry. Then we have the times across the top in hourly increments from nine in the morning until six, though usually they knock off at five. In the columns we have the job number.' She showed them a second sheet. 'This is the list of jobs we were doing that day. Nine in all. No installations; they were all maintenance.'

Tracey scanned the list of addresses. Two of the jobs were within a few miles of the Grenvilles' house. She looked back at the staff spreadsheet. Daisy and Don were at one of the houses for four hours, Henry was at the other on his own for three hours. 'Do the technicians use their own vehicles?' asked Tracey.

'Not any more,' said Mrs Connolly. 'We used to, but people started taking advantage. They'd turn up late and leave early and we couldn't keep track of people. Now we use Sam for all transport and we have a GPS on his van so we can see where he is.' She pulled out a sheet that was a map of the local area with a dotted line that zig-zagged back and forth.

Tracey looked at it and then handed it to Lulu. The dotted line was never closer than a couple of miles to Hepworth House.

Mr Connolly returned with a plate of chocolate digestive biscuits. He put it on the coffee table and sat down next to his wife. She patted him on the thigh. 'Thanks, babe.'

'Your wish is my command,' he said. He nodded at the sheets. 'Does that answer all your questions?'

'I think so,' said Tracey. 'So Sam drops the technicians off and then picks them up when they're finished?'

'They phone him when they're done,' said Mr Connolly. 'We tried letting them use their own vehicles but it didn't work out.'

'Yes, Mrs Connolly explained that.'

'Our people are completely trustworthy,' said Mrs Connolly. 'They might not be the best timekeepers, but they're not thieves. And they're definitely not killers.'

Connolly nodded. 'We run Disclosure and Barring Service checks on all our staff,' he said. 'We have to because many of the homes with pools have children. Also we look after a lot of indoor pools in second homes, so some of the owners leave the keys with us, so we have to trust our people. They're all as honest as the day is long.'

'Did you have a key for the Grenville house?'

Connolly shook his head. 'No. They were always in when we went round.'

Tracey nodded as she studied the spreadsheet. 'This all looks fine,' she said. 'Can we take these with us, for our records?'

'Of course,' said Mr Connolly.

'So what happened on Monday?' asked Mrs Connolly as she picked up a biscuit. 'There wasn't much detail in the papers. Just that there had been a robbery and someone had died.'

'Yes, that's pretty much it,' said Tracey. 'An insurance assessor was killed.'

'Beaten to death with a poker, they said on the TV,' said Mr Connolly. 'And Mr Grenville took a beating too.'

'I don't know what the country's coming to,' said his wife. 'We thought we'd got away from all that by moving out of London. We were mugged, in Westbourne Grove. On the way back from the cinema. Two men who said they had guns. We never saw the guns but you can't take the risk in London, can you, so we gave them our watches and my rings.'

'And my wallet,' said Mr Connolly.

'That was when we decided we'd had enough, and we moved here. But now? Okay, you don't get mugged in the streets, but masked men breaking into houses, that's scary.'

'I think you're still unlikely to encounter violence here,' said Tracey.

'Tell that to the Grenvilles,' said Mrs Connolly. 'And there have been other robberies in the area, you know?'

'Yes, we are aware of that,' said Tracey.

'You need to put more bobbies on the beat,' said Mr Connolly.

'Well, I'm not sure that helps in rural areas,' said Tracey.

'We're starting to worry about what we should do,' said Mrs Connolly. 'We already have an alarm system and CCTV; we're thinking of getting a dog. A pit bull or a Rottweiler.'

'Dogs can certainly deter burglars,' said Tracey.

'Meow!' said Conrad.

The Connollys burst into laughter. 'That's funny,' said Mr Connolly. 'It's as if he's talking.'

'He is,' said Lulu. 'Probably telling you that guard dogs are overrated.'

Tracey finished her coffee and stood up. She gathered the sheets of paper together, folded them, and put them in her handbag. 'Thank you so much for your time.'

Lulu bent down and Conrad jumped up onto her shoulders. 'That is amazing,' said Mrs Connolly. 'I've never seen a cat do that before.'

'Conrad is one of a kind,' said Lulu.

Mr Connolly took them to the front door. 'I hope you catch those bastards,' he said as they stepped outside.

'We'll do our best,' said Tracey.

Connolly closed the front door as Tracey and Lulu walked over to the Mondeo.

They noticed a large Triumph motorcycle parked at the side of the Range Rover. Lulu raised an eyebrow and Tracey nodded. 'I assume it's Connolly's. But he said he wasn't at the party, and I don't remember seeing him there.'

'Me neither. It was just a thought.'

'I suppose someone could have borrowed the bike? Driven it from here to Hepworth House.'

'We need to take a closer look at the worksheets,' said Tracey. 'See who was here close to the time of the party. Obviously anyone who was out working isn't a suspect, but anyone here at the house would have been able to ride the bike to the party.'

Tracey unlocked the car and they climbed in. Lulu put Conrad on her lap. Tracey flicked through the sheets of paper that Mrs Connolly had given her. Eventually she shook her head. 'There is no one who isn't accounted for, which means only Mr and Mrs Connolly were here. And we didn't see either of them at the party.' She put the papers away. 'To be honest, I think we're getting close to stopping our suspension of disbelief, don't you? The only people who might have known where their key was stored were otherwise engaged at the time of the robbery. That leaves just Julia and Bernard, and Julia wasn't in the house.' She started the car and slowly drove towards the road. 'So you know what this means, don't you? Bernard is the only one who could have taken those paintings to the filter room.'

Lulu nodded. 'That's what it looks like.'

'And if you take that line of thought to its logical conclusion, there was no robbery.' She frowned. 'But if there was no robbery, then Bernard must have killed Billy Russell.'

'But that makes no sense at all,' said Lulu.

'Well, it would if Russell was there to steal from the house and Bernard discovered him. Russell attacked him and Bernard lashed out with a poker.' Tracey frowned. 'But then why fake the robbery? Why not just tell the police what happened?'

'Maybe he thought he'd be in less trouble if the police thought there had been a robbery.' Lulu sighed and shook her head. 'But you realize what it means if there were no intruders? It means that Bernard must have hurt himself! He must have hit himself with the poker. I can't believe he did that.'

'Maybe Russell hit Bernard first? Maybe Russell grabbed the poker and hit Bernard, Bernard grabbed the poker and killed Russell, then hid the paintings.'

'But again, if Bernard was attacked, why didn't he go to the police?' said Lulu. 'Why did he fake the robbery?'

'You're sure that their company is making money?'

'That's what Julia and Bernard have been saying. You think this is about money? Some sort of insurance scam?'

'Why else make it look as if the paintings had been stolen?'

Lulu grimaced. 'If it was about the insurance, wouldn't he have hidden more valuable paintings? If anyone knew the value of the artwork, it would be Bernard. And none of this explains why Billy Russell was in the house.'

Tracey accelerated down the road. 'Maybe Bernard called Russell and asked him to come to the house. Maybe Bernard was planning some sort of insurance fraud and wanted Russell to help him. When Russell said no . . .'

'What, Bernard whacked him with a poker? That's a bit extreme.'

'Maybe Russell threatened to go to the police?'

'His word against Bernard's, surely,' said Lulu. 'It's no reason to kill him.' She shook her head, trying to clear her thoughts. 'None of this makes sense.' She looked over at Tracey. 'What about talking to Mrs Russell? We know that he was at the house on his day off, so maybe he told her why he was going.'

'That's not a bad idea,' Tracey said. 'I'll drop you off at the house and then pay her a visit.'

'Why not strike while the iron's hot?' said Lulu. 'Besides, if she was at the birthday party, maybe I'll recognize her.'

'Why would she be at the birthday party?' Tracey's jaw dropped. 'Oh, you think that she might have killed Bernard out of revenge?'

'If Bernard really did kill her husband, then it's a possibility, isn't it?'

25

The Russells lived in a small bungalow in the leafy residential suburb of Headington, on the east side of Oxford. There was a low wooden fence around a garden that had been concreted over to allow a grey Volvo to park. Lulu realized it was the same car that had been in front of Hepworth House. Tracey parked her Mondeo in the street and she and Lulu walked to the front door. Conrad was sitting on Lulu's shoulders, looking around.

Tracey pressed the doorbell and after a few seconds they heard feet shuffling along the hallway. The door was opened by a woman in her fifties, her eyes red from crying, her greying hair in disarray. She was wearing a white bathrobe and pink fluffy slippers that might once have looked like rabbits. She blinked at them and gathered the robe around her neck. 'Mrs Russell? It's me again, Inspector Calder. I'm sorry to bother you but we want to talk to you about your late husband.'

'Have you found the man who killed him?'

Tracey shook her head. 'I'm afraid not.'

Mrs Russell looked at Lulu for the first time and smiled when she saw Conrad. 'Oh my goodness. A cat!'

'Yes,' said Lulu. 'His name is Conrad.'

'He's such a handsome boy.'

'Can we come in and have a chat, Mrs Russell?' said Lulu. 'We won't be long.'

'I suppose so,' said Mrs Russell, her eyes staying on Conrad as she shuffled to the side. Tracey and Lulu stepped into a small hall. There was an open door to their left and Mrs Russell nodded at it. 'In there,' she said. 'It's cold, I'm afraid. I can't afford to have the heating on during the day.'

Tracey and Lulu walked into a small sitting room with a low sofa facing a television, a pine coffee table and two small armchairs either side of a fireplace which had been blocked off with a piece of painted board. A vase of plastic flowers had been placed in the middle of the fireplace. There was a copy of a caravan magazine on the coffee table, next to some glossy brochures. They sat down on the sofa and Mrs Russell took one of the armchairs. There was a box of tissues on a small table next to her chair, and a yellow mug of what looked like tea. The room was cold and Mrs Russell sat with her arms folded.

'Are you having problems with the power companies?' asked Tracey.

'Everyone is,' said Mrs Russell. 'It costs an arm and a leg to keep the place warm these days.'

'I thought your husband was on a good salary at the insurance company?'

'He used to do quite well but most of his earnings are bonuses and they've not been good the last few years. He never gets the good clients, that's the problem. And his ex-wife takes half of everything he earns before I even get to see a single pound.'

'Oh, is he still supporting them?'

'Yes, even though it was a long time ago. Almost twenty years. She got pregnant so he had to marry her. He tried to make it work but she was a whore, forgive my language.

She was unfaithful three or four times that he knew about and they had another child that I'm sure isn't even his but when they divorced the court said she got to keep half his wages. I ask you, how is that fair?'

'She never remarried?' said Lulu. 'His ex-wife?'

'She's too smart for that,' said Mrs Russell. 'She's had a string of men friends but they never stay over. She knows that if they move in, the money will stop. She got the house, you know that? The house and half of his salary. How is that fair?'

'It's not fair,' said Lulu.

'No, it's not. Billy kept going back to the court but they wouldn't listen: he has to pay for her and for the two kids even though one of them . . .' Tears brimmed in her eyes and she bent forward to pull a tissue from the box. 'Well, there's no more salary for her to take now, so more fool her.' She dabbed at her eyes. She looked over at Tracey. 'Do you think she'll get half of Billy's pension?'

'I don't know, Mrs Russell,' said Tracey. 'I'm sorry.'

'It just isn't fair,' she said. 'The court isn't fair and life isn't fair. And now Billy has gone and I'm on my own. I don't understand why any of this has happened.'

Conrad jumped down off the sofa and padded across the carpet to Mrs Russell. He looked up at her and meowed. 'What is it, boy, you want to sit on my lap?' Conrad meowed again and she patted her knee. 'Come on, then.' Conrad jumped smoothly onto her lap and curled up. Mrs Russell smiled down at him and began to stroke his fur. Conrad purred and Mrs Russell's smile widened. 'He likes it.' She looked over at Lulu. 'He likes it!'

'He's a people person,' said Lulu. 'Well, a people cat.'

Mrs Russell relaxed as she stroked Conrad, and the smile stayed on her lips.

'I wanted to ask if your husband had any enemies, Mrs Russell,' said Tracey. 'Anyone who might have wanted to hurt him?'

'Billy? No, everyone loved Billy. No one had a bad word to say about him.'

'No problems with the neighbours?'

Mrs Russell shook her head. 'No. Never.' She took her eyes off Conrad and looked at Tracey. 'It was a robbery, those other police said. There was a robbery and one of the robbers killed my Billy.'

'That's what it looks like, Mrs Russell. But we need to make sure.'

Mrs Russell frowned. 'Make sure of what?'

'Well, just to make sure that Billy didn't know the men who killed him.'

'Well, that doesn't make sense, does it? Why would he know burglars? And if they knew him, why would they kill him?'

'We're just making enquiries, Mrs Russell. That's all. Had he fallen out with any of his friends recently?'

'Billy didn't have many friends. He wasn't what you'd call social. He was happy enough here at home, with me.' She frowned. 'The man who owned the house, he was attacked, too, wasn't he?'

'He's dead now, Mrs Russell. That's why we are making more enquiries.'

Mrs Russell looked back at Conrad and smiled. 'He is a lovely boy.'

Conrad purred loudly.

'Did your husband say where he was going, the day he died?' asked Tracey.

'I thought he was going to work. He had his suit on and everything. But then the day after it happened his boss Mr Drummond phoned and asked where he was. I had to tell him that Billy was dead and I got very confused because I was sure that Billy was working but Mr Drummond said no, he'd taken sick leave and that didn't make any sense because Billy wasn't sick.'

'Had he done that before, taken sick leave when he wasn't sick?' asked Lulu.

Mrs Russell nodded. 'Sometimes. I said he was being naughty but he said that everyone did it and that you were allowed so many days a year. And it's not as if they were paying him well: his salary has stayed the same for more than five years.'

'Did Billy sometimes do work outside the company?' asked Tracey. 'Like freelance work?'

Mrs Russell shook her head as she continued to stroke Conrad. 'No. He said his home time was his home time. Work was nine to five, he said. That's what they paid him for, and that's what they got.'

Lulu leaned forward and picked up the brochures that were lying on the coffee table. They were from caravan companies. 'Oh, you like caravans?' said Lulu.

'Billy always wanted to buy one,' said Mrs Russell. 'We could never afford one, but he said we should start looking.'

'He was planning to buy one?' said Lulu.

'He said he was but I don't know where he thought he was getting the money from. Money has been tight and it gets tighter every year.'

'When did he say he might buy a caravan?' asked Lulu.

'A few days ago, I suppose. Last week, maybe.'

'Just before he was killed?'

Mrs Russell nodded. 'Just before, yes.'

'And what did he say, exactly?'

Mrs Russell continued to stroke Conrad. 'He just brought the brochures home with him and said I should tell him which I liked. I just laughed, there's no way we could afford a caravan, not in a million years.'

'And what did he say?' said Tracey.

'He said that maybe he'd win the lottery, but that didn't make any sense because we can't afford to waste money on lottery tickets.'

Lulu flicked through the brochures. The cheapest caravan on offer cost just under twenty thousand pounds, but some models were three times that price. 'They look nice,' she said.

'It was just a dream of mine,' said Mrs Russell. 'My dad had one when I was little and we had some great holidays. "The freedom of the road", Dad always used to say.' She forced a tight smile. 'It'll stay a dream until the day I die.'

'Do you think Billy was serious, about wanting to make your dream come true?' asked Lulu.

'How could he have been? We don't have that sort of money.' She smiled down at Conrad. 'You are such a good boy,' she said.

'Meow!' he replied.

Mrs Russell laughed. 'He understands every word, doesn't he?'

'Oh, yes,' said Lulu.

'Mrs Russell, did your husband have an office here? Somewhere he worked when he was at home?'

'Billy never worked from home. He said that's what the office was for; he never brought work home with him.'

'Did he have a diary, then? Somewhere he'd keep a track of his meetings. I know they make him put all his meetings on the computer at work, but if he's anything like me he'd have it written down too.'

'Yes, he never trusted the computer. He always used a Filofax – it's in the bureau.' She gestured at the bureau in the corner of the room. Tracey went over and opened it. There was a stack of opened mail, mainly bills, and a black leather Filofax. As she picked it up she saw a glossy magazine underneath it. It was the Sunday magazine with Julia's photograph on the cover. Tracey picked it up, showed it to Lulu and raised an eyebrow.

Tracey put down the magazine and took the Filofax over to the sofa. She sat down and opened it, then went through the diary section. It was one page per day, and Tracey went through to the day that Russell had died. There were several entries for that day, but all had been crossed out. At the top of the page were two capital letters. BG. Obviously Bernard Grenville.

'Did Billy have any visitors on the days before he died?' asked Tracey.

'Visitors?'

'Did anyone come to the house that you didn't recognize? Strangers?'

'No,' said Mrs Russell.

'What about these people? Did you ever see him talking to them?' Tracey opened her handbag and took the pictures that Mrs Connolly had printed. She showed them to Mrs Russell, one at a time. Mrs Russell looked at them and solemnly shook her head.

Tracey smiled and put the pictures back into her handbag. 'Could you give me your husband's phone number, Mrs Russell?'

Mrs Russell looked up at her, blinking in confusion. 'You want to phone Billy?'

Tracey couldn't help but smile. 'No, Mrs Russell, I just want to check his phone records. Can you give me the number?'

Mrs Russell reached over to pick up her mobile phone. 'I can never remember his number. Isn't that bad? My own husband and I don't know his number.'

'Everybody's like that these days,' said Lulu. 'It's because all our numbers are stored in the phone.'

Mrs Russell scrolled through her address book, then read out her husband's number. Tracey wrote it down in her notebook and thanked her. She and Lulu stood up. Lulu picked up Conrad and put him on her shoulder.

'He's a lovely cat,' said Mrs Russell.

'He is,' said Lulu.

'We could never have pets because Billy was allergic. He came out in a rash if he even went near a cat or a dog.' She forced a smile. 'I suppose now I can get a cat, can't I?'

'You can, and you should,' said Lulu. 'Cats are terrific companions.'

'Meow!' said Conrad.

'He agrees with you!' said Mrs Russell, excitedly.

'Conrad is a very agreeable cat,' said Lulu.

26

Tracey dropped Lulu outside Hepworth House but kept the engine running. 'Don't you want to come in?' asked Lulu.

'I need to get back to the office. We're briefing the investigation team later this afternoon.' The inspector smiled uncomfortably. 'Lulu, I need you to do something for me.'

'Okay,' said Lulu.

'Please don't mention to Julia that we went to see Mrs Russell. Or the Connollys.'

'Why ever not?'

Tracey shifted uncomfortably in her seat. 'I just don't want her worrying unnecessarily, that's all.'

'Oh my goodness, you think she's a suspect!' said Lulu, shocked.

'No, I'm not saying that,' said Tracey. 'She was listening to the musicians when her husband was killed and I don't think for one minute that she hit Billy Russell with the poker, but I think she might well know more than she is telling us about the robbery. So let's just say that I see her as a person of interest.'

'You think she might have paid someone to kill Bernard?'

'It's a possibility, yes.'

Lulu shook her head. 'She loved him. And what possible reason would she have for killing him? They had no money worries, they were so happy in their new house. And I very much doubt that either of them were having affairs.'

'There are just too many unanswered questions,' said Tracey. 'I'm checking her alibi for that Monday.'

'Her alibi? Now she needs an alibi?'

'She says she was out of the house running errands when Bernard was attacked, and until I've confirmed that she was where she says she was, she needs to remain a person of interest. All I'm asking is that you don't tell her anything about my lines of investigation.'

'Tracey, you're asking me to lie to one of my oldest friends.'

'Not lie, no. Don't ask, don't tell, maybe. I was taking a risk by involving you in the investigation, I really don't want that decision to come back and bite me.'

'Fine. I won't raise it, but I'm not going to lie.'

'That's okay, I can't ask for more than that.'

'And I can tell you that Julia doesn't have a bad bone in her body.'

'I'm sorry I mentioned it,' said Tracey. 'It's just that at some point I'm going to have to raise some issues with her and I don't want her to be prepared, that's all. But I don't think for one minute that she killed Billy Russell or her husband.'

Lulu nodded. 'I get it,' she said. 'Okay, so when will you be back? Or are you planning a surprise dawn raid with armed officers?'

Tracey grinned. 'Probably late afternoon tomorrow,' she said. 'I have a SOCO meeting in the morning.'

Lulu held Conrad to her chest as she got out of the Mondeo, then lifted him up onto her shoulders. She closed the door and waved as Tracey drove off down the driveway.

'It sounds as if she doesn't trust Julia,' said Conrad.

'That's just good protocol,' said Lulu. 'Police work isn't about trusting people, it's about considering all the evidence and then coming to a conclusion.'

'If this was your investigation, what would you do differently?'

'She's young and relatively inexperienced, that's true. But these days homicide investigators all have to follow the Murder Investigation Manual. So I probably would be doing exactly what she's doing.'

'There's a manual?'

'There are several manuals. And any good detective will know them all by heart.' The Mondeo turned onto the main road and drove away. 'Plus she'll have a boss who will keep an eye on the decision log to make sure that she's covering all the bases.' She sighed. 'If it was up to me, though, I'd have gone to see Mrs Russell earlier. When you're looking for a killer, usually the victim is the key. I get the feeling that Tracey was concentrating too much on the robbery. She obviously felt that the robbery was the cause of the murder, but in fact it was the opposite. The murder came first, and with a murder it's usually all about the victim.'

'So the key to this is to ask why was Billy Russell killed?'

'Exactly.'

'But his widow said that he didn't have problems with anyone and that everyone liked him.'

'People usually say that about their loved ones. And if he did have a problem with someone, then it's perfectly possible that he kept it from his wife.'

'And maybe Bernard kept something from Julia.'

'It does seem strange that two men – neither of whom

apparently had an enemy in the world – were both killed. And killed so violently.'

'What do you think happened?'

Lulu smiled. 'Hand on heart, Conrad, at the moment I just don't know.'

'Sounds like you need a glass of wine.'

Lulu laughed and looked at her watch. 'Well, it is wine o'clock.' She reached for the doorbell and then pulled back her hand. 'I don't want to disturb Julia if she's sleeping. Let's go around the back.'

They walked around the side of the house and up onto the terrace. Lulu turned the handle of the French windows. It opened.

'You'd think she'd get into the habit of locking it,' said Conrad. He jumped down and walked into the study, taking care to avoid the bloodstains.

'It's the countryside,' said Lulu. 'People generally don't lock their doors here.' She followed Conrad across the study and down the corridor to the main hall. 'I don't think I could live in a house as big as this,' said Lulu.

'It's too big, isn't it?' said Conrad. 'It would have been too big for the two of them, but one person would get lost here.'

'I wouldn't be able to relax; you'd never know who else was in the house with you. They were never meant for couples or people on their own, they were for families and a big staff.'

'I prefer *The Lark*.'

'So do I,' said Lulu. 'But I do love a big bath.'

They headed up the right-hand branch of the stairs. 'And I don't understand this double stair thing,' said Conrad. 'What's the point?'

'It's a design thing. It's aesthetically pleasing.'

'It's a waste of stairs,' said Conrad. He nodded at the massive chandelier. 'And don't get me started on that thing. How many man-hours did it take to make, do you think?'

'Thousands,' said Lulu. 'Julia said it was handmade.'

'By vegan artisans, no doubt.'

'So you're not a fan of vegans?'

'I'm a cat, Lulu. Carrots and lettuce are for rabbits.'

They reached the top of the stairs and headed towards Julia's bedroom. Conrad was right, the house was simply too big. Just getting from room to room took forever. Before she had lived on *The Lark*, Lulu's home had been a four-storey Victorian townhouse in Maida Vale, more than enough space for her and her husband. She had moved out after Simon had died, partly because the constant reminders of what she had lost were too upsetting, but also because the house was simply too big for one person. *The Lark* was perfect for her: everything within a few steps, cosy and warm at night, lots of fresh air, and the comforting rocking as another boat went by.

'*The Lark* is perfect, for both of us,' said Conrad.

Lulu stopped and looked at him in amazement. 'Did you just read my mind?'

He chuckled. 'No, I just saw the faraway look in your eyes and followed your train of thought.'

'It's very disconcerting when you do that.'

Conrad looked up at her, an amused smile on his face. 'Really? I would have thought it was quite reassuring to have someone know you so well that they can guess what you're thinking.'

Lulu wrinkled her nose. 'I suppose it is. It just catches me by surprise when you do it, that's all.'

They started walking again and eventually reached the door to Julia's bedroom. Lulu gently eased it open. Julia was lying on the bed, cuddling her pillow and snoring softly. 'She's still sleeping,' she whispered.

'She's in shock,' said Conrad. 'You should let her sleep.'

'You're right,' said Lulu. She gently eased the door closed and they started the long walk to the kitchen.

27

'What would you like to eat?' Lulu asked as she opened the refrigerator door and peered inside.

'That smoked salmon was delicious,' said Conrad. He was standing on the kitchen island.

'It was, wasn't it?' She looked down the shelves and found a pack on one of the lower shelves. 'There we are,' she said. 'And I'll have some salad.' She picked up a bag of M&S mixed-leaf salad.

Lulu put a slice of smoked salmon onto a small plate and cut it up. She put it down in front of Conrad, then poured some Evian water into a bowl for him before making a smoked salmon salad for herself.

'Today was an interesting day,' said Conrad.

'It was, yes.'

'We know that there was no one from the pool company at the house when Russell was killed,' said Conrad. 'So the only people who could have put the paintings in the filter room are Bernard and Julia. Do you think Julia really was out of the house when Russell was attacked?'

'Why do you ask that?'

'I was just wondering if she was here or not,' said Conrad. 'We can be fairly sure that there were no intruders and that Bernard was lying about that. We know that Russell wasn't at the house on business. Not company business, anyway. So if Bernard lied about that, maybe he told other lies.'

'Tracey can check that.'

'Or you could ask Julia yourself.'

'Oh, I don't want to start interrogating Julia. She's my friend. And I'm not a detective any more.'

'No, but you want to know the truth, don't you?'

'Yes, of course. At least, I suppose I do.'

Conrad tilted his head on one side. 'What do you mean?'

'Well, if they did both lie to me and they did kill Billy Russell, then I guess that would end my friendship with Julia, wouldn't it?'

'Because she lied?'

'That, and the fact that she'll be in prison. Oh, I don't know. My mind is in a whirl.'

'It is confusing, isn't it? And even if Bernard and Julia killed Russell, who killed Bernard?'

'Well it obviously wasn't Mrs Russell, was it?' said Lulu. 'I can't see her sneaking into the party and stabbing Bernard in the back. And you could see how distraught she was. I don't think she was lying.'

'She has a good aura, I know that much,' said Conrad. 'Lots of blue which shows that she has a strong, intelligent personality, but almost as much pink which shows that she is kind, caring and loving. She doesn't have a liar's aura. I'm sure she has no idea why her husband was killed.'

'It was interesting that he had that magazine with the article on their company.'

'Yes. Very interesting.'

'Suppose Russell read the magazine and realized that Bernard was rich now. Really rich. And suppose Russell thought he could get money from Bernard.'

'Why would Bernard give him money?'

'Blackmail, maybe,' said Lulu.

'Because his shop burned down? But the police have already said it wasn't arson. They're not going to change their minds now, are they?'

'I suppose not. But it can't be a coincidence, can it? Russell sees the article in the magazine and then turns up at the house.'

'No,' said Conrad. 'Cause and effect, obviously.'

'So did Russell phone first? Did he tell Bernard he wanted to talk and Bernard invited him to the house?'

'Tracey said she was checking the phone records, didn't she?'

'She did, yes.'

'And we still don't know if Julia was in the house when it happened.' He sighed. 'I really hope that Julia hasn't been lying to you.'

'You and me both.'

'Cats never lie.'

'Really?'

'I said it, so it must be true.'

Lulu laughed and shook her head.

'What are you laughing at?' asked Julia, appearing at the kitchen door. She had changed into a baggy sweatshirt, track-suit bottoms and Chanel slippers.

'Oh, just the way Conrad was grooming himself,' said Lulu. 'He was having a good old go at his paw.' She stood up, wondering if Julia had heard anything else.

'You want to be careful,' said Julia.

Lulu frowned, not understanding what she meant.

Julia grinned. 'You'll be known as the crazy cat lady of Little Venice if you carry on like this.'

'Do you want me to get you some salad and some salmon?' Lulu asked. 'Or I could cook for you.'

'Maybe later,' said Julia. 'How long was I asleep for?'

Lulu looked at her watch. 'Five or six hours,' she said. 'We popped in to check on you and you were fast asleep.'

'We? Oh, you and Conrad? Yes, I was having all sorts of dreams.'

'Sita gave you an injection; she said you needed to sleep.'

Julia frowned. 'I don't remember that. Sita was here?'

'I called her. You remember fainting?'

'I suppose so. I mean, I remember talking to you and everything whirling around and the next thing I remember is being in bed.' She held out her arm. 'That accounts for the sore arm, I suppose.'

'You came around after you fainted and we walked you to the bedroom, but you seemed out of it,' said Lulu. 'It's understandable, you've been under a lot of pressure. Sita talked about PTSD.'

'Oh, don't be silly. PTSD is what soldiers get.'

'Julia, you saw your husband die. That's going to have an effect on you.'

'Yes, you're right. You're always right.' She sat down on one of the stools.

'And Sita said no alcohol.'

'Doctors always say that. And I'm a doctor and I say alcohol is absolutely fine.'

'You're a PhD. Not a doctor doctor. And Sita the doctor doctor was quite adamant that you shouldn't drink. She said that you should eat.' She put the blister pack onto the island. 'And you need to take these, one every twelve hours.'

Julia picked up the pack and squinted at it. 'What are these?'

'To relax you.'

Julia laughed. 'Wine will relax me.'

'She said no alcohol.'

Julia sighed. 'Just kill me now.'

'Let me make you something to eat,' said Lulu.

'I'm not hungry.'

'Julia, you barely picked at your croissant this morning and you've had nothing all day.'

'Why do I have to keep repeating myself, Lulu? I'm not hungry.'

'That's because of the stress. Even if you don't feel hungry, you need to eat something.'

Julia sighed theatrically. 'Fine. I'll eat. If it stops you nagging me, I'll eat.'

'Meow!' said Conrad.

'See, Conrad agrees with me.'

'Lulu, he's a cat. He's just saying meow. That's what cats do.'

'Meow!' said Conrad.

'There you go, that proves my point,' said Julia.

'The doctor said protein rather than carbs,' said Lulu. 'How does scrambled eggs sound?'

'If it shuts you up, fine,' said Julia with a grin.

Lulu shook her head in exasperation, then slid off her stool and went over to the fridge. She took out a box of eggs, and the pack of cold cuts. 'You do remember what Tracey was talking about when you passed out?'

Julia frowned. 'Not really.'

'Tracey was explaining that Russell's blood was all over Bernard's clothing, and that Bernard had probably trans-ferred the blood to the loungers in the pool room.'

'Oh, that's ridiculous,' said Julia.

Lulu broke three eggs into a bowl and whisked them with a fork, then added a knob of butter and a splash of milk and put the bowl into the microwave.

Julia laughed. 'Don't let Bernard catch you . . .' she began, and then tailed off as she realized what she'd said.

'It's how I do them on the boat,' said Lulu. She cooked the eggs for a minute, took out the bowl and stirred the eggs, then microwaved them for another minute. She put the cooked eggs onto a plate, added several slices of ham, chorizo and salami, and put it down in front of Julia.

'Now that is fast food,' said Julia. 'Did that even take you two minutes?'

Lulu gave her a knife and fork. 'Eat,' she said.

Julia threw her a mock salute. 'Aye, aye, sir,' she said.

Lulu put the bowl in the sink and then sat back at the island. Julia began to pick at her food.

'The day of the robbery, you said you were out arranging for Bernard's birthday cake?' said Lulu.

Julia nodded. 'And finalizing the flowers, yes. Why do you ask?'

'I was just wondering. You didn't see Billy Russell arrive, did you? So I thought that maybe he was waiting for you to leave.'

Julia nodded. 'I didn't see him, no. When I got back the grey Volvo was here. And the police had arrived. A patrol car, anyway.'

'Who'd called them?'

'One of the cleaning team. Bernard had come to and had crawled into the hall. He shouted and one of them came down to see what was wrong. So you think Russell didn't want me to see him?'

'I think he might have waited until you left. Or maybe he already knew you were out.'

'How would he know that?'

'He could have spoken to Bernard on the phone.'

'You think that's likely?'

'I really don't know. Tracey will be checking Russell's phone, I'm sure. I was just wondering where you went, that's all?'

'There's no mystery, I went to Oxford to check on Bernard's birthday cake. And the flowers. And to do some shopping. And I got my nails done. Full mani-pedi.'

'So you would have made an appointment for the mani-pedi?'

'Yes, of course.' She frowned. 'Lulu, are you asking me if I have an alibi?'

Lulu laughed. 'No, of course not. Why would you say that?'

'I don't know, it just feels as if you're checking up on me.'

'No, not at all. But if Russell knew in advance that you wouldn't be here, it means that he wanted Bernard to be on his own. And that could be significant.'

'Once a detective, always a detective?'

Lulu chuckled. 'I suppose so.'

'Can you stay here tonight?'

'Of course, I was planning to.'

'Thank you. Thank you for everything.'

'You don't have to thank me,' said Lulu.

'Meow!' said Conrad.

'Conrad says we're happy to be here. Now, how are the eggs?'

'Surprisingly good,' said Julia. 'All that wasted time cooking them when all I had to do was nuke them. Who knew?'

'A DI I used to work with taught me. He had microwaved scrambled eggs for breakfast in the office.'

Lulu picked up her knife and fork and tucked into her salmon and salad. 'I know it's early days, Julia, but what are your plans? Do you have any idea what you're going to do?'

'About what?'

'Are you going to stay here? In this house?'

'I hadn't even thought about it.'

'It's just that it's so big. I don't like the thought of you rattling around in it on your own.'

Julia nodded. 'Me neither. I keep expecting to see Bernard come into the room at any moment. Then I remember that he's gone and I'll never see him again.' Her eyes widened. 'We've got to arrange the funeral, haven't we? How do we do that? I've never arranged a funeral before.'

'There's no rush, Julia. The police have Bernard's body and when they're done they'll release it to the funeral director. They'll handle all the arrangements.'

'I suppose we should have the funeral reception here, but how can we do that when this is where he died? That wouldn't be right, would it?'

'You can use a hotel near the church. The funeral director will know all the choices. Did Bernard want to be buried, or cremated?'

'We never talked about it. Who talks about things like that, really? Bernard loved life, he never talked about death.'

'But it'll be in his will, surely? Along with what he wants at the funeral, and so on?'

Julia snorted softly and shook her head. 'He never made a will. Neither did I. Our lawyers asked us a couple of times but Bernard always said there was no need. He said neither of us were going to die, and in the unlikely event of one of us dying, the other would get everything. Husband and wife. Till death do us part.' She finished her food and put down her knife and fork. 'That was lovely. I didn't think I was hungry but I obviously was.' She yawned. 'I feel so tired. I think I'll go back to bed for a while.'

'Conrad and I will escort you to your room.'

Julia laughed. 'You two are so sweet together,' she said. She slid off her stool and swayed unsteadily.

Lulu stood up quickly and took her arm. 'Are you okay?'

'I just feel a bit woozy.'

'You have to move slowly. I don't know what was in the injection Sita gave you, but it must have been strong.'

'I'm okay, really. I'm just sleepy.'

'Come on, let's get you to bed.' She put her arm around Julia's waist and took her slowly along the corridor to the hall, then up the stairs on the right. Conrad padded along behind them, his tail straight up in the air.

When they reached Julia's bedroom, Lulu helped her into bed. Julia rolled onto her side and hugged a pillow. 'I'll stay here with you,' said Lulu.

'No need,' said Julia. 'I'll be fine. I'll sleep. And Bernard always said I snored like a train when I was really tired. Enough to rattle the windows. You and Conrad go and have fun. I'll see you in the morning.'

'Are you sure?' asked Lulu, but Julia had already closed her eyes and was snoring softly.

'Come on,' Lulu said to Conrad. 'Let's let her sleep.'

They left the room and Lulu pulled the door closed. They went back downstairs to the conservatory. Lulu dropped down onto one of the sofas and Conrad jumped up to sit next to her.

Lulu sighed. 'It has been a crazy few days, hasn't it?'

'A rollercoaster,' agreed Conrad. 'Her nails did look nice, didn't they?'

'Yes, they did.'

'So she was out getting her nails done.'

'It would appear so. I'm assuming Tracey will be checking, but yes, she definitely had them done recently.'

'But not the pedi part.'

'The pedi part?'

'Her toenails. They hadn't been painted.'

'When did you notice that?'

'She kicked off her slippers when she got into bed.'

'Are you sure? She might just have had them polished and not painted.'

Conrad shook his head. 'I'm closer to the ground than you so I get a better look. There might have been a mani but there was no pedi.'

'That's interesting. But she might have just been using "mani-pedi" as an expression.'

'I suppose so.'

'You think she was in the house when it happened?'

Conrad shrugged. 'I don't know.'

'That would be quite something, wouldn't it? If she was there and Bernard hit Russell with the poker. And now they're covering it up.'

'But why?' asked Conrad. 'Why would they want to kill Russell?'

'That's a very good question,' said Lulu. 'And at the moment I have absolutely no way of answering it.'

28

Something soft patted Lulu on the cheek and she turned her face away. There was another pat, this time on her nose. 'Lulu, wake up!' It was Conrad.

'I'm sleeping,' murmured Lulu.

'You have to wake up,' said Conrad.

Lulu opened her eyes. It was dark. Conrad was sitting on the bed next to her. 'What's wrong?'

'I heard a noise downstairs.'

'What sort of noise?'

'I don't know. Just a noise.'

'What time is it?'

'I don't know. I'm a cat. We don't have watches.'

Lulu lifted her arm and looked at her watch, but it was too dark to make out the time. She rolled over and picked up her phone. It was just after two o'clock in the morning. She sat up and listened intently. 'I don't hear anything.'

'You're not a cat.'

'Can you hear something?'

'Not now. But I did before.'

'Are you sure?' Lulu switched on the bedside lamp.

Conrad's eyes narrowed. 'Lulu, I wouldn't have woken you up if I wasn't sure.'

Lulu ran a hand through her hair and blinked to clear her eyes. 'Could it be Julia?' She had checked on her friend at midnight and she had been fast asleep.

'The noise was downstairs.'

'What sort of noise?'

'A cracking sound. Like glass breaking.'

Lulu frowned. 'Like glass breaking? Was it glass breaking or wasn't it?'

'I just heard a crack. And after that, footsteps. Do you think you should call the police?'

'It'll take them half an hour to get here. And they might not even send a car. What do I tell them? My cat heard a noise?'

'You could tell them that you heard it.'

'But I didn't. And they're unlikely to come out just because I heard a noise.'

'You could phone Tracey. After what happened to Bernard, she would send someone out, wouldn't she?'

'Yes, she would. But she wouldn't appreciate it if we wasted her time.' Lulu swung her legs over the side of the bed, still holding her phone. She padded across the carpet to the door and eased it open, then stood listening for a while.

Conrad joined her. 'Can you hear anything?' he asked.

'No,' she whispered. She stepped out into the corridor and turned on her phone's torch. She shone the beam up and down, then started walking towards the stairs.

'I really think we should call the police,' muttered Conrad.

Lulu stopped and listened again. 'I don't hear anything.' She turned to look at him. 'What about you?'

'Well, not now, no. But I did before.'

Lulu shone the phone torch towards the stairs and started walking again. Conrad followed, his tail twitching from side to side. They reached the top of the stairs and the light from the phone glistened on the massive chandelier. She played the beam down the right-hand stairs, then the left. She realized that her heart was pounding in her chest and she took several deep breaths.

'Are you okay?' whispered Conrad.

'I'm just a bit tense.'

'Call the police.'

'But I can't hear anything. It could have been the wind before. Or a cat.'

'It was most definitely not a cat,' whispered Conrad. 'I know what a cat sounds like and it did not sound like a cat. Or a dog. Or a fox. Or anything on four legs.'

'Okay, okay,' said Lulu. She played the beam along the ground floor but there was nothing to be seen. 'I'm going to switch on the lights,' she said.

'I think you should call the police and let them switch on the lights,' Conrad persisted.

'Can you hear something? Anything?'

Conrad tilted his head from side to side, his ears pricked up and moving independently. 'No,' he said eventually.

Lulu put a bare foot on the top stair and kept her left hand on the banister as she played the torch beam up and down. As she moved down to the second step, a scream pierced the night air. The hairs stood up on the back of Lulu's neck and her mouth fell open in surprise as she looked at Conrad.

'Well, I heard that, obviously,' said Conrad archly.

Lulu stepped back off the stairs just as a second scream, even louder than the first, came from the direction of Julia's room.

'Call the . . .' started Conrad, but Lulu was already running down the hallway, the beam from her phone jerking from side to side.

'This is not a good idea,' hissed Conrad, then he started running after her.

Lulu's breath was coming in ragged gasps as her feet slapped against the carpet. There was a third scream, if anything even louder than the first two. She skidded to a halt outside Julia's bedroom and grabbed for the door handle.

'Lulu, no!' shouted Conrad, but it was too late, Lulu had already twisted the handle and pushed the door open. What she saw filled her with horror. Julia was standing with her back to the wall, a bloodstained pillow in front of her. A figure in dark clothing and a ski mask was stabbing at her with a long knife. The bedside lamp was switched on and it cast long shadows as the attacker lunged at her. Julia screamed again as the knife sliced into the pillow. There was blood dripping from both of her arms where previous blows had struck home.

'Leave her alone!' screamed Lulu at the top of her voice. The figure turned to look at her. It was a man, she realized. Not too tall, and slightly built, but it was definitely a man. His eyes and mouth were all that was visible through the ski mask, but they were in shadow and she couldn't make out any details.

'I've called 999!' She held up her mobile phone as if that was somehow proof. 'The police are on their way.' She stepped to the side so that he had a clear escape route. He could run if he wanted to. 'You need to get out of here now!' shouted Lulu.

The man turned back to Julia, who was staring open-mouthed at Lulu. The knife lashed out and caught Julia on the side of the neck. She screamed and kicked out with her leg but she missed him and he lunged with the knife again.

This time she managed to block it with the bloodstained pillow.

Lulu frantically looked around for something, anything, to use as a weapon. She spotted a jade statue standing on a low chest; it looked like a dragon or a snake curved around a rock. She dropped her phone onto the chest and picked up the statue. It weighed several pounds and she grunted as she raised it over her head and walked towards the man. He heard her coming and turned to face her, the knife held above his head.

'Bitch!' he shouted and pulled back the knife.

There was a blur of brown, black and white to her left as Conrad raced across the room, jumped onto the bed and then leaped again, towards the man, his paws out and his claws extended. Conrad made a squalling sound that Lulu had never heard before as he hit the man in the chest. One of his paws raked the ski mask and it split and the man yelped in pain as Conrad's claws scratched him.

Conrad twisted around in the air and landed on all four paws. He looked up at the man and hissed. The man drew back his leg and tried to kick Conrad, but Conrad was already jumping to the side and the blow missed.

'Don't you dare kick my cat!' shouted Lulu and she threw the statue at the man. It was heavier than she thought, but it hit him on the left knee and she could tell from the way he yelled that it had hurt. The material of the man's mask had split across his left cheek and Lulu was sure she could see blood.

Julia moved away from the wall and pushed the man with the pillow, hard. He stumbled towards the bed and yelped again as he put his weight on his injured knee. Lulu moved out of his way.

The man straightened up. He was still holding the knife. It was long and thin and slightly curved. Lulu was certain it was the knife that had killed Bernard.

'Get out of my house!' shouted Julia, and she pushed him in the back again, sending him stumbling towards the door. Lulu bent down quickly and picked up the jade statue. She raised it above her head, ready to throw it at him again.

Conrad jumped back onto the bed and arched his back, all his fur standing up straight as if he'd been electrocuted. He hissed at the man and snarled and was clearly bracing himself for another attack.

The man cursed and ran towards the door. He had his head down so Lulu couldn't get a good look at him but she was sure that Conrad had torn his flesh.

The man ran into the hallway and headed for the stairs. Lulu hurriedly put the jade statue back onto the chest and started after him. 'Lulu!' shouted Julia.

Lulu stopped. 'What?'

'Where are you going?'

'I'm going to chase after him, see if he had a car or a motorbike, he must have got here somehow.'

'Lulu, he's got a knife. And look at me. He's clearly not afraid of using it.'

'Meow!' said Conrad, whose fur had now returned to normal.

Julia dropped the bloodstained pillow to the floor and held out her arms so that Lulu could see the damage, and there was blood dripping from the cut on her neck. 'Oh, I'm so sorry, I don't know what I was thinking,' said Lulu, hurrying over to her friend. 'Sit down and I'll get you a towel.' She looked at the cut on Julia's neck and nodded when she saw that it wasn't very deep. She took Julia over to an easy chair, sat her down and hurried into the bathroom. There was a stack of small hand towels by the sink, neatly folded. Lulu picked up three of them and ran them under the tap. She hurried back into the bedroom and placed one of the wet towels against the cut in Julia's neck. 'Keep some pressure on it,' she said.

Julia nodded and did as she was told. 'Do you think I need an ambulance?'

'Maybe, but let's do some first aid now because with the best will in the world it's going to be at least half an hour before an ambulance gets here. And, to be honest, the cuts don't look too deep.' She dabbed at the slice on Julia's left arm with a second towel, then wrapped it around the wound. Then she used the third towel to clean the cut on Julia's right arm. When she had finished, she asked Julia to take the towel away from her neck so that she could have a second look at the wound there. The bleeding had almost stopped. 'I think this is going to be fine. It might not even need stitches,' she said. 'But keep the pressure on it for a while longer.'

'Yes, doctor,' said Julia, and pressed the towel to her neck.

The cut on the right arm had started to bleed again so Lulu dabbed at it and then wrapped the towel around it.

She bent down and picked up her mobile phone and tapped on the screen. 'What are you doing?' asked Julia.

'I'm doing what I should have done in the first place,' said Lulu. She looked at Conrad, who was sitting on the bed watching them. 'I'm calling 999.'

29

Sita Patel got up from the bed, patted Julia on the shoulder and walked over to Tracey and Lulu, who were standing by the window. Conrad was curled up on the sofa, watching them. 'If we carry on like this, I should set up an office here,' she said.

'Is she okay?' asked Lulu.

'She's fine,' said Sita. 'She was very lucky. Most of the cuts are superficial and will heal on their own. The cut to her neck could easily have been fatal if it had been a bit deeper, but as it is I've closed it with surgical glue. She might end up with a slight scar but it'll barely be noticeable. I've just cleaned the superficial cuts and used steri-strips on the bigger ones. I've given her a tetanus shot to be on the safe side.'

'She doesn't need to go to hospital?' asked Tracey.

'She's better off here,' said Sita. 'The way our hospitals are at the moment, there's every chance she'll pick up something more serious. I hope you catch the guy, Tracey. He could easily have killed her.'

'That was his plan.'

Sita picked up her medical bag. 'Right, I'm off,' she said and headed out of the room, waving goodbye to Julia as she went.

Tracey and Lulu went over to the bed. Julia was propped up with pillows and her arms were dotted with steri-strips.

The closed wound on her neck was barely visible. 'How do you feel?' asked Lulu, sitting on the side of the bed.

'Lucky to be alive, frankly,' said Julia.

'Tell me again what happened, right from the start,' said Tracey.

'I was asleep, half asleep anyway,' said Julia. 'I heard a door open and close down the hallway. So I sat up and switched on the light. Then I heard another door open and close, it sounded as if someone was walking along the hall. I thought maybe it was Lulu and that she'd forgotten what room I was in.'

'There are a lot of bedrooms,' said Lulu.

'Then the door opened and it was a man in a ski mask with a knife. I screamed and tried to run to the bathroom but he was too quick and he blocked my way. I grabbed a pillow and used that to fight him off, but it wasn't much use. Then Lulu appeared.' She forced a smile. 'You saved my life.'

'I think it was Conrad who did the saving.'

'Conrad?' said Tracey.

'Conrad attacked him,' said Julia. 'It was amazing, I've never seen anything like it. He was fearless. He jumped at him and clawed his face. Well, his mask anyway.'

'No, I'm pretty sure he drew blood,' said Lulu. 'When will SOCO be here? They might be able to get the attacker's DNA.'

'SOCO won't be out until the morning, unfortunately,' said Tracey. 'There are overtime issues. Plus it's not a murder case so I can't plead priority.'

'Well, it sort of is a murder case,' said Lulu. 'It's obviously the same man who killed Bernard. And from the look of it, I'd say it was the same knife.'

'Really?'

Lulu nodded. 'The blade was about ten inches, long and thin, curved with a sharp tip.'

'That does sound like it,' said Tracey. 'But even so, SOCO won't be out until after nine. But I can get a head start.' She opened her handbag and took out a small plastic evidence bag, a sealed swab and a pair of latex gloves.

'You are well prepared,' said Lulu.

'It comes with the job these days,' said Tracey. She pulled on the gloves. 'Can you hold Conrad for me?'

'Sure.' Lulu sat down on the bed and Conrad jumped onto her lap.

'Was it just the front paws?'

Lulu nodded. 'Yes, and I think it was the right paw that did the damage. The cuts were on the left side of his face.'

Tracey opened the pack and took out the swab. Lulu held Conrad's paws and he obligingly extended his claws. There were spots of blood on two of the claws on his right paw. Tracey carefully swiped the swab along the claws and then popped it into a small plastic tube and sealed it. 'Job done,' she said, pulling off the latex gloves. 'So, the glass was smashed in the French windows of the study, the same as last time.'

Lulu nodded. 'Yes, this time they were locked. I made sure everything was locked before I went to bed.'

'And it looks as if he left the same way.'

'I don't know,' said Lulu. 'I didn't try to follow him, he still had the knife.'

'Did you hear him drive off?' Tracey took a notebook and pen from her pocket.

Lulu shook her head. 'No. Nothing. And I didn't hear anyone drive up. But then I was asleep.'

'What woke you up?'

Lulu looked at Conrad and smiled. She could hardly tell Tracey that Conrad had woken her. 'I guess it must have been Julia's scream.'

'So a car or a bike could have driven up and you wouldn't have heard it?'

'True. But I definitely didn't hear a car drive away. Or a bike.'

'Me neither,' said Julia.

'He must have parked some distance away and walked here,' said Tracey. 'And it's clear he wasn't familiar with the layout of the house.'

'Why do you say that?' asked Julia.

'Because he had to try several doors before he found your room,' said Tracey. 'I know he was wearing a mask and gloves, but can you remember anything about him – anything at all?'

'He was young, I think,' said Julia. 'And I think he was white.'

'I think so, too,' said Lulu. 'I could see a patch of skin where Conrad had ripped the mask. White and clean shaven.'

'Did he say anything?' asked Tracey, scribbling in her notebook.

'He shouted "bitch" at me, that's all.'

'Did he have an accent?'

'It was just the one word and he shouted it,' said Julia.

'And there was nothing familiar about him, about the way he moved or the way he held himself? He didn't remind you of anyone?'

'No one,' said Julia. 'No one at all.'

'Okay,' said Tracey, putting her notebook away. 'I think that's all I need for the moment. Now, there are four uniformed officers downstairs with DC Collier. They've checked the house and the grounds and we're sure he's gone. But obviously what's happened is a worry.'

'You think he might come back?'

'He killed Bernard and he came back to kill Julia. He's clearly driven by something so I don't think he'll give up, but I don't think he'll be back tonight. Having said that, I'm going to leave two officers here overnight, one at the front door and one by the terrace. We found the switches for the outside light so we'll keep the gardens illuminated. But with the best will in the world I don't think you should be staying here until we've caught the guy.'

'It's my home,' said Julia.

'Yes, I understand that. But it's very big and it's in the middle of nowhere. I can't give you a twenty-four-seven police guard, I'm afraid. I can use the excuse that they're securing a crime scene tonight, but once SOCO have come, they'll have to go. You saw how easy it was for him to break in last night. He could come back again, and next time you might not be so lucky. I do think we will catch this guy sooner rather than later, but until we do I think you'd be safer staying somewhere else.'

'Come and stay with me on *The Lark*,' said Lulu. 'The bed is big enough for two, or I can sleep on the sofa. It'll be cosy and only the three of us will know that you're there. I'll have to move her again soon but that's a good thing, too.'

'How secure is the boat?' asked Tracey.

'I'm still moored at Jericho and there are lots of other boats around. I can lock all the doors and windows and anyone would be sure to hear someone trying to break in.'

Tracey nodded thoughtfully. 'It sounds like a good idea,' she said. 'If there was an issue, a patrol car can get to Jericho a lot more quickly than it can get here.'

'So that's agreed,' said Lulu. 'Once SOCO have finished, we can pack a few things and head to *The Lark*.'

'I'll be here later today, so I can drive you.' Tracey looked at her watch. 'Well, if I'm lucky I'll be able to get a few hours' sleep still.'

'I'll walk you to the front door,' said Lulu.

'In case I get lost, you mean?'

Lulu chuckled as she bent down so that Conrad could jump onto her shoulders, then she took Tracey out of the bedroom and along the hall.

'So your bedroom is along there?' said Tracey, pointing towards the other hallway.

'Yes. The guest wing.'

Tracey looked back the way they had come. 'You must have run like the wind.'

'The adrenaline must have kicked in,' said Lulu. 'To be honest, if I had been thinking straight I probably should have phoned the police first.'

'Meow!' said Conrad.

'Well, Conrad obviously agrees with you,' said Tracey. She looked back towards the guest wing. 'You must have amazing hearing, to have heard the noise from Julia's room, all the way down there.'

'It was the middle of the night and I guess the sound carried.'

'Well, either way she was very lucky. If you hadn't heard her cry out, I dread to think what might have happened.'

They went down the stairs together. 'Oh, I spoke to the

chief financial officer of the vaccine company today,' said Tracey. 'He was very helpful, very forthcoming. He even showed me some very impressive spreadshects that I couldn't make head nor tail of. But what I took away from him was that the company is in very good shape financially, and has been for a couple of years. The Grenvilles were always going to make a great deal of money from the flotation, and their shareholding looks set to be worth tens of millions of pounds. Maybe as much as a hundred million.'

'Wow,' said Lulu.

'Yes, that's what I said. It's a lot. But the company hasn't always been as successful as it is now. The chap I spoke to was brought in after the partners had all chipped in funds to keep it afloat. His name is Jeremy Wilkinson.'

They reached the bottom of the stairs and walked across the marble floor to the front door. 'Anyway, Jeremy says about five years ago the partners – including Julia – had a great idea for their medical company but they needed to put it into practice before they could get outside investors interested. They needed to set up a lab, employ technicians and run a number of clinical trials. There were six partners in all and they needed three million pounds to get up and running. Half a million pounds each. Three of the partners came from wealthy families, so they had no problem coming up with the cash, one took out a second mortgage and the other sold one of their buy-to-let properties. Apparently Julia and Bernard were struggling to find the money: their shop was ticking over but the bank wouldn't give them a loan. Then their shop caught fire and the insurance company paid up and they had the money they needed to invest.'

'So you think it was arson?'

Tracey shrugged. 'The fire investigators say no, but at the time they didn't know that Bernard and Julia needed the cash urgently. Setting fire to their business wouldn't have made sense if it was ticking over, which it was, but it makes perfect sense when you know that they needed half a million pounds. And that's pretty much what they had in the bank once they'd paid off their mortgage and their debts.'

'I can't see them deliberately setting fire to their shop, Tracey. I really can't.'

'Well, at some point I'm going to have a chat with the lead investigator,' said Tracey. 'Get it from the horse's mouth.'

'Can I come?'

'I don't see why not.'

Lulu opened the front door. A uniformed constable in a high-vis jacket nodded at Tracey and stepped to the side to allow them out. They walked towards Tracey's blue Mondeo.

'They knew that if they didn't come up with the money they'd risk losing millions,' continued Tracey. 'They needed Julia's scientific expertise, but she wasn't the only scientist on the team.'

'The magazine article made it sound as if she was the power behind the company.'

Tracey smiled. 'Yes, it did. But Jeremy says that was just PR. There are four scientists on the team and none is irreplaceable. If Julia and Bernard hadn't come up with the money, they would have gone ahead without Julia. Or used her as an employee, paid her a salary for her work. A good salary, sure, but nothing compared with what she got as a director and shareholder.'

Tracey opened the door to the Mondeo. 'And again, please

don't say anything to Julia. It's perfectly possible that she's an innocent party in all this.'

'Bernard did it without telling her, you mean?'

'I'm going to take a look at the fire scene and see if anything was missed at the time. Until then, I'd be grateful if you kept it to yourself.'

'I will,' said Lulu.

Tracey got into the car and Lulu and Conrad watched her drive away.

'What do you think?' asked Conrad. 'Do you think they deliberately set fire to the shop for the insurance money?'

'On a gut level, no. Absolutely not. I wouldn't have thought either of them could possibly do something like that.'

'But you have to look at the evidence. That's what you always say.'

'Yes. Exactly. And in this case, it's all circumstantial. If there had been anything at all suspicious about the fire, the fire investigators would have found it. They're professionals – not much gets past them.'

30

Lulu and Conrad spent the rest of the night in Julia's bedroom. Conrad slept curled up next to Julia on the bed and Lulu lay on the sofa by the window. Several times during the night Conrad opened his eyes and his ears twitched if he heard a noise outside, but he soon settled down again. Lulu woke up at eight. She drew back the curtains and looked out. The sky was a cloudless blue. She let the curtains fall back and went into the bathroom and showered, then chose a blue and white Karen Millen dress from Julia's collection. Julia was still sleeping when she went back into the bedroom.

'I'll stay with her,' whispered Conrad.

'Thank you,' said Lulu.

She went downstairs. She was about to head to the kitchen but then had a change of heart and opened the front door instead. A young constable was standing there, a high-vis jacket over his uniform. He had his back to the door and was staring down the drive. 'Good morning, officer,' she said.

'Good morning, ma'am,' he said. He was in his twenties, fresh faced and stick thin, wearing gold-framed spectacles. He looked more like a librarian than a thief-taker, was Lulu's first thought.

'Can I interest you in a bacon sandwich and a cup of tea?' said Lulu.

'It sounds amazing but I really shouldn't, ma'am.'

'Nonsense, I used to be in the job and I know that the police thrive on strong tea and bacon sandwiches. The only decision you need to make is, red or brown sauce and how many sugars in your tea?'

The constable grinned. 'Brown, please, ma'am. And two.'

'Good choice. So everything was quiet last night?'

'Very quiet,' said the constable. 'You've got foxes on your land, I heard them barking. And there's a tawny owl off in the woods. But no visitors.'

'Excellent,' said Lulu. The constable guarding the terrace was older and heavier and needed no persuading to place his breakfast order.

Lulu walked around to the kitchen and spent the next twenty minutes making bacon sandwiches and mugs of strong tea. She served the two constables and then sat in the conservatory and ate her own sandwich – liberally covered in Heinz tomato ketchup – and drank her tea. She stared out over the garden as she ate, trying to process everything that had happened the previous night. She had faced violence before in her thirty years as a police officer in London, it went with the turf. She had encountered criminals carrying knives and once a sawn-off shotgun, but in her police days she had always had backup. When she had burst into Julia's bedroom there had been no one supporting her, it was just two women and a cat against a man with a very deadly knife. It could have so easily ended badly; if it hadn't been for Conrad launching himself at the man, both Lulu and Julia could have ended up dead on the floor.

And who was this man who hated the Grenvilles so much that he had killed Bernard and broken into the house to kill Julia? Knives were a very personal weapon. They had to be used up close and repetitively. Generally one stab wasn't fatal, unless the first blow struck the heart or severed a major artery. Knives had to be used several times and the killer had to be right next to the victim. Guns killed at a distance, and a poisoner could be miles away when his victim died, but knives meant that the killer was there to hear the last gasp and see the life fade from the victim's eyes. It took passion or hatred to kill with a knife, so who could possibly have hated Bernard and Julia so much? They didn't appear to have any enemies, and no one would gain financially from their deaths. She frowned, wondering what would have happened to Julia's money if she had died. Neither she nor Bernard had made a will, which meant that when Bernard died everything went to Julia. But what would happen if Julia then died – who would inherit her estate? It would be worth millions of pounds, and people had killed for much less. Was it as simple as that? A relative had seen how much money the Grenvilles had and they had decided they wanted it for themselves. Was the man in the mask a hired killer, then? Had someone paid him to kill Bernard and Julia? But he had seemed so young. The mask had hidden his face but there was no disguising the fact that he had the body of a teenager, a man in his early twenties at most. And professional killers rarely used knives. Guns were the weapon of choice. Knives were for amateurs.

The killer's lack of experience had shown when he had fled following Conrad's attack. He'd still had the upper hand, he was bigger and stronger than Julia and Lulu, and he had the knife, but he had panicked and fled. Professionals didn't panic. So it was personal: the man hated them with such a passion that he wanted to stab them to death. That brought her around full circle to her original question – who could possibly have hated them that much?

She finished her sandwich and tea and washed her plate and mug and the frying pan in the sink, then took out two frozen croissants and popped them into the oven. As they cooked, Lulu made a fresh cup of tea for Julia. When the croissants were piping hot, Lulu put them on a tray with jam, honey, butter and a cup of tea. She carried it carefully to the hall and up the stairs. By the time she reached Julia's bedroom, her arms were aching. The house was ridiculously large; a simple breakfast delivery was a major undertaking and it made no sense that Bernard and Julia had chosen to live there. It was a house that cried out for a large family and an even larger staff.

She balanced the tray on her left arm and opened the door. Conrad sat up immediately, his ears up, but he relaxed as soon as he saw it was Lulu. Julia was still fast asleep, hugging one of her pillows. Lulu used her foot to close the door and carried the tray over to the bed.

'She's been dreaming a lot,' said Conrad. 'She keeps saying Bernard's name.'

'Did she say anything else?'

'Just his name.'

Lulu put the tray on the bedside table and sat down on the bed. She gently touched Julia on the shoulder.

'Maybe you should let her sleep,' said Conrad. 'She seems happy.'

'She has to face the real world,' said Lulu.

'There's value in sleep,' said Conrad. 'That's why cats nap so much.'

'I suppose so,' said Lulu.

'Who are you talking to?' murmured Julia. Her eyes fluttered open. 'Were you talking to me?'

'I was just telling you that I'm delivering breakfast in bed.'

'What time is it?'

'Just after nine.'

Julia rolled onto her back and smiled up at Lulu. 'Breakfast in bed?'

'And service with a smile. Come on, sit up.' Lulu helped Julia up and put a pillow behind her back.

'I'm really not hungry, Lulu.'

'Humour me.'

'Yes, doctor doctor.' She sipped her tea and then looked at the plasters on her arms. 'It feels like a dream, doesn't it? As if it never really happened. If it wasn't for the plasters I'd think that I had imagined it all.'

'A nightmare, more like,' said Lulu.

'Who was he? Why does he want to kill me?'

'I was asking myself the same question,' said Lulu. 'Can you think of anyone, anyone at all, who would want to hurt you or Bernard?'

'I told you before, we don't have enemies. We really don't. Everyone at the company wants the same thing; we barely see our neighbours, never mind talk to them; we don't get into arguments with people. There are no love triangles, I'm with Bernard . . .' Her face fell and she corrected herself. 'I was with Bernard every night of our marriage. We never slept apart. Not once. We actually made it a rule. Not that we needed it to be a rule, we just wanted to always say goodnight in person. Face to face. So there are no spurned lovers, nothing at all like that.'

'And I know this sounds morbid, but what would happen to all your money if you did die?'

'My money?'

'The shares in the company, this house, the paintings, everything. You said you and Bernard never drew up wills.'

'That's right.' She frowned. 'I see what you mean. Wow, I hadn't thought of that. Bernard has two brothers and they have children, but of course when he died everything came to me. My parents are dead and my sister died ten years ago, so I guess it would go to her children.'

'How many children?'

'Three. Two boys and a girl. They're all grown. My brother-in-law remarried and he lives in Spain with his new wife now.'

'I know this is going to sound crazy, but is there any way that the guy from last night could be one of your nephews?'

'Of course not. Michael is in his mid-thirties and Paul is just a few years younger.'

'Do they have sons?'

'Lulu, seriously, what are you suggesting?'

'It's the detective in me,' said Lulu. 'Once a copper, always a copper.'

'You think one of my relatives might have done this?'

'It's all down to motive, Julia. And money, or greed, they're prime motives. It occurred to me that someone – a distant relative maybe – might have realized that if you and Bernard died, they would get tens of millions of pounds. People have been killed for a lot less than that.'

'I'm sure they have, but it's not generally known that Bernard and I never drew up wills. For all anyone knows our money goes to the RSPCA.'

'Bernard might have mentioned it at a family party. Then when there was all the publicity about the IPO, maybe someone saw an opportunity.'

'Well, Michael is in Los Angeles. He married an American and he's a dentist. No children. Paul is gay, he and his husband adopted a lovely little girl from China.'

'And the man from last night – I know he was masked and we didn't get a look at his face – but did he remind you of any of your relatives?'

'Categorically, absolutely, not,' said Julia.

'Okay, I'm sorry, I had to ask,' said Lulu.

'Well that's not strictly speaking true,' said Julia with a smile. 'You could just have let Tracey carry out her investigation. But it's like you said: once a copper, always a copper.'

'I know, I'm sorry. I just want this guy stopped, whoever he is. I worry that if they don't catch him, he might try again.'

'Oh, Lulu, please don't say that.'

'We have to consider that possibility, Julia. He killed Bernard and he came back to kill you. I don't see that he's simply going to shrug and forget about it. He must have a reason for doing what he did and that reason hasn't suddenly gone away.'

'You're starting to scare me now.'

Lulu patted her on the shoulder. 'I don't mean to, but equally I don't want anything to happen to you.'

Julia forced a smile. 'Thank you.'

'Now eat your breakfast.'

'Yes, doctor doctor.' She broke off a piece of croissant and nibbled it.

They heard the doorbell ring in the distance. 'That'll be Tracey,' said Lulu. 'I'll go and let her in.'

Conrad mewed and stood up, arching his back and then relaxing. 'Sounds as if he wants to go with you,' said Julia.

'It does, doesn't it?' Lulu bent down so that Conrad could scamper up onto her shoulders. Lulu pointed at the tray. 'And make sure you finish that!'

'I will, ma'am,' said Julia, flashing her a mock salute.

Lulu walked to the hall, took the stairs on the left, and opened the front door. It wasn't Tracey, and it took her a few seconds to realize that it was Dr Patel. She was wearing a beige overcoat and a black beret and carrying a medical bag. 'Sita, sorry, I wasn't expecting you.'

'I thought I'd better pop in bright and early to check Julia's dressings,' said the doctor. She grinned at Conrad. 'Good morning, Conrad.' She stepped to the side so that Lulu could see Tracey, who was standing by her Mondeo as she pulled blue shoe covers over her black pumps. A SOCO van was parked behind the Mondeo and two technicians were pulling on forensic suits. Lulu waved at Tracey and Tracey waved back. 'How was Julia overnight?' asked Sita.

'She slept right through,' said Lulu. 'I just took her up some breakfast.'

'I can't imagine how she must feel, seeing Bernard die like that and then to be attacked herself.'

'She's quite strong. Resilient.'

'She is, yes,' said Sita.

'Can you find your own way up to her room?' asked Lulu.

'Is there a map?'

Lulu grinned. 'Unfortunately not.'

'I left a trail of breadcrumbs last time I was here, so with any luck that'll help.' Sita headed into the hall and up the stairs.

The young constable was standing to the side of the door. He smiled and nodded at Lulu. 'Thanks for the sarnie, ma'am,' he said. 'It hit the spot. I'll drop the mug in the kitchen when I leave.'

'No problem,' said Lulu. She walked over to Tracey, who was still adjusting her shoe covers.

'How's Julia?' Tracey asked.

'I was just telling Sita, she seems fine.'

'That's good,' said Tracey. 'I gave them the swab I took from Conrad's claws and I've requested that it be fast-tracked. If we're lucky his DNA will be in the system.'

'Fingers crossed,' said Lulu.

'But even if it isn't, it'll help when we finally get a suspect,' said Tracey. 'And there's something else I want to show you.' She straightened up, walked around to the rear of the Mondeo and opened the boot. She leaned in and took out a painting inside a large evidence bag. Lulu realized it was the oil painting of Bamburgh Castle. 'Best we do it in the study. You'll need shoe covers.' She handed Lulu a pack of blue shoe covers.

'Of course,' said Lulu. She opened the pack, pulled the covers over her trainers, and took Tracey into the house. They went through the main hall and down the corridor to the study.

There were already two SOCOs in the room. A man was photographing the broken glass by the French windows, while a woman was examining the floor close to the coffee table. They were both wearing white forensic suits and blue shoe covers. Lulu recognized the photographer as Robbie, who had been there when they had found the missing paintings.

'Hi Robbie, hi Gemma,' said Tracey.

Robbie nodded and smiled, the woman stood up and

grinned at Tracey. 'This is the third time I've been out here, maybe I should move in,' she said.

'Sita was saying the same: she was here last night looking after Mrs Grenville.'

'How is Mrs Grenville?'

'Surprisingly well, considering what happened,' said Tracey. 'I'll take you up when you're ready. There's quite a bit of blood in the room but it's all Mrs Grenville's. Conrad scratched the assailant, but there didn't seem to be any of his blood on the carpet. I swabbed Conrad's claws and booked the sample in last night.'

Gemma frowned. 'Conrad?'

Tracey gestured at Conrad, who was wrapped around Lulu's neck.

'Oh my gosh, how did I miss that?' said Gemma. She laughed and shook her head. 'You'd think a SOCO would have better powers of observation, wouldn't you? So Conrad is a he? Most calicos are female, aren't they? That makes him a very special cat indeed.'

'Meow!' said Conrad.

'Oh, listen to him. He agrees with me.' She held up her gloved hands. 'I'd stroke you but I know most cats really don't like the feel of latex.'

Tracey held out the picture. 'So, I wanted to run this by Lulu and get her thoughts.'

'Ah, yes, the mysterious spatter.'

'Would you hold it in position? It was over there behind the desk.'

'No problem,' said Gemma. She took the painting and walked carefully behind the desk.

'Lulu, can you stand in the middle of the room, just

about there.' She looked over at Gemma. 'That's where Billy Russell would have been standing, right? Based on where the body was found.'

'That's about right. Maybe facing a bit more this way.'

Lulu shuffled around. 'Like this?'

'A bit less.'

Lulu moved again. 'That works for me,' said Gemma. She was holding the picture against the wall. Tracey went to stand in front of Lulu, then looked over at the fireplace. 'Let's make this more realistic,' she said. She went over to the fireplace and picked up a set of brass tongs. She went back to Lulu. 'So, Billy Russell was hit three times on the head, from the front,' she said. She raised the tongs.

'Tracey, do you want me to take some pictures?' Robbie asked. 'For posterity?'

'That would be great, Robbie, thank you.'

'I'll maybe put a soft filter on, to make you more attractive.'

'Would you? That is so sweet.' Tracey looked at Lulu. 'So, from the spatter pattern it looks as if Mr Russell was hit here, with a downward blow.' She slowly brought down the tongs so that they almost brushed Lulu's hair. 'The poker was then brought back, causing some spatter on the floor, and then Mr Russell was hit again, harder this time, causing more spatter. The poker was then placed on the floor.' Tracey pointed at the spot on the floor where the poker had been found. Robbie clicked away with his camera as Tracey carefully put the tongs down and straightened up. 'So, we had Mr Russell's blood on the floor from where he had been struck, and more blood that had come off the poker.'

'That all makes sense,' said Lulu.

'It does,' said Tracey. 'But what doesn't make sense is the blood spatter on the painting. You can see how far away we are from it. There's no way Mr Russell being hit here could end up with blood spatter on the wall. Am I right, Gemma?'

'You're absolutely right,' said the SOCO. She took the picture away from the wall and held it out. 'And of course it wouldn't explain how blood got on the back of the painting, would it?'

'Really?' said Lulu. 'The back?'

'Yup,' said Gemma. She walked around the desk and over to Lulu.

Lulu took the painting from her. Even through the plastic of the evidence bag she could see the spots of blood on the back. The frame had also been dusted for fingerprints.

'Now hold the painting in front of you. As if you were showing it to me.'

Lulu did as she was told. Tracey bent down and picked up the tongs. Robbie moved to the side to get a better view for his camera.

Tracey raised the tongs above her head. 'Now when I hit you, the blood spatters down on both sides of the painting.' She mimed hitting Lulu on the head. 'One. Two. Three. Now there is blood on the floor where you're standing. And there is blood behind me that has fallen off the poker. And there's spatter on the front and the back of the painting. And if you look carefully, you can see spatter on top of the frame. Now, there's other blood on there, smears from when it was picked up and carried, but there's only one way the spatter could have got here.'

'So Billy Russell was holding the painting when he was killed?'

'Exactly,' said Tracey. 'And to confirm it, we found Russell's prints – and Bernard's – on the frame.' She took the painting from Lulu and gave it to Gemma. 'Can you take that back with you?'

'Of course,' said Gemma.

'But if Billy Russell was killed while he was holding the painting, why didn't Bernard mention that?' said Lulu. 'He can't have forgotten, can he?'

'I think we've reached the point where we have to accept the fact that Bernard killed Russell,' said Tracey. 'That's why there was so much of Russell's blood on his clothing. So we can pretty much discount everything he told us. The robbery, the break-in, the masked men: he made it all up to cover up the fact that he killed Billy Russell.'

Tracey's phone rang. She handed the tongs to Lulu, then took the phone out of her pocket and looked at the screen. 'I have to take this,' she said. She walked to the far end of the study.

Lulu replaced the tongs on the rack by the fireplace. Gemma put the Bamburgh Castle painting onto Julia's desk.

'If Bernard is lying about the attack – and I'm starting to accept that he was – then what about his injuries?' said Lulu. 'Is it possible he was fighting with Russell?'

'Both of their blood was on the poker, there's no doubt about that. But once Russell had been hit he'd have been in no state to hit Bernard. The second blow killed him, it cracked the skull and there was massive internal bleeding.' She shrugged. 'Bernard must have inflicted the injuries on himself. That's the only thing that makes sense.'

'He was really hurt,' said Lulu.

'Well, was he?" said Gemma. 'I mean, I was here on the

day and yes, there was a lot of blood, but he was checked out at the hospital, scans and everything, and he was basically okay. No serious damage. What happened to Russell shows you the sort of damage that a poker can do in the right hands.' She grimaced. 'I suppose I should say in the wrong hands, shouldn't I?'

'You think he hit himself with the poker?'

'Why not? His blood is all over it.' Gemma mimed holding a poker and hitting herself on the head with it. 'It takes commitment, but if he had just killed Russell then he'd be high on adrenaline. It's doable. And of course the black eye came from when he hit the coffee table.' She pointed at the coffee table in front of the sofa where Conrad was sitting. 'He made it sound as if he fell against it after he was hit but it would be easy enough to kneel down and just fall forward. That would give you a shiner, guaranteed. It would explain the two marks the poker made on the floor. He could have hit Russell, put the poker on the floor while he took away the paintings as part of his robbery story, then he came back, picked up the poker, walloped himself, put the poker down, then throws himself against the coffee table.'

Lulu shook her head. 'I still can't believe that Bernard would do all that.'

'I guess you do whatever you have to if you want to stay out of prison,' said Gemma.

'Who's staying out of prison?' said Tracey as she walked towards them, slipping her phone back into her pocket.

'We were just talking about everything Bernard must have done to paint the scenario he did,' said Lulu. 'The wounds to his head and eye, he had to have done it to himself.'

'And it would have worked if we hadn't found the paintings in the filter room,' said Tracey. 'Okay, that was the fire investigation guy. He can give us half an hour at the scene. Do you still want to come?'

'Sure,' said Lulu.

'Which crime scene is this?' asked Gemma.

'It's a fire, from five years ago,' said Tracey. 'It may or may not be connected to this, we're still not sure.'

'And Dishy Dave is where? He's still your bag carrier, isn't he?'

'Dental appointment. He lost a crown biting into a kebab. We'll be back in an hour or so.'

'We'll still be here.'

'Can you make your own way up to Mrs Grenville's bedroom? Take the stairs and go left along the hallway, it's the fourth room on the left.'

'Fifth,' said Lulu.

'I stand corrected,' said Tracey. 'Dr Patel is up there with Julia. Tell her I'll call her later.'

'To be honest, I'm not sure how much forensics there will be up there,' said Lulu. 'He was wearing a mask and gloves and the only contact he had with her or the pillow was the knife.'

'Pillow?' Gemma repeated.

'Julia used a pillow to fight him off,' said Lulu. 'There's a lot of blood on it but it's all hers.'

'We'll check anyway,' said Gemma. 'So far it's not looking good. No footprints in or outside. It's been dry for the last few nights, so no mud. It looks as if he might have trodden in the broken glass, though, so if we do catch the guy we might find traces in his shoes that will tie him to the crime scene.'

'Right, well my mobile is on, so call me if you need me, otherwise we'll be back here in less than an hour and a half.'

Lulu went over to the sofa and bent down so that Conrad could jump onto her shoulders.

'That's a great trick,' said Robbie. 'I wish I could try that.'

'I'm not sure I could take your weight, Robbie,' said Lulu.

31

'There he is,' said Tracey, nodding at a red van with OXFORDSHIRE FIRE AND RESCUE on the side and INVESTIGATION UNIT on the door. It was parked in front of a line of shops. The parking was metered and there were no spaces free, so she drove further down the road. She managed to find a space and reversed in, then she and Lulu walked back along the pavement. Conrad was wrapped around Lulu's neck. She barely felt his weight any more, it was as if he became part of her when he was on her shoulders.

As they approached the van, the driver's door opened and a big burly man with dishevelled ginger hair climbed out. He was wearing a fireman's tunic, fireproof leggings and heavy boots. As he turned to face them Lulu could see he had a sprinkling of freckles across a nose that looked as if it had been broken a couple of times. He had a broad chin with a large dimple in the centre, and when he smiled at Tracey he revealed large slab-like teeth. 'Long time no see, Tracey,' he said.

'This is good of you, Ricky, I know how busy you guys are.' Ricky held out a massive fist and Tracey pumped hers against it. 'This is Lulu, a former Met detective superintendent who's riding shotgun on this one.'

'Nice to meet you, Lulu,' he said. He nodded at Conrad. 'And friend.'

He looked to Lulu as if he would have no trouble carrying an entire family out of a burning building. 'His name's Conrad,' said Lulu. 'We're a team.'

'Well, I can see that.' He was holding a large plastic file in his left hand, and he used it to wave at a Thai restaurant close to the end of the parade of shops. 'This is where it happened,' he said. 'I was actually part of the investigation. I'd only been with the unit for six months or so and I was shadowing the number two, a guy called Ronnie Crawford.' He took them along to the front of the restaurant. It was called SIAM KITCHEN and the name was spelled out in ornate gold letters. By the door was a framed menu along with a phone number and web address. 'There's no point in going inside because it was totally rebuilt after the fire,' he said. 'But back in the day, this front area was an antiques shop. It had an entirely different frontage, which was all destroyed. Behind the shop was a small bathroom, and a storeroom, and stairs leading up to the flat. Then beyond the stairs was a large room that was used as a workshop. The woman who died in the fire restored paintings and furniture. She and her family lived upstairs rent-free as part of the deal she had with Bernard.'

'Victoria McBride?' said Tracey.

'That's right. You heard the story, yeah? She was due to go to Exeter with her husband and their son. It was her in-laws' wedding anniversary. Their fortieth, I think. Anyway, the day they were due to go, she was sick. A bad cold, her husband said. She insisted that they go without her, and they did. They went on the Saturday and they were due back on Sunday afternoon. The fire broke out just after midnight and she died of smoke inhalation. The main bedroom was directly above the workshop.'

'And there was no smoke alarm?'

'No, there were two. One in the shop and one in the workshop.'

'So why didn't they wake her up?'

Ricky smiled thinly. 'I asked the same question. Ronnie said it was probably because the lady was doped up on Night Nurse. But nobody outside heard the alarms go off, either. Ronnie said that it was because it was late at night so there wouldn't be many people around.'

'But the people next door, on either side – wouldn't they have heard the alarms?'

'Ronnie said the party walls were thick.'

'It sounds as if Ronnie had an answer for everything,' said Lulu.

'Yes, well, I can't argue with that,' said Ricky. 'Both smoke alarms were badly burned in the fire, but both had batteries in. Ronnie took them away for analysis and later we got a report saying that they were both fully charged, but . . .' He gestured vaguely but didn't finish the sentence.

'But what?' said Lulu.

'I don't know. Maybe nothing.'

'Tell us,' said Tracey.

'Well, I did see the batteries a few weeks later. They were in evidence bags. See, I don't think they were the batteries that we took from the alarms. They were the same brand, but the smoke damage didn't look the same to me. By then Ronnie had sent in his report, that it was an accident, and we were working on other cases, so I just let it be. I was still on probation and I didn't want to rock the boat.'

'And what did Ronnie's report say?'

'The fire was accidental. The workshop was used to restore paintings and furniture so it was full of flammable materials. The lady used all sorts of alcohol-based fluids to clean oil paintings, and there were containers of paint and thinners and varnish all over the place. And she used an electric fire to keep the room warm, one of those twin-bar things. She had finished varnishing a bookcase and the weather had been cold, so she kept the fire on all day and night. Ronnie thought the radiant heat from the fire had been enough to ignite an oil painting that had been left too close to it. And once the fire had started, it ripped through the workshop and then into the shop. Antiques, right? You can imagine how quickly it burned, it was all wood and paper and canvas. There was some metal and pottery, but the rest of it . . .' He frowned as he remembered. 'It tore through the shop in minutes, and by the time the appliances got there it was well ablaze.'

'But the upstairs flat wasn't burned?'

'No, the appliances got there in time to stop it spreading upstairs, but by then the lady was dead from smoke inhalation.'

'And what did you think about the cause of the fire?'

'Oh, it was the electric fire, no question. It ignited a painting close to the bookcase. You could see how the fire had spread out from the bookcase and there was only the one point of origin.'

'So it was an accident?' said Lulu.

'Well, that's up for debate,' said Ricky. 'The point of origin was the painting in front of the fire. But according to the lady's son, there wasn't a painting in front of the fire when he checked, and he was the last person in there.'

'You spoke to the boy?'

'We spoke to the boy and his father, and to Bernard. The father didn't see anything, he was out fetching his car. Parking is a nightmare around here. But the boy was adamant that there wasn't a painting in front of the fire.'

'What did Bernard say?'

'He hadn't been in that day. Weekends were usually quiet so the shop was shut with a telephone number on the door if anyone wanted Bernard to come around and open up the shop. But he said that Victoria was always careful with the materials she used and that she had been in the business for a lot of years. He was very . . . plausible.'

'But you didn't believe him?'

'I was never asked at the time. But looking back, no, I didn't. There was a burglar alarm fitted and it hadn't gone off and there were no signs of forced entry other than the damage done by the firefighters. So if it was arson, then the perpetrator must have had a key, and that narrowed it down to just a handful of people.'

'Why was the boy in the workshop?' asked Tracey.

'His mum had sent him to make sure that the heater was on because the cold would have ruined the finish on the bookcase she was working on.'

'And why didn't Ronnie believe him?'

'Ronnie said you couldn't trust teenage boys to do anything, they only had one thing on their mind. Fair enough, I've got a boy, so I know what he means. But he seemed fine to me. Distraught about his mum, obviously, but quite clear on what had happened the last time he saw her.'

'So Ronnie just ignored what the boy said?' said Tracey.

'Pretty much.' He looked up and down the street as if

checking that they wouldn't be overhead. 'Look, Tracey, this is all off the record, right? I mean, obviously my meeting with you is in my diary and I expect you to do the same, but I'd prefer what is said here to be just between the two of us.' He looked at Lulu. 'Sorry, Lulu. Three.'

Lulu stroked Conrad's hair. 'Four,' she said.

Ricky laughed. 'Right, four. Can we keep the conversation just between the four of us?'

'Of course.'

'The thing is, I always thought there was something a bit off about the way Ronnie handled this investigation. There were a couple of red flags that I saw, but he ignored them. And it happened again with another suspicious fire a few months later. It was a garage, and it screamed arson to me but Ronnie said it was spontaneous combustion of some oily rags.'

'Does that happen?' asked Lulu.

'Well, yes, it does, under the right circumstances. It's the result of oxidation. As the oil oxidizes, it can raise the temperature of the rag through its ignition point. If there's a pile of rags, then the heat can't escape and eventually they can ignite. Garages always know they have to be careful when they dispose of their waste, but mistakes happen. Anyway, Ronnie was adamant that this fire was an accident, but it looked to me as if the fire had started in two places. Now, yes, you can get spontaneous combustion, but it's very, very unlikely to happen twice in the same premises at the same time. Ronnie brushed off my concerns, he said that the second incident was a result of the fire spreading, and he was my boss so I couldn't disagree with him. But he was wrong, Tracey. The fire had started in two places and that meant it was arson. The following year he bought a villa out in Spain. On the Costa Brava. Big place with its own pool.'

'And where is Ronnie these days?'

'He retired about a year after the fire but he's dead now. Died six months ago. Bile duct cancer.' He shrugged. 'Who knew that was a thing? Anyway, his wife sold the villa in Spain and she moved back to the UK. She bought a very nice place in Chipping Norton, I'm told, not far from where David Cameron has a house.'

'That was quick.'

'Well, it was always Ronnie who wanted to live in Spain.'

'You think he was paid off?' said Tracey.

Ricky put his head closer to hers and lowered his voice. 'That's the thing, Tracey. I can't be seen to be saying that, it opens up a whole can of worms. But there were at least three fires that I thought were wrong.' He gestured at the Thai restaurant. 'Including this one. And if he was deliberately ignoring signs of arson, there had to be a reason for that.'

'Pay-offs?' said Lulu.

'I couldn't possibly make that allegation,' said Ricky. 'Not without hard evidence, and that I don't have. The thing is, fire investigation isn't an exact science, even though the textbooks pretend that it is. And the science is changing all the time, the goalposts keep moving. Things that were taken as gospel ten years ago we now know are completely wrong. So there's no way I could ever really prove that he made some bad calls. But there's no doubt that he bought a villa that he really couldn't have afforded on a firefighter's salary. And his wife always drove a top-of-the-range BMW.'

'Maybe his wife had money?'

Ricky shook his head. 'She never worked, not once the kids were born. They have three, two boys and a girl, and the youngest had just finished university when Ronnie retired. He was always moaning about the fees and the way he had to support them while they were studying. He was adamant that he didn't want them saddled with student loans, so he paid for it all.'

'That's a lot of money,' said Tracey.

'Tell me about it,' said Ricky. 'My boy has just started at Reading University and I'm helping as much as I can, but he's still taken out a hefty loan and he's having to flip burgers at McDonald's at the weekend.'

'How easy would it be to bribe an investigation officer?' asked Lulu.

'It's doable,' said Ricky. 'We have to check out the fire scene, obviously, and usually we'd want the owner there because we've always got questions that need answering. It would be the easiest thing in the world for the guy to see if you're amenable to a bribe.'

'Has it happened to you?' asked Lulu.

'A few times. It's usually very subtle: they'll ask if there's any way the investigation can be speeded up, and suggest that maybe they could pay a commission for faster service. They wait until you're on your own and they keep it vague so that you can never prove that a bribe was offered.'

'And did Ronnie talk to Bernard on his own?' asked Lulu.

'A few times. And this was a big claim. A million pounds or so. A bribe of say fifty grand would barely make a dent in the claim.'

'I don't think Bernard had access to fifty thousand pounds

back then,' said Lulu. 'They were living hand to mouth, pretty much. The shop was making money, I'm told, but not enough for Bernard to get his hands on that much cash.'

'I doubt it would have been cash,' said Ricky. 'Ronnie mentioned Bitcoin a few times.' He held up his file. 'Or Bernard might have promised him a cut of the insurance payout. So the fact that he didn't have access to cash wouldn't be an issue. But all this is just chit-chat, right? We're off the record?'

'Absolutely,' said Tracey. 'But answer me this. If someone came forward now with evidence – real evidence – that the fire was arson, could something be done?'

Ricky frowned. 'In what way?'

'Reversing the decision, maybe getting back the insurance payout?'

'Well, that's going to be difficult, isn't it, with Bernard Grenville being dead and all?'

'But before he died? If someone came forward and they could prove that the fire was deliberate, you could redo your report and the insurance company would be able to get its money back?'

'Hypothetically, yes. It's happened before.'

'But that would need new evidence, wouldn't it?'

'Oh, yes. That would be a given. Even the suspicions I had – have – wouldn't be enough. It would need something like an arsonist coming forward and admitting that he had done it and that Bernard had paid him, something like that. But I don't see that happening, do you?'

'I guess not,' said Tracey.

Ricky looked at his watch. 'I've got to go,' he said. 'I'm actually giving evidence in court in an hour.'

'You're a star, Ricky, thanks so much for your time.' Tracey put out her fist and Ricky bumped his against it.

'Nice meeting you, Lulu,' said Ricky. 'And Conrad.' He walked away to his van.

Tracey and Lulu headed back to the Mondeo. Several passers-by spotted Conrad and smiled. 'Well that was interesting,' said Lulu.

'Wasn't it?'

'But just because the fire was arson doesn't mean that it was Bernard who did it.'

'He benefited from it,' said Tracey. 'He and Julia. Everything they have today comes from the insurance payout.'

'Yes, I get that. But he might not have actually done it himself.'

'Even if he didn't, he is the only one who could have bribed Ronnie Crawford. That makes him culpable. But knowing that he was behind the arson attack on his shop five years ago doesn't help us identify his killer, does it? And that's my main concern at the moment.'

They reached the car. Tracey unlocked it and they both climbed in. Conrad curled up in Lulu's lap. His eyes were closed and his breathing was slow and steady but Lulu was sure he was listening to every word. 'So, Bernard set fire to his own shop,' said Tracey. She saw Lulu open her mouth to protest and raised a hand to stop her. 'Or got someone to set fire to it. Either way, the end result was him getting a massive insurance payout. The claims assessor, Billy Russell, was sure that the fire was deliberate but the fire brigade investigator said it was accidental, and was presumably paid for not identifying the fire as arson. Then five years later, Billy Russell goes to see Bernard, and Bernard kills him. Obviously totally unplanned on Bernard's part because he used a poker and frantically tried to cover it up by faking the robbery.'

Lulu nodded but didn't say anything. She knew that Tracey was speaking out loud so that she could get her thoughts in order and she didn't want to interrupt the flow.

'So Billy Russell must have said something to Bernard, something that angered him so much that he grabbed a poker and beat him to death. Now, the only connection they had was the insurance policy, so it had to be connected to the fire and to the insurance payout.' She frowned. 'But what could Billy Russell have to say five years after the fire? Had he found out something? Something that could result in Bernard losing his money – and his liberty? I just don't see what that could have been. As Ricky said, it would have had to have been something dramatic to get the fire brigade to reverse its verdict on the fire.' Tracey sat back in her seat and gripped the steering wheel so tightly that her knuckles whitened. 'So why didn't Russell take the information to the police? Blackmail? Is that what happened? He wanted money from Bernard? Maybe he figured that Bernard had paid off the fire investigator and that he'd pay again. He saw the magazine article that said Bernard was now worth millions and figured he'd tried to get a piece of it.' She turned to look at Lulu for the first time. 'Does that make sense?' she asked.

'It all makes perfect sense,' said Lulu. 'Unfortunately. But it doesn't get us any closer to identifying Bernard's killer, does it?'

'Well, in a way it does,' said Tracey. 'Whoever killed Bernard presumably did it as revenge for Bernard killing

Billy Russell. It must have been someone who knew that Bernard's story of a robbery was made up, and that despite what was in the papers and on TV, Bernard had killed Russell. Which means they must have known why Russell had gone to see Bernard.'

'An accomplice?'

'A friend. A relative. A colleague. But yes, an accomplice.'

'Well, we know he didn't have many friends, right? That's what his wife said. And I don't see Mrs Russell sneaking into the house to stab Bernard, do you?'

Tracey shook her head. 'You saw him, Lulu. So did Julia. We know he's a young man. Currently sporting wounds on his left cheek, courtesy of Conrad the cat.'

Conrad opened his eyes. 'Meow!' he said.

Tracey chuckled. 'He's been listening to everything we said.'

'So, if he's not a relative and not a friend, maybe he's a colleague of Billy's,' Tracey continued. 'Maybe Billy spoke to a colleague about his suspicions and they cooked up this plan together. Then when Bernard killed Russell, the colleague wanted revenge. He kills Bernard and then he goes back to kill Julia.'

Lulu grimaced. 'I don't know about that,' she said, gently stroking Conrad's back. 'Would a work colleague be so driven by revenge that he'd kill? It seems unlikely.'

'There's an easy way to find out,' said Tracey. 'We can go and see Mr Drummond again and persuade him to let us take a walk around his offices. If the killer is there, you'll be able to spot him, with any luck.'

'Meow!' said Conrad.

Tracey laughed. 'Conrad says he's a witness, too.'

'Yes, he is,' said Lulu. 'In fact Conrad got much closer to him than I did.'

'Then we'll make sure he walks around with us,' said Tracey.

32

Tracey pulled up outside the offices of Oxford Insurance Services, parking in between two near-identical BMWs. She switched off the engine. 'We're still trying to get access to the phone records of Bernard and Billy Russell,' Tracey said. 'I marked the requests as priority but I think every investigating officer does that now as a matter of course. It used to take a few days to get phone records, but now it can be weeks or even months. Ours is a murder investigation so we should get put to the top of the pile, but even so I have to make sure they're phoned every day to make sure they know it's urgent.'

'I heard it's the same getting ATM details nowadays. Constant bottlenecks.'

Tracey nodded. 'When we first started to realize how CCTV and phone data could help us solve crimes, it seemed like a godsend. And they still do help solve the majority of crimes. But accessing the data means we have to deal with companies, and the speed of response comes down to how many staff they have. They resent the fact that they have to pay their staff to do our work for us, and quite frankly they have a point. When it was a handful of enquiries a day they could cope, but now it's hundreds if not thousands of requests every day from all over the country.'

They climbed out of the Mondeo and walked into the building. Conrad rode on Lulu's shoulders. He was looking left and right as they walked up to the reception desk. They were greeted by the same red-headed receptionist, but it was clear she didn't remember them. She asked them for their names and it was only when she saw Conrad that she realized they had been there before. 'Oh, you're the policemen,' she said. 'Policewomen, I mean.'

'Police officer is the preferred term,' said Tracey. 'Or detective.'

'And you don't like wearing name tags,' said the receptionist. 'I remember now. Have a seat and I'll see if Mr Drummond is available.'

They sat on the sofa and watched people go back and forth to the stairs and the lifts. Lulu didn't see anyone who looked like the man she had seen in Julia's bedroom.

After five minutes Mr Drummond's secretary came down the stairs and walked towards them with the grace of a catwalk model. He was wearing a tight blue suit and gleaming black shoes with the most pointed toes that Lulu had ever seen. 'I'm so sorry,' he said, wringing his hands together as if to demonstrate just how sorry he was. 'Mr Drummond is out of the office today and almost certainly won't be back.'

'That's not a problem,' said Tracey. 'We don't actually need to talk to him. All we really need to do is to take a walk around the office.'

The secretary frowned. 'Excuse me?'

'We are looking for a man who may have been at a house where a woman was attacked,' said Tracey. 'We have a rough description but we really need to assure ourselves that it wasn't someone from your company.'

The handwringing stopped and the secretary smiled. 'Well, that's easy enough,' he said. He pointed off to the left. 'Brianna in human resources can show you our full staff list, including photographs. Her office is over there. I'll walk you over.'

'We were planning on talking to human resources, but it would be a huge help if we could actually see the people in person, as it were. The problem is that our facial description is a bit vague so it's more about body type, the way they walk, things like that. So what we'd like to do is just walk around, very discreetly, and see with our own eyes.'

The secretary nodded. 'I don't suppose that will be a problem.'

'We won't be interviewing anyone, we probably won't even have to speak to anyone, you won't even know we are here,' said Tracey. 'From what we saw last time, most of your offices are open plan and any cubicles are glass-sided, so we should be able to get a look at everyone. And then, when we've done our walkaround, we'll go and talk to Brianna.'

'That sounds fine,' said the secretary. 'Why don't you get started and I'll tell Brianna to expect you.'

'That would be so sweet of you,' said Tracey. 'I'm sorry, I didn't get your name last time.'

'Gary,' he said.

'Well thank you for all your help, Gary,' said Tracey, patting him on the arm.

'While we're here, Gary, could you give us a list of everything that was destroyed in the fire at Bernard Grenville's shop, five years ago?' asked Lulu. 'That was the fire that we came to talk to Mr Drummond about last time.'

'Yes, that's easily done,' he said. 'Can I ask why?'

'We're taking another look at the fire in the light of everything that's happened.' She looked over at Tracey, who was frowning. 'I just thought it might help.'

Tracey nodded. 'Yes, I suppose so.'

Lulu looked back at Gary. 'Any idea how long it will take?'

'Oh, no time at all,' he said. 'I'll do it while you're doing your walkaround and then I'll leave it with Brianna.'

'You're too kind,' said Lulu.

'Do you plan to start at the top and work down, or start here and work up?' asked Gary.

'I think top down works best,' said Tracey.

'Well, you know the way. You could start outside Mr Drummond's office. I'll talk to Brianna. If there's anything else you need, just give me a call.'

'Gary, you've been wonderful,' said Tracey.

Gary smiled and walked away, hips swaying and his left hand out to the side. Tracey turned to Lulu. 'Definitely not him?'

'The attacker was more assertive. More aggressive. And a couple of inches shorter.'

'Good to know,' said Tracey. 'So now you're thinking there was some sort of fraud involved with the fire?'

'I really hope not, but if Bernard did actually bribe the fire investigator, and if he did kill Billy Russell, then who knows what else he did?' said Lulu. She shook her head. 'It's as if I never knew him. If he did do all this, he's not the man I thought he was. And what about Julia? Did Bernard lie to her all these years?'

'Or did she know?' said Tracey. 'That's the more important question.'

'Meow!' said Conrad.

Tracey smiled. 'See! He agrees with me.'

'He's a very agreeable cat,' said Lulu.

They went up the two flights of stairs to the top floor and along to Mr Drummond's office. It was in the far corner of the building and it made sense to start there. There were five smaller offices, each with a floor-to-ceiling window to the side of the door. They checked them all as they walked by, looking casually left and right. There were women in two of them and the three men were all middle-aged and overweight. The rest of the top floor was open plan with two dozen desks, each with two computer monitors and an orthopaedic chair. There was a water cooler by a window overlooking the car park and they stopped and each drew themselves a paper cone of water. They stood with their backs to the window as they surveyed the staff. Half were women and so could be immediately discarded as possibilities. That left twelve men. One was very short, only a little over five feet tall, and one was basketball-player tall. Of the remaining ten, four were in their forties or older.

Two of the younger men were standing together at the far side of the office, deep in conversation. The unmarked left cheek of one was clearly visible and when they eventually went back to their desks, they could see that the other man was also unmarked.

'Your two o'clock,' said Tracey.

Lulu looked to her right. A young man in a grey suit was standing at his desk, his phone against his left ear. He was the right height and build but after a minute or so he changed hands on the phone and they were able to get a good look at his left cheek. There was no cut.

After a few minutes by the water cooler, they were satisfied that the attacker wasn't there, so they took the stairs down to the floor below. The whole floor was open plan with about thirty workstations, but most of the desks were unoccupied. There were fewer than ten people working and most of them were women. There were two men, both in the right age group, but even from a distance it was obvious that one was too short and the other too overweight to be the man they were looking for.

They went down to the ground floor. There were six small offices at one end, all with floor-to-ceiling glass panels that allowed them to look inside. Three were empty; middle-aged men were sitting at their desks in the others. They walked back through reception. The door to the human resources office was open. Tracey knocked and they went inside. There were two desks but only one was occupied, by a chestnut-haired lady in her thirties wearing a pale green dress and with a small crucifix hanging over her throat. 'Are you Brianna?' asked Tracey.

'I am, yes.' Brianna frowned when she saw Conrad sitting on Lulu's shoulders. 'OMG,' she said. 'Is that a cat?' She shook her head. 'What a stupid question. Of course it's a cat.'

'His name is Conrad,' said Lulu.

'Meow!' said Conrad.

'And he says he's very pleased to meet you,' said Lulu.

'OMG, he talks.'

'Yes, he does.'

Tracey held out her warrant card. 'I'm Inspector Calder with Thames Valley CID,' she said. 'Did Gary tell you we'd be dropping by?'

'He did, yes. You're looking for somebody, right?'

'It's more about eliminating people from our enquiries. We've just walked through the office space and I noticed that there were a lot of empty desks on the floor above us.'

'Ah, yes, that's where the claims adjusters and sales team work,' she said. 'They're in and out all the time.'

'Ah, okay,' said Tracey. 'That makes our life a little harder, unfortunately. How easy would it be for us to see photographs of your staff?'

'Very easy,' said Brianna. 'We need everyone's photo for their company IDs. They're all on the computer.'

'And how many employees are there?'

'As of today? One hundred and twenty-seven.'

'Can you sort them by age and sex and so on?'

'We use gender, these days. Self-described gender. But, yes, we have to keep records like that to ensure that we meet our diversity quotas.'

'So you could call up all the photographs of men under thirty, say?'

'People who identify as male, yes.'

'I think we could drop that to twenty-five,' said Lulu. 'I'm sure he was early twenties.' She looked at Brianna. 'By the way, has anyone called in sick today?'

'Let me check.' She tapped on her keyboard and squinted at the monitor. 'We've got three off sick, and one on maternity leave.'

'The three off sick, how many are men? I mean, how many identify as male?'

'Two,' said Brianna. 'There's Ted Donaldson, but he's forty-six, and there's Neil Rawlings, he's thirty-four.'

'Okay, can you show us the men aged up to twenty-five? People who identify as male, I mean.'

'Sure,' said Brianna. She tapped on the keyboard again. 'We have eleven who fit that criterion,' she said. She rotated her screen so that they could see the photographs. Lulu had seen eight of the men in the office. She pointed at the three men she hadn't seen. 'Who are these guys?'

'The one on the left is Tim Sutter. He's on annual leave at the moment. Spain, I think. The one in the middle is Dennis Collins, he's a claims adjuster and most of his clients are in north London, so he's out of the office a lot.' Collins had a beard and Lulu was fairly sure she hadn't seen facial hair when Conrad had slashed the man's ski mask. 'And the one on the right is Charlie Brett. Charlie broke his leg a few weeks ago and it's still in plaster. It's been easier for him to work from home.' She turned the screen back. 'Is there anything else I can do for you?' she asked brightly.

'Did you know Mr Russell?' asked Tracey. 'The man who died?'

'Billy? Yes, of course. He's been here for ever. We were so shocked when we heard. I mean, how awful, right?'

'Really awful,' said Tracey.

'Have you found who did it?'

'Enquiries are ongoing,' said Tracey. 'Did Mr Russell have any close friends here at the company?'

'Billy? No, not really.'

'No one he had lunch with sometimes? Or went to the pub with?'

'No, Billy was very much nine to five. We've organized a few team-building exercises over the years. Pub quizzes, treasure hunts, after-work yoga sessions, that sort of thing, but Billy never attends.'

'And lunchtimes?'

'Billy would always have his lunch at his desk.'

'Always alone?'

'Don't get me wrong, Billy wasn't antisocial. He was perfectly nice to everyone and would always sign birthday cards or leaving cards with a sweet remark, and he would always ask about people's families or offer them words of advice if they were having a hard time. But I think that Billy felt that the workplace was just that, a place for work. He did his job and then went home and that was where he did his socializing. But he was well liked here; people are always asking me about his funeral because they want to go. Speaking of which, do you know when it will be?'

'I'm not sure,' said Tracey.

'I'd like to know so that I can send an email round.'

'I'll make sure you're told,' said Tracey. 'And thank you for your help today.'

'By the way, Brianna, did Gary give you an envelope for us?' asked Lulu.

Brianna frowned and shook her head. 'He didn't, no. Do you want me to call him?'

Before Lulu could answer, Gary appeared at the door, red-faced and flustered. 'Oh, I am so sorry, I had a paper jam,' he said. He held up an A4 manila envelope. 'It took me forever.'

Lulu took the envelope from him. 'You're an angel, thank you.'

Gary's cheeks flushed at the compliment. 'Did you find what you were looking for?'

'We were just telling Brianna, we didn't see anyone who fits the description in the building, and she was good enough to show us photographs of the staff, so we are confident we are not looking for anyone employed here,' said Tracey.

Gary patted his chest over his heart. 'Well, that's a relief. I'll be sure to tell Mr Drummond.'

'Please do,' said Tracey. 'And thank you again for all your help.'

Gary took them to reception and waved as they walked back to the Mondeo.

'Wouldn't it be nice if everyone in the world was as sweet and helpful as Gary,' said Lulu as they climbed into the car.

'No question,' said Tracey. 'It would certainly make my life much easier.'

33

Gemma was standing next to the SOCO van, struggling out of her white forensic suit, when Lulu and Tracey arrived back at Hepworth House. Robbie was sitting behind the wheel, talking on his mobile.

'Sita left half an hour ago,' said Gemma as Tracey climbed out of the Mondeo. 'She told me to tell you that Mrs Grenville is healing nicely.'

'That's good to know.'

Gemma rolled up the forensic suit and stuffed it into a black rubbish bag, along with her latex gloves and shoe protectors. 'Forensics-wise, the news isn't so great,' she said. 'Nothing at all in the study that will be of any help. Though, as I said before, you'll almost certainly find glass fragments embedded in the perp's shoes. Nothing on the stairs or the corridor leading to the bedroom. We found lots of hairs in the bedroom, but even a visual examination says it's female, just because of the length. Or cat. There's a lot of cat hair on the bed and the sofa. There's plenty of blood spatter and a lot of blood on the pillowcase and on Mrs Grenville's clothing. We'll check it all, obviously, but it's pretty clear that it's Mrs Grenville's blood.' She shrugged. 'I really don't think we'll be much help. Sorry.'

'That's a shame,' said Tracey. 'Maybe we'll have more luck with the DNA sample from Conrad's claws.'

'Fingers crossed,' said Gemma. 'Or claws crossed, I suppose.'

She tossed the rubbish bag into the van and closed the door. 'Right, we're done here. Let's hope third time's a charm and we won't be back.'

'I'm with you there,' said Tracey.

Gemma got into the front passenger seat and the van headed down the driveway.

The uniformed constable was still standing at the front door, his arms folded across his chest. 'Right, we'll be taking Mrs Grenville to a safe house,' Tracey said to him. 'You and your colleague can head on back to the station.'

'Yes, ma'am.'

'I hope it wasn't too boring.'

The constable nodded deferentially. 'Happy to be of service,' he said. 'And I need the overtime, ma'am.'

Lulu and Tracey went inside and up to Julia's bedroom. She had changed into a baggy Fair Isle sweater and black leggings and was sitting on the sofa by the window, checking her mobile phone. 'Is everything okay?' she asked.

Conrad jumped down off Lulu's shoulders and landed silently on the bed.

'Everything's fine, we're all done here,' said Tracey. 'Do you want to get your things ready and I'll drive you to Lulu's boat?'

'All done,' said Julia. She pointed at a small Louis Vuitton wheeled suitcase standing next to the doors to the dressing room.

'Let's go, then,' said Tracey. 'The police guard is standing down so you'll need to lock up and set the alarm.'

'How long do you think I'll be away?'

'That depends on how much help we get from the DNA on Conrad's claws,' said Tracey. 'I really wouldn't be happy about you staying here on your own until we have the man in custody.'

They went back outside, just as the police patrol car was driving away. Tracey put Julia's bag in the boot of her Mondeo while Julia and Lulu walked around the house checking that the doors were locked. Julia locked the French windows in the study and looked down at the dried blood-stains. 'We need to get that cleaned,' she said.

'There's plenty of time for that,' said Lulu.

'And what about the window? The broken glass?'

'We can send a carpenter around to board it up,' said Lulu. 'And this time the alarm will be on, so that should deter anyone from breaking in. But if you're worried, you could arrange for a private security firm to keep an eye on the place for you.'

They went to the kitchen, checked that the conservatory was secure, then locked the kitchen door and went back to the hall. Julia tapped the security code into the burglar alarm console and they both hurried outside as the system began to beep. Lulu got into the back of the Mondeo with Conrad. Julia locked the door and climbed into the front seat. Tracey put the car into gear. As they drove away, Julia watched the house through the wing mirror.

'Are you okay, Julia?' asked Tracey.

Julia sighed and folded her arms. 'I know it sounds crazy, but I feel as if I'm abandoning Bernard. I mean, I know he's not there, he's in the mortuary, but it feels as if he's still in the house and I've left him.'

'I understand, and it's not crazy,' said Tracey, 'but at the moment it's not safe for you to stay there.'

Julia nodded tearfully. 'I know.'

The Cat Who Solved Three Murders

Conrad dropped down off Lulu's shoulders and made his way carefully across the centre console and onto Julia's lap. Julia began to stroke him softly as she blinked away the tears.

34

Lulu directed Tracey to a car park about a hundred yards away from where she had parked *The Lark*. Jericho was just outside the old Oxford city wall. In days gone by it had been a place for travellers to rest if they had arrived at the city after the gates had closed for the night. These days it was a popular area for students and tourists, with buzzing restaurants, vegan cafes, vinyl record shops and independent bike shops. The area was bordered by the Oxford Canal and there were always narrowboats chugging up and down.

Tracey pulled Julia's case for her and Lulu walked with her arm around Julia. Conrad stuck to Lulu's heels. They reached the towpath and headed towards *The Lark*. 'You know, in all my years in Oxford, I've never walked by the canal,' said Tracey. 'I've eaten here often and drunk in the Old Bookbinders Ale House a few times, but I've never walked along the canal.'

'It's a different world,' said Lulu. 'You're in the city but separate from it. It's a community but people are coming and going all the time.'

'It's a slower pace of life, isn't it?'

'It has to be. Narrowboats weigh twenty tonnes and travel at three miles an hour. There isn't much rushing.'

They reached *The Lark* and Conrad jumped up onto the rear deck.

'He certainly knows where home is,' said Julia.

Lulu climbed on board and opened the double doors, then she helped Julia onto the boat. 'Watch the steps,' said Lulu as Julia went carefully down.

Lulu took the bag from Tracey. 'Would you like a coffee or tea?' asked Lulu.

Tracey looked at her watch. 'Actually, I will, thank you.'

She climbed on board and followed Lulu down the steps. 'It's a bit cramped for three, but you two grab the sofa and I'll take the steps,' said Lulu. She lit one of the gas hobs and filled the kettle from the sink tap.

'This is amazing,' said Tracey, looking around. 'It's a real home, isn't it?'

'It's got everything I need,' said Lulu.

'What about electricity and the water – where do they come from?'

'There are batteries that are charged whenever the engine is running. And there's a tank that holds enough water for a fortnight. And the toilet waste goes into a cassette which is emptied every week or so.'

'And you can go anywhere in the country?'

'Anywhere there's a canal. And there are almost five thousand miles of canals and rivers which are navigable in the country.'

'And they're easy to sail? Or drive? Which is it?'

'It's drive,' said Julia. 'That's one of the first things I asked.'

Lulu laughed. 'Yes, you literally just point them in the direction you want to, and generally there isn't much choice. There are no gears, just forward and backward, and the top speed is four miles an hour.'

'And what about those things that move you up and down hills?'

'The locks? Well, yes, they can be challenging when you're

on your own, but it's doable. Keeps you fit, too. And usually there's someone around who'll give you a hand. Canal people are friendly folk. You can rent one really easily.'

'I'll talk to my husband. See if I can persuade him.'

The kettle boiled and Lulu made tea for them all. She took out a packet of Jaffa cakes and put them on a plate. Tracey laughed. 'I haven't had a Jaffa cake for years.' She took one, bit into it, and sighed with pleasure.

'Oh, go on then,' said Julia, taking one.

Lulu laughed, put the plate on the sofa between them and sat down on the steps.

'Lulu suggested I should get a private security firm to guard the house,' said Julia. 'What do you think?'

'To be honest, whoever it was wasn't there to steal,' said Tracey. 'I'm not sure they'll try again.'

She looked at the plate of Jaffa cakes, and then over at Lulu. Lulu laughed. 'Help yourself.'

Tracey took another Jaffa cake and ate it in two quick bites. She was about to take a third when her phone rang. She fished it out of her pocket and looked at the screen. 'I've got to take this, sorry.'

Lulu moved off the steps and Tracey hurried outside.

'Do you think they'll catch him?' asked Julia.

'I do,' said Lulu. 'We've got his DNA thanks to Conrad. And he'll have cuts on his face.'

'I just wish I could figure out who hates me so much,' said Julia. 'And Bernard? Who would want to kill Bernard?'

'We'll catch him,' said Lulu.

Tracey appeared at the doorway. 'We've had a break with Russell's phone records,' she said. 'He didn't phone Bernard, but his GPS puts him at your house on the day he died.'

'Well, we know that he was there,' said Lulu. 'So that doesn't move us forward.'

'Let me finish,' said Tracey. She grinned. 'I bet you gave your detectives hell when you were a superintendent.'

'I was firm but fair,' said Lulu. 'I'm sorry, please continue.'

'Russell made and received several calls from another mobile during the days before he went to your house. My guys have got a name and a place of work, so I'm heading out there now. Do you want to come? You could help with identification.'

'Try and stop me,' said Lulu. She gulped down her tea and put the mug in the sink.

'I'll come too,' said Julia.

'No, not with those cuts,' said Lulu. 'Sita said no exertion for you, just rest.'

'I'm fine.'

'Julia, your throat was slashed,' said Lulu. 'Seriously, I can identify the guy, you just take it easy.' She pointed towards the front of *The Lark*. 'The bed's that way. And there's food in the fridge if you're hungry. And wine.'

Julia grinned. 'Now you're talking.'

Lulu and Tracey headed out onto the rear deck. Conrad ran up the steps after them. Lulu bent down for him to jump onto her shoulders and then she stepped off *The Lark* and onto the towpath to join Tracey.

'I'm assuming there's a reason you didn't say who this person was who phoned Russell?' said Lulu as they walked down the towpath.

Tracey nodded. 'His name is Oliver McBride. He's the son of Victoria McBride, the lady who died in the fire.'

Lulu's mouth fell open in surprise. 'Wow,' she said. 'That can't be a coincidence. Motive and opportunity.'

'Normally I'd check on McBride's GPS to see where he was last night, but considering who he is, we can do that later. He works at a fishmonger's in Jericho. We can walk from here.'

35

A large brass fish – a plaice, or maybe a sole – was hanging above the window of the fishmonger's. A painted sign proclaimed that the seafood within was 'fresh daily from Cornwall and Billingsgate' and there was a blackboard on the pavement with a list of prices of crabs, prawns and a variety of fish.

Lulu and Tracey slowed as they approached the shop. 'Have you called for backup?' asked Lulu. Conrad was lying across her shoulders, his ears pricked up.

'I want to check it's him first,' said Tracey. 'I don't want to have a whole team out to discover he was phoning Russell about a fish delivery.'

'Are we going to go in?'

Tracey smiled. 'I don't think you can with Conrad on your shoulders,' she said. 'I'm pretty sure Health and Safety means cats aren't allowed into fish shops.'

'We could always say that he's a seeing-eye cat,' Lulu joked. 'I guess we'll get a look at him through the window.'

'That's the plan,' said Tracey. 'And if it is him, I'll call for a car.'

The shop door opened and they both caught the smell of fish and crab. A woman in a leopard-print coat emerged, clutching a carrier bag with the shop's logo on it.

'I tell you what – you stay here and I'll pop in and take a look around,' said Tracey. 'If I see anyone who fits the bill

I'll tell you. He doesn't know me but there's a good chance he'll remember you, and he'll definitely remember Conrad.'

'Good idea,' said Lulu.

'Right, I'll put my housewife face on,' said Tracey. She smiled, grimaced, smiled again, and headed towards the door. She pushed it open and disappeared inside.

'I hope it's him,' said Conrad.

'So do I,' said Lulu. 'Julia can't carry on like this, knowing there's someone out there who killed her husband and who wants her dead.'

'If he is the son of the woman who died in the fire, he has a motive, doesn't he?'

'Yes,' said Lulu. 'Revenge. People will do anything to get revenge, especially when a loved one dies. And Oliver McBride lost his mother. If he blames Bernard and Julia, yes . . .' She fell silent as an old couple walked by. The man was bent over a walker as he shuffled along, the woman, probably his wife, had her arm looped through his and was whispering words of encouragement. Lulu was just about to continue her conversation when the shop door opened and Tracey stepped out onto the pavement. Tracey hurried over to her, holding a carrier bag. 'It's him,' she said excitedly.

'Are you sure?'

'He's the right height and build and he has a plaster on his left cheek.' Her face was flushed with excitement. 'And the knife he's using to fillet the fish is exactly as you and the pathologist described: long and thin and curved. It's him, Lulu.' She pulled out her phone. 'I'm going to call for backup.'

Lulu moved sideways to peer through the window. There was a huge display of seafood in the window, with various varieties of fish and crustaceans laid out on crushed ice, and to the left was a long marble counter. On the wall behind the counter was a blackboard on which the prices had been chalked by hand, along with colourful drawings of the seafood on offer. A red-faced man in his forties, his stomach bulging against a blue and white apron and wearing a straw boater, was scooping fresh prawns into a plastic bag. Lulu frowned. He clearly wasn't the man who had attacked Julia.

Tracey was talking into her phone now, her hand cupped over her mouth.

There was a second man further along the counter. Lulu moved to the side to get a better look. He was also wearing an apron and a boater, but he was younger and thinner, a good-looking lad with short blond hair. He was filleting a salmon with a long, thin, knife. Tracey was right. It was exactly the same as the one the attacker had used in Julia's bedroom.

McBride leaned forward and said something to his customer, an old lady wearing a floral headscarf, then he turned to look at the window, revealing the strip of flesh-coloured plaster on his face. His eyes widened when he saw Lulu, and widened even further as he spotted Conrad. He stared at them for several seconds and then turned and ran to the rear of the shop, his boater dropping onto the floor behind him.

'He's running!' shouted Lulu. She headed for the door and felt Conrad's claws tighten on her shoulder.

'Lulu, no!' said Tracey. 'Wait!'

Lulu had already pushed the door open and rushed into the shop. There were half a dozen customers and they all looked in her direction. Conrad jumped down and landed on the tiled floor. There was a door at the far end of the shop and no sign of McBride. She hurried towards the door.

'Oy, you can't go in there!' shouted the fishmonger, but Lulu had already pushed it open. She dashed through, followed by Conrad.

'Lulu, no!' shouted Tracey, who had run into the shop. It was too late: the door was already closing behind Lulu.

She was in a large kitchen area with two massive walk-in freezers to her left and a long stainless-steel table to the right. A woman in a white coat and a blue hairnet was taking oysters from a large Styrofoam box and arranging them on a metal platter. 'Oliver? Which way did he go?' shouted Lulu.

The woman pointed a yellow-gloved hand at another door marked FIRE EXIT. Lulu ran towards it, with Conrad at her heels. As she reached the door she heard a motorcycle fire up outside. She pushed the door open. Beyond the shop was an alley running the full length of the parade of shops and cafes. There were several skips filled with rubbish and wheelie bins every few yards.

She heard the roar of the bike again and looked to her left. McBride was sitting astride a large motorbike and as she stepped into the alley he sped off.

Lulu stood in the middle of the alley, gasping for breath. Conrad was at her feet. 'What is it with you and chasing bad guys?' he said.

'He's getting away.'

'I can see that. But what would you do if you caught him?'

'He left the knife in the shop.'

'Lulu, he's bigger and stronger than you. He doesn't need a knife to hurt you.'

'What can I say? The adrenaline kicked in.' The motorcycle had almost reached the end of the alley, when suddenly its way was blocked by a police car. McBride hit the brakes and screeched to a halt, then turned on the spot with a squeal of rubber. He twisted the accelerator and the bike leaped forward, heading straight for them.

'Well, this isn't good,' said Conrad.

Lulu stepped into the middle of the alley and raised her hands. 'Stop!' she yelled.

'Are you serious?' said Conrad.

'Stop, police!' shouted Lulu as the bike roared towards her, the engine noise echoing off the alley walls.

'You're not police, Lulu! Good grief!' Conrad dashed towards the bike, then stopped and reared up onto his back legs, his front paws up, hissing and snarling. For one awful moment Lulu was sure that the bike was going to go straight over him but at the last second McBride leaned to the right and the bike crashed into an overflowing skip. McBride flew through the air and hit the ground with a thump as the bike fell on its side, its engine still roaring.

Conrad dropped down onto all fours and turned to look at Lulu. 'And that is how you stop a motorcycle,' he said.

36

'You'll be able to see and hear everything from here,' said Tracey. They were in a room on the second floor of Thames Valley Police HQ. It was small, with just enough space for a desk on which stood two screens, and four chairs. The blinds were down and the overhead fluorescent lights were on. Lulu was sitting on one of the chairs and Conrad was next to her.

One of the screens was from a camera pointed at Oliver McBride, who was sitting in an interview room on the ground floor, just along from the custody suite. McBride was no longer wearing his apron, and his shirt sleeves were rolled up to reveal bandages on both elbows and a plaster cast on his right hand and wrist. There was a can of Coke in front of him. 'The police doctor says he's okay and doesn't need painkillers, so we'll go ahead with the interrogation,' said Tracey.

The second screen showed DC Collier sitting at the table, with a bottle of water in front of him. There was a tape recorder with two tape slots against the wall.

'He's been charged with the murder of Mr Grenville and the attempted murder of Julia. He's been asked if he wants a solicitor but he's declined. I'll go down now and start the interview.' She patted Lulu on the shoulder. 'What you did was foolhardy in the extreme, you know that?'

Lulu smiled. 'Yes, I do.'

'Well done.'

'You should thank Conrad. He's the one who made him swerve.'

'Well done, Conrad,' said Tracey.

Conrad looked up at her and meowed.

Tracey laughed. 'I love it when he does that. Okay, so I'll come back up when we're done. Wish me luck.'

'I'm sure you don't need it,' said Lulu. 'But break a leg.'

Tracey chuckled and let herself out of the room.

'Why wouldn't he want a solicitor?' asked Conrad, looking at McBride on the screen.

'Either he isn't going to say anything, and is going to take the "no comment" route. Or he's going to unburden himself and doesn't want a solicitor to get in the way.'

'Which do you think?'

'I think he swerved rather than hit you,' said Lulu. 'He could have run you over, but he didn't.' She shrugged. 'But I don't know, I really don't.'

'He doesn't look like a killer, does he?'

'Oh, most killers are just ordinary people who made a bad choice,' said Lulu. 'There aren't many monsters around, not real monsters, anyway.'

'He doesn't have a bad aura,' said Conrad. 'I see reds and indigos but the colours are murky.'

'Murky? What does that mean?'

'A murky red is a sign of holding on to anger or trauma. Obviously the death of his mother. And a murky indigo suggests self-doubt and uncertainty. He's clearly a very troubled boy. But not evil. Definitely not evil.'

On the left-hand screen, the door opened and Tracey appeared, carrying a mug. She closed the door and sat down, then nodded at DC Collier, who started the taping.

Tracey gave the date and the time, then said her name. DC Collier gave his name.

'So, Oliver, could you please confirm your full name and your date of birth, for the tape,' said Tracey.

McBride did as he was told, then slouched in his chair with his injured arms stretched out on the table.

'You have been charged with the murder of Bernard Grenville and the attempted murder of Julia Grenville. I have asked you already if you want a solicitor and you have refused. So I will ask you again, would you like a solicitor to be with you while we interview you?'

McBride shook his head.

'You have to say it out loud, Oliver. For the tape.'

'No,' said McBride. 'I do not want a brief.'

'Oliver, can you tell me why you did what you did? Why did you kill Mr Grenville? And why did you try to kill his wife last night?'

'They killed my mum,' said McBride, his voice a low whisper.

'Who did?'

'That bastard Grenville. And his bitch of a wife.'

'Why do you say they killed your mother?'

'Because they did. They set fire to their shop and my mum died. It was an insurance job.'

'How do you know that, Oliver?'

McBride sneered at her with contempt. 'You want the whole story, do you? Like you care.'

'I do care, Oliver. I want to know what happened.'

McBride sighed. 'Okay, fine. I saw the article in a magazine. I recognized her immediately. She'd been at my mother's funeral with her husband and they both came up to me afterwards and said how sorry they were and that if I ever needed anything I was to talk to them. They said the same to my dad. Mr Grenville even put his arms around my dad and hugged him and said something about us all getting through this together. That was the last time we heard from them. The building was sold and me and my dad moved out. Dad never got over what had happened. In a crazy way he blamed himself. He kept saying that he should have stayed home with Mum and that it was his fault that she'd died. But it wasn't his fault at all. She insisted we go.'

McBride sat back in his chair and picked up his can of Coke. He raised the can to his lips, but then changed his mind and put it back on the table.

'I'm not a big reader, but I wondered what she'd done so I started reading the article. All that money they'd come into, right? A fortune. Millions of pounds, right?'

Tracey nodded. 'Their company is going public, that's correct.'

'I didn't really understand where the money was coming from. Anyway, I was reading the article when I saw the photograph of her in her study. That's when I saw the painting.'

'This painting?' asked Tracey. She slid a sheet of paper across the table towards McBride. 'For the purpose of the tape, I am showing Mr McBride a photograph of exhibit 26B, a photograph of a painting that used to hang in Julia Grenville's study.'

Lulu leaned forward to get a closer look at the screen. It was the Bamburgh Castle painting.

McBride picked it up, looked at it, and nodded. 'Yes. This is the one.'

'And what was special about this painting?'

'It was in my mother's workshop the night she died. At least it should have been. So it should have been destroyed in the fire.'

'How do you know it was in the workshop, Oliver?'

'Mum sent me down to check that the heater was on before Dad and I left. She was doing some work on a couple of paintings and she had varnished a bookcase. It was going to be a cold night so she wanted to be sure that the heating was on.'

'And was it?'

McBride nodded. 'Yeah. It was a twin-bar electric fire and it was on. And on the table by the door was the painting of the castle. Mr Grenville had asked my mum to clean it and put it in a new frame. That was going to be her next job before she got sick.'

'How do you know that?'

'I used to hang out with my mum after school. I'd do my homework while she worked. So I always knew what she was working on.'

'So you saw the painting on the table?' Tracey pointed at the sheet of paper he was holding. 'The painting of Bamburgh Castle.'

'Yes. Definitely.'

'So when you saw that painting in the magazine, what did you think?'

'Well it's obvious, innit? It meant that bitch or her

husband had been in the workshop that night and taken the painting with them. They must have started the fire. They killed my mum.'

'But you don't know that for sure, Oliver,' said DC Collier.

'I know that the painting was there when I checked. The door was locked, so only someone with a key could have taken it. I left my mum's keys with her when Dad and I left. Dad had his key. That only leaves the Grenvilles. One of them must have let themselves in and taken the painting – how else could it end up on the wall of her study five years later?'

'What did you think had happened, Oliver?' asked Tracey.

'It's obvious, innit?' said McBride. 'Whoever came in to set the place on fire, took the painting with them. You're supposed to be the bloody detective – can't you work that out for yourself? They set the fire that killed my mum and they took their precious painting with them. They cared more about their painting than they did about my mum.'

'Okay, Oliver, but once you realized that the painting in the magazine photograph was supposed to have been destroyed in the fire, why didn't you come to us? The police?'

McBride sneered at the detective. 'Are you serious? They're rich. Stinking rich. Have you seen the size of their house? And the magazine said they were worth millions.'

'So?' said DC Collier.

'So the rich never go to prison, do they? Everyone knows that. And who am I? A bloody fishmonger. So it'd be my word against theirs, and who's going to believe me? I'd be wasting my breath.'

'We would have listened to you, Oliver,' said Tracey.

McBride shook his head fiercely. 'Bollocks,' he said. 'No one listened to me about the fire, did they?'

'You spoke to the fire investigators?'

'Yes, but they wouldn't listen to a word I said. They said it was an accident right from the start. The only person who would listen to me was Billy.'

'Billy Russell?'

McBride nodded. 'Yeah, Billy Russell. He was working for the insurance company. I told him that I checked the electric fire before I left and that there was nothing nearby that could have caused a fire. He said he'd talk to the fire people, but they wouldn't listen to him either.'

'So you spoke to Mr Russell?'

'Loads of times. He said he was sure that the fire wasn't an accident but the fire investigation officer was a prick and didn't believe him. Billy argued with his bosses but they didn't believe him either and eventually they paid the Grenvilles more than a million quid. And you know how much they paid me and my dad for the death of my mum? Sweet fuck all.' He folded his arms. 'So, no, I didn't think of talking to the feds. What would have been the point?'

'So, what did you do, Oliver?' asked Tracey. 'When you saw the painting in the magazine and knew that someone must have removed it before the fire, what did you do?'

'I talked to Billy. That was the only thing I could do. He knew right from the start that there was something suspicious about the fire.'

Tracey and DC Collier looked at each other, then back to McBride.

Conrad was sitting up, his head moving between the two screens, his ears pricked up and twitching independently. He turned to look at Lulu. 'It was Oliver who told Billy?' he said.

'That makes sense,' said Lulu. 'And that's how the magazine ended up in the bureau. Oliver must have given it to him.' She was staring at the screen on the left, the one showing Tracey and DC Collier. Tracey was doing a great job: she had opened McBride up and he seemed happy to tell her everything. It was still a worry that he didn't have a solicitor with him, but Tracey had offered him the chance to have one several times.

'How did you get in touch with Billy?' asked Tracey.

'I phoned him. He'd given me his number ages ago and said that I could always call him. He was a good guy, a really good guy.'

'And you went to see him?' asked Tracey.

McBride nodded. 'He didn't want me to go to his house, so I met him in a pub.'

'Which pub?'

'The Coach and Horses. It's not far from where he lives.'

'And how did you get there?' asked Tracey.

'My bike.'

'You cycled?'

McBride sneered at her. 'As if,' he said. 'Motorbike. A Triumph. It's a classic.'

'That was the bike you were riding today when you were arrested?'

'Who's going to pay for the damage to my bike, that's what I want to know?' He held up his bandaged arms. 'And look at this. Look what you did to me. This is police brutality, this is.'

'When was this meeting?' asked Tracey patiently.

'The Sunday before last. In the afternoon. About three.'

Tracey took back the sheet of paper. 'And how did it go? The meeting?'

'It went okay. I showed him the magazine and explained that I'd seen it in the workshop before Mum died. He said he didn't recognize the painting and that he remembered everything that the Grenvilles had claimed for. He kept asking me if I was sure. And I kept saying yes. He said he'd talk to the police. I let him have the magazine, for evidence. And I went home, and waited.' He reached out, picked up his Coke and took a sip.

'And then what happened?' asked DC Collier.

McBride sneered at him. 'You know what happened. It was in the papers. Grenville killed Billy. Smashed his head in with a poker.' He shook his head scornfully. 'And you guys fell for his story that it had been robbers and that they attacked him, too. Bollocks. For all I know, they both killed Billy. Him and his wife.'

'Why didn't you go to the police then, Oliver?' asked Tracey quietly.

'Are you serious? How can you ask that? He got away with killing my mother and now he's getting away with killing Billy. You lot aren't interested in putting guys like him in jail.'

'So what did you do, Oliver?' asked Tracey quietly.

'You know what I did.'

'I know why you did it, but I'm not sure how you managed to pull it off.'

'I wasn't trying to pull anything off. I just wanted him

dead. He killed my mother and he killed Billy so he got what was coming to him.'

'How did you know about the birthday party?'

'We supply fish to the sushi company that was doing the catering. They'd ordered salmon and tuna from our shop so I said I'd deliver it fresh on the day. I got to the house as they were setting things up. I handed over the fish and then hid in a bathroom and waited. I spotted a spare wig and put that on. Nobody pays the servers any attention.'

'What about the knife?'

'I brought it with me. One of my filleting knifes. It has a sheath to protect it. I had it tucked into my belt. I waited until there were a lot of people there and I left the bathroom. Nobody even looked at me. Then I saw Grenville going into a bathroom. I waited for him to come out and then I followed him as he walked to the study. I realized there was no one else in the hallway so I pulled out the knife and stabbed him in the back, three or four times. I thought he'd go down straight away but he didn't, he kept on walking through the study. There were people there so I turned around and put the knife back in the sheath. Then I didn't know what to do. I really didn't have a plan. I wanted to kill them both but I knew if I stayed I'd get caught so I went outside and got on the bike and drove away.' He shook his head. 'I was sure that they'd catch me, that somebody had seen me but they didn't and I realized I was home free.' He grinned wolfishly. 'That's when I figured I should go back and kill the wife. I figured they'd hear the bike so I parked by the gate and walked to the house. I was better prepared that time, I had a mask and gloves. I broke in and crept up to her bedroom. Took me a while to find it. So many bloody bedrooms. But I did find it and I would have killed her if some bitch and a cat hadn't stormed in.' He reached up and touched the plaster on his face. 'The cat went for me. Leaped at me and almost took my eye out.'

Lulu looked across at Conrad. 'He asked for it,' said Conrad.

'Most definitely.'

'But it sounds as if he's making himself out to be the victim.'

'Criminals often do that,' said Lulu. She looked back at the screens.

'I should sue,' said McBride, still touching the plaster. 'I could have lost an eye.'

'You should talk to a lawyer about that,' said Tracey. 'In fact, if you want a lawyer, you can call one now or we can get a duty solicitor for you. That's your right – I told you that when we cautioned you.'

'A lawyer isn't going to help me,' said McBride. He folded his arms. 'I did it. I killed him. And I'm not sorry I did it. He had it coming.'

'Do you want me to call someone for you? Your father?'

McBride's eyes narrowed. 'My father? Don't you know?'

'Know what?'

'Dad killed himself. Well, drank himself to death, really. Died a year ago. He never got over Mum dying. I wish he'd lived long enough to see that I got our revenge.'

'By killing Bernard Grenville?'

'Exactly.'

'And do you regret anything?' asked DC Collier. 'Do you regret doing what you did?'

'He murdered my mum,' said McBride. 'He deserved it.'

'And Mrs Grenville?'

'Yes, you're right,' said McBride. 'That's the one thing I regret. I regret not killing her. And if it hadn't been for that bloody cat, I would have.'

37

Lulu waved as the Toyota Prius pulled away from the kerb. Julia twisted around in the back of the car and blew a kiss. Lulu and Conrad stayed on the pavement until the car was out of sight. With Oliver McBride in police custody, Julia had wanted to get back to the house to arrange to have the study cleaned and the glass repaired in the French windows. Lulu was going to move *The Lark* to another mooring and then get an Uber to the house either later that evening or first thing the following day.

The towpath was busy so Conrad stayed silent until they were on *The Lark* and Lulu was uncorking a bottle of Chardonnay.

'What's the plan?' said Conrad as he sat next to her on the sofa.

'What do you mean?'

'Are we going back to London?'

'I think we should wait for Bernard's funeral. At some point I want to go travelling but not just yet.'

'Travelling?'

'I thought I might take *The Lark* up to Birmingham. Or Manchester. Maybe even further. But at the moment Julia needs me, so I think we should stay in Oxford.'

'Do you think that Julia knew what Bernard had done?' Conrad asked. 'Do you think she knew that he started the fire in his shop?'

'I'm not sure.'

'Yes, you are,' said Conrad quietly.

Lulu looked at Conrad and he met her stare with unblinking green eyes. 'Why do you say that?' she said.

He tilted his head on one side as he stared at her. 'It's true, though, isn't it?'

'Are you reading my mind?' She poured wine into a glass. She stopped at the halfway point, but then had a change of heart and added more.

'No, but I know how you think. And I know how much you love Julia. So your heart is trying to overrule your head. You want to ignore the evidence.'

Lulu didn't answer.

'I'm right, aren't I?' said Conrad. He butted her arm with his head.

Lulu sighed and reached for her handbag. She opened it and took out the envelope containing the printed sheets that Gary had given her in the insurance company's office. Conrad moved closer to Lulu to get a better look as she slid out the sheets of paper. 'The painting of Bamburgh Castle was supposedly burned in the fire, but of course it wasn't and it ended up on the wall by Julia's desk,' said Lulu. She flicked through the sheets and showed him a photograph of a small watercolour painting, a view of Christ Church cathedral in Oxford. 'I saw this in one of the guest bathrooms, near the kitchen.'

'Oh, wow,' said Conrad.

Lulu flicked through a few more sheets and stopped at a red and gold abstract painting based around black Chinese characters. 'This is in their bedroom.'

She showed him another page, this one with a framed antique map of Oxford. 'I'm pretty sure that this is in the library.'

She gathered the pages together and sighed. 'There might be others, I don't know. It's a big house.'

'So Bernard took more than the Bamburgh painting?'

Lulu nodded. 'Yes. It could well have been a spur-of-the-moment thing. He was about to start the fire when he saw the painting and realized he didn't want it destroyed. He decided to save it, but then maybe figured he could take some more. He grabbed what he could carry before he started the fire.'

'And you think he told Julia?'

'They talked about everything. Literally everything. And I don't see how Julia couldn't have noticed that some of the paintings that had supposedly been burned in the fire had turned up in the house. But then, she wasn't especially interested in the shop. I suppose it's possible she hadn't seen them. But the Bamburgh painting was important to her, so she must have noticed that one, if nothing else.' She shrugged. 'I really don't know.'

'Are you going to tell Tracey?'

'About what?'

'About the paintings not being destroyed in the fire. That's evidence, right? It's evidence of fraud if nothing else.'

'It is, yes.'

'So are you going to tell the police?'

'If I do, what then? Bernard's dead – he can't be punished now, can he? And if they do decide that she knew about the fraud, what will they do? Send her to prison for a few years? Her husband is dead, Conrad. She saw him die. Hasn't she been punished enough already?'

'But what about the lady who died in the fire? Doesn't she deserve justice?'

'Well, in a way Mrs McBride got justice, didn't she? Her son killed Bernard.'

'An eye for an eye?'

'I'm not saying it's right. I'm just saying that Bernard killed Mrs McBride, unintentionally, and her son killed Bernard, deliberately. Even if she knew that the fire was being set, does Julia deserve to be punished more than she already has been?'

'So what are you going to do?' asked Conrad.

'I don't know,' said Lulu. 'I really don't know.' She put the pages back into the envelope.

'I think I know what you're going to do.'

'What?'

'I think you're going to let sleeping dogs lie.'

Lulu nodded. 'You might be right.'

Conrad sighed and shook his head. 'Dogs have got a lot to answer for, they really have.'

The Cat Who Caught a Killer

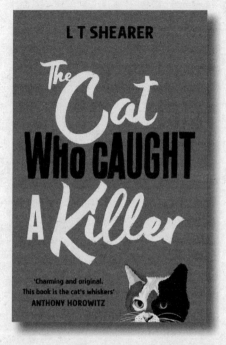

Find out how Lulu and Conrad met in the first book in the charming cosy crime series, perfect for cat lovers!

'A charming, offbeat story with some great characters and wonderful London locations. I'm sure it will make readers long for their own canal boat, and quite possibly – if they don't already have one – their own talking cat. Conrad is a delight'
S. J. Bennett

OUT NOW

1

It was a gorgeous summer's day when Conrad walked into the life of Lulu Lewis. The sky was a cloudless blue, birds were singing in the distance and the water of the canal was just starting to turn green from the warm-weather algal bloom.

Lulu was about to go out and cut some fresh mint from the small strip of land on the other side of the towpath. The mooring was hers, courtesy of the Canal and River Trust, but she had squatter's rights on the narrow piece of land between the towpath and the hedge, where she grew a selection of herbs including mint, rosemary, chives and thyme. She had just started experimenting with garlic, but hadn't been having much luck.

As she looked out of the galley window she saw a cat heading her way, walking in the middle of the towpath as if he owned it. Lulu could tell it was a tom, just from the way he strutted along with his tail in the air, but she knew right away that he was special because he was a calico – a mixture of black, white and orangey brown – and most calicos were female.

The cat stopped in his tracks and began sniffing the air, his ears up. The right side of his head was mainly black with a white patch around the nose and mouth, and the left side was brown and white. His eyes were a vibrant green. He seemed to be looking right at Lulu and she felt a slight shiver run down her spine. He started walking again.

Lulu leaned forward over the double gas hob to get a better view. His front legs and chest were white, his body and tail were thick stripes of black and brown, and his rear legs had white socks. He reached the prow of the boat. *The Lark*. She hadn't named it; the boat had been ten years old when she had taken it on. The previous owner, a retired teacher, had owned it from new and had bought it as a lark, he'd said. Lulu had quite liked the name, and anyway it would have been bad luck to change it. It was a traditional narrowboat, painted dark green with black trim and with *THE LARK* in gold capital letters over a painting of the bird.

The cat walked slowly along the towpath. Past the double cabin, past the toilet, and then he drew level with the galley. He stopped and looked up at her, moving his head slightly and sniffing. His tail was upright like an antenna.

'Well, good morning,' whispered Lulu. 'What a handsome boy you are.'

The cat's ears flicked forward as if he had heard her, and he made a soft mewing sound. He wasn't wearing a collar but he looked too well fed and clean to be a stray. He started walking once more and reached the rear of the boat. He stopped again, then jumped smoothly onto the back deck.

Lulu turned away from the window. The cat appeared at the doorway and sat down.

'Welcome aboard,' said Lulu. The cat stared at her for several seconds and then mewed. 'You're welcome to come in,' said Lulu. 'You'll be my first visitor.'

The cat stayed where he was at the top of the four wooden steps that led down into the cabin.

'Well now, Mr Calico Cat, I'll get you something to drink

– let's see if that tempts you to come in.' Lulu bent down and opened the small fridge that was barely big enough to hold a carton of milk and half a dozen bottles of wine and water. She took out the milk and picked up a white saucer from the tiny draining board.

She was just about to pour milk into it when the cat coughed politely. 'Actually, I'm not much of a milk drinker.'

Lulu gaped at the cat in astonishment. 'What?'

'Most cats are lactose intolerant. They don't have the enzyme that digests the lactose in milk. No enzyme, so no digestion, so the lactose just passes through our system. It can be messy. So best avoided.'

'What?' repeated Lulu.

'So maybe pour me a nice, crisp Chardonnay instead.'

'What?'

The saucer slipped between her fingers and seemed to fall in slow motion to the floor, where it shattered. She stared at the cat, her mind whirling as she tried to come to terms with what had just happened.

'Well, that wasn't the reaction I expected,' said the cat.

'What?'

The cat put his head on one side. There was an amused look in his piercing green eyes. 'You do speak English, don't you? You can say something other than "what", or am I wasting my time?'

'What? Yes. Of course. English. What?'

'I think you should pick up the bits of the saucer before someone gets hurt,' said the cat.

'What? Right. Yes. Okay.' Lulu shook her head in bewilderment. She put the milk carton back in the fridge and then went slowly down on one knee and carefully picked up the pieces, placing them in a pedal bin to the side of the fridge. Her knee cracked as she stood up again. 'How did you know I had Chardonnay?' she asked.

'I won't lie, that was a guess. I did see the wine bottles, but it could have just as easily been Pinot Grigio. I didn't really want wine to drink, obviously. It was just a joke, I didn't think you'd go all Greek on me.'

'Greek? What?'

'They smash plates, right? The Greeks. It's what they do.'

'Right, yes, okay. I'm sorry, I'm a bit confused here.'

'I can see that. Could I have some water?'

'Water?'

'Water. H_2O. Tap water is okay. Do these boats have tap water or do they have tanks?'

'I have a mains water supply,' said Lulu. 'It's a residential mooring. Electricity, too.'

'Excellent,' said the cat. He looked expectantly at Lulu.

'So, water?' Lulu said.

'Perfect.'

'I have Evian.'

'Well, that will be a treat,' said the cat.

Lulu opened the fridge again and took out a bottle of Evian. She opened an eye-level cupboard, took out a Wedgwood saucer and poured water into it. She put the saucer at the bottom of the steps, then replaced the bottle of water in the fridge. She went and sat on the sofa as the cat padded down the steps. He sniffed the water cautiously and then began to lap.

Lulu watched as the cat drank, then she sighed. 'This is a dream, right?'

The cat looked up from the saucer. 'Are you asking me, or telling me?'

Lulu pinched her own arm, so hard that she winced.

'What are you doing?' asked the cat.

Lulu shook her head. 'If it's a dream, why can't I wake up?'

The cat finished drinking and jumped gracefully up onto the sofa and sat looking up at her. 'You need to relax.'

'What?'

'Let's not start that whole "what" thing again.' He rubbed his head against her arm. 'I'm real. This isn't a dream. Deal with it.'

'But cats can't talk,' sighed Lulu.

'Says the lady who is talking to one.' He gently headbutted her. 'You can hear the lack of logic in your statement, right? If cats can't talk, then we couldn't be having this conversation, could we?'

'Maybe I'm going crazy.'

'Well, that's a whole different conversation, isn't it?'

'If you can talk – and I'm not discounting that this is all a figment of my imagination – but if I'm not crazy and you are talking to me, then why?'

'Why? I suppose that's a step up from what.'

'I mean, why me? Why are you talking to me?'

'You mean of all the canal boats in Little Venice, why did I jump onto yours?'

'If you like. Yes.'

The cat shrugged. 'You seemed like a nice person. And you have a good aura. Lots of bright yellow and indigo.'

'That's good, is it?'

'It's perfect.' The cat chuckled. 'I suppose I should say purr-fect.'

'So I suppose black is bad? For auras.'

The cat nodded. 'It can mean there is anger that's being held inside. Or it could be that the person is sick. Of course, sometimes it's the anger that causes the sickness. Or the other way around. Dark blood red also points to a lot of anger. We tend to keep away from blood-red auras but with black auras we can sometimes help.'

'We? Who's we?'

'Cats. We see auras. Cat auras and human auras. The auras of all living things, actually.'

'I didn't know that.'

The cat snorted softly. 'Why would you? You're a human.'

Lulu frowned. 'You said you could help people whose auras are black.'

'We can make it easier for them, when they pass.'

'When they die, you mean?'

The cat gave the slightest twitch of its whiskers. 'We prefer to say pass. But, yes, if we see someone with a black aura, we can sit with them and help calm them.'

'That I have heard of,' said Lulu. 'There used to be a cat at a nursing home I visit. She was friendly enough but never got onto anyone's bed. Unless they were dying. Then she would jump up and lie next to them.' Her eyes widened and her hand flew up to cover her mouth. 'Oh, my. Oh no. Is that why you're here?'

The cat's eyes narrowed. 'What? No. Of course not. I told you already, your aura is fine. Better than fine.' The cat purred. 'What do I call you?'

'My name? It's Lulu. And you?'

'Conrad.'

'Conrad? Conrad the Cat? Conrad the Calico Cat?'

'That's my name, don't wear it out.'

'It's unusual.'

Conrad snorted softly. 'Says the lady called Lulu.'

Lulu chuckled. 'My dad gave me the name Lulu. There was a singer, a little Scottish girl, who had the number one song when I was born – "Shout" – and Dad said I was shouting all the time from the moment I was born. Who gave you your name?'

'I chose it myself.'

'Good choice.'

'That's what I thought. It means brave counsel. It's German. Originally.'

'And are you brave?'

'Fearless.'

'And you give good advice?'

'I try.'

Lulu turned to look at him. 'Is that why you're here? To give me advice?'

Conrad squinted at her quizzically. 'You keep looking for a reason as to why I'm here,' he said.

'Because it's strange. It's not every day I get approached by a talking cat.'

'Don't overthink it, Lulu. Sometimes paths just cross, that's all there is to it.'

'But why me, Conrad? Why talk to me?'

'You seem like a nice person.'

Lulu couldn't help but smile. 'Well, thank you,' she said. 'You seem like a nice cat, too.' She sighed. 'I need a drink.'

'A nice crisp Chardonnay?'

Lulu chuckled. 'I was about to make myself a glass of fresh mint tea.'

'That does sound rather good.'

'I think that's what I'm going to do,' she said. She stood up, filled the kettle at the sink and then used a match to light one of the hobs. She put the kettle on the flames and went up the steps to the back deck. Conrad followed her. Lulu stepped carefully off the boat and onto the towpath. She heard a whirring sound off to her right and turned to see a young man in a grey hoodie and tight jeans hurtling towards them on an electric scooter. She stood back, as the man clearly had no intention of slowing. 'Idiot,' she muttered under her breath as the man whizzed by. An increasing number of people were using electric scooters along the towpath and several people had been injured. The main problem was that they were practically silent so you couldn't hear them coming. Lulu smiled. Actually the main problem was that they were driven by morons who cared nothing for their fellow man – or cats.

'Aren't you just so tempted to push them into the canal?' said Conrad from the safety of the deck.

Lulu laughed. 'Definitely,' she said. She looked right and left again and walked over to her tiny vegetable plot. Conrad jumped off the boat and joined her. He sniffed the plants, one by one.

'How long have you lived on the boat?' he asked.

'Just two months.'

'I thought you'd been here for years, you seem so comfort-able on her.'

'I am, I love it.' She pointed across the road. 'I used to live down there, on Warrington Crescent.'

Conrad nodded. 'Warrington Crescent is nice.'

'It's lovely, but . . .' She shrugged. 'It doesn't matter.' She bent down and ran her hand through the mint plants, then sniffed her fingers. The aroma took her back to her childhood, when she would pick fresh mint from the garden whenever her mother cooked roast lamb. Half a century vanished in a flash and she was a child again.

'Smells always take you back, don't they?' said Conrad. 'More than any of the other senses. Smell just goes straight to the olfactory cortex in the temporal lobe and triggers memories that you never thought you had.'

Lulu looked across at him. 'Did you just read my mind?'

Conrad chuckled. 'Mind-reading isn't in my skill set,' he said. 'You smelt the mint and then you had a faraway look in your eyes as if you were remembering something.' He tilted his head to one side and blinked. 'Elementary, dear Lulu.'

Lulu picked four stems, one from each mint plant. She took them back to the boat. This time Conrad ran ahead of her and jumped onto the deck first. There was a grace to his movements that reminded her of a cheetah she'd once seen on safari in Botswana, many years ago. He turned to watch her walk to the boat. 'Do you ever take her out, along the canal?' he asked.

'Not yet, but I will do,' she said. She stepped onto the deck. 'The engine has been serviced and there's fuel on board. But so far I'm just enjoying living on her. But one day, I plan to go travelling.' She went down the steps. The kettle was already boiling and Lulu turned off the gas. She washed the mint under the tap, placed it into a glass and poured on the hot water. The minty aroma filled the galley. Lulu took the glass over to the sofa and sat down. Conrad gracefully jumped up and sat next to her. She sniffed at the glass, then held it out for Conrad to smell. He nodded his appreciation. 'Nice,' he said. 'But I prefer catnip.'

'What is it about cats and catnip?' asked Lulu.

'We love it,' said Conrad. 'You know how you like Chardonnay? I guess it's the same. The leaves contain an oil called nepetalactone and it stimulates the pheromone receptors.'

'So you get high?'

'We feel euphoric, yes. Happy.'

'So probably more like cannabis than alcohol.'

'Do you smoke cannabis?'

Lulu shook her head. 'No.'

'I didn't think so. I would have smelt it.'

Lulu sipped her tea and looked at the cat over the top of her glass. A talking cat? It had to be a dream. There was no other explanation. Cats didn't talk. End of. But she was clearly hearing this one speak and the only way that made any sense was if she was asleep. At some point she would wake up and everything would be back to normal. She had been having some strange dreams recently. They were often about her husband and, under the circumstances, that was to be expected, she knew. But the chances of her ever having a conversation with Simon again were on a par with her meeting a talking cat. Dreams were dreams, and that was the end of it.

'Penny for your thoughts?' asked Conrad.

Lulu just laughed and shook her head.

2

Lulu finished her mint tea and washed the glass. Conrad sat on the sofa, grooming himself. She turned to look at him, wondering when exactly the dream would end and she would wake up. It was a detailed dream, no doubt about that – probably the most realistic she had ever had – but there was no way any of this could be real. Cats did not talk. They simply didn't.

Conrad stopped grooming and sat up. 'You look as if you want to say something,' he said.

Lulu looked at her watch. It was a gold Rolex. Simon had bought it for her on their tenth wedding anniversary and she had worn it every day since he'd died. 'I should be going.' She wondered if now was the time for her to wake up.

'I'll come with you,' said Conrad. 'Is that okay?'

'Yes, sure, I guess. But there are quite a few roads to cross. Are you okay with roads?'

'I can ride on your shoulders.'

'What?'

'And we're back to "what" already,' said Conrad. 'I thought we'd moved past that.'

Lulu laughed. 'I'm sorry, it's just that I've never heard of that before.'

'It's quite common,' he said.

'I've heard of parrots on shoulders. Long John Silver and all.'

'Same principle,' said Conrad. 'Sit down. I'll show you.'

Lulu walked over to the sofa and sat down. Conrad arched his back and stretched his legs, then smoothly jumped up onto her shoulders. He wrapped his tail around her neck and sat on her left shoulder. 'This is the side position,' he said. 'It's fairly comfortable but it's slightly less secure. He moved slowly, until he had wrapped himself around the back of her neck, his head on her right shoulder, his back legs on her left. 'I call this the scarf position,' he said.

'I can see why,' said Lulu. She was surprised at how little he weighed; it was almost identical to wearing a fur scarf. Not that she would wear anything made of fur, of course. Not these days.

'Try standing up,' said Conrad.

She did. He was perfectly balanced and within seconds it felt completely natural. 'I love this,' she said.

'Walk up and down.'

She walked past the shower to the main cabin door, then slowly turned. 'This is amazing,' she said. She walked back through the galley and did a twirl. 'You're so light.'

'Why, thank you.'

'And you feel so warm against my neck. Seriously, we can walk around like this? You won't fall off?'

'Not unless you decide to spin around suddenly,' said Conrad. 'So, where exactly are we going?'

'To see my mother-in-law. She's in a nursing home.'

'Is she sick?'

'Actually she's quite strong. But she has a few issues with her memory, so she has to be in a place where she can be looked after.' She picked up her handbag and walked carefully up the steps, then onto the towpath.

The nursing home was close to Lord's Cricket Ground, just over a mile from the canal. There were two ways to get there: along Warrington Crescent or down Clifton Road. Warrington Crescent was slightly shorter but Lulu tended to go the longer way.

Walking with a cat on her shoulders was a novel experience. She walked slightly slower than normal, but there was never any sense that Conrad was uncomfortable or about to fall off. Most of the time he purred softly in her ear.

She got a lot of smiles from passers-by as she walked, especially from children. She headed down Clifton Road, past Tesco and the Venice Patisserie, and walked by Raoul's Deli, a Maida Vale institution that had long been one of Lulu's favourite food shops. Their duck eggs were out of this world. She smiled to herself. Talking cats were also out of this world.

She stopped at the traffic lights at the top of Clifton Road. A postman pushing a cart of letters and parcels stopped and grinned at the cat. 'Did it take a lot of training to do that?' he asked.

'No, he taught me in a couple of minutes,' said Lulu.

The postman frowned, then opened his mouth to reply, but then the lights changed and Lulu walked across the road, chuckling to herself.

'That was funny,' said Conrad.

'Yes, I thought so,' said Lulu. Their route took them from Maida Vale into St John's Wood. St John's Wood was usually regarded as being slightly more posh than Maida Vale, with its high street chock-a-block with trendy cafes and overpriced delis, and its whitewashed villas with Bentleys and BMWs parked outside. It was where The Beatles had made many of their albums in the Abbey Road recording studio, and where Sir Paul McCartney still lived.

Lulu had always preferred the edgier Maida Vale, where three-quarters of the homes were mansion block flats and houses were owned by the likes of Paul Weller and Ronnie Wood. Earl Spencer used to live there, but he had moved.

It took another five minutes to reach the nursing home, a four-storey block built around a central courtyard with a small lawn and shrubs and rockeries, with benches for the residents to sit on and paved areas where wheelchairs could be parked.

The main reception area was small but functional, with two low sofas and an armchair around a glass coffee table. There were two employees behind a teak counter, a young man in his twenties with blue-framed spectacles and curly hair whom Lulu knew only as Gary, and an older woman in a dark blue suit who was one of the home's duty managers, Mrs Fitzgerald. The area was overseen by two domed CCTV cameras and all visitors had to be signed in and given a stick-on badge.

Mrs Fitzgerald smiled brightly when she saw Lulu, but then her eyes widened in surprise when she saw the cat lying across her shoulders. 'Oh my goodness,' she said. 'Will you look at that?'

Gary peered through his glasses. 'Is it real?'

Lulu laughed. 'Yes, of course it's real. Do you think I'd walk around with a fake cat around my neck?'

Gary's cheeks reddened and he shrugged.

'Is it yours?' asked Mrs Fitzgerald.

'He's sort of adopted me. Is it okay if I take him in to see Emily?'

The Cat Who Caught a Killer

'Of course. We're animal friendly here. We always have been. Animals have a calming influence. Well, most of them. We had one of our residents who wanted to bring his venomous snake collection with him; we had to draw the line there.'

She handed Lulu a paper badge with the date and LULU LEWIS on it. Lulu stuck it on her jacket. 'Does Conrad need a badge?'

'I think he probably does,' said Mrs Fitzgerald. She wrote CONRAD on another badge and gave it to Lulu, who stuck it onto her shoulder, just below Conrad's head.

There were glass doors to the left and right; Lulu went through the ones on the right. The door slid open electronically and she walked down a corridor and then up a flight of stairs to the first floor. There was a lift but Lulu always preferred to use the stairs.

'These places always smell the same,' said Conrad. 'Pee and disinfectant. I'm told that prisons smell the same.'

'Who told you that?'

'A cat who had been into a prison, obviously,' said Conrad.

They reached the first floor and Lulu walked along another corridor to Emily's room. To the left of the door was a small frame and inside it was a typed card. EMILY LEWIS. The typed card and the frame always worried Lulu. It was nice that everyone would know who was inside, but there was a lack of permanence about it: it would be all too easy to slide out the card and slip in another one.

She knocked quietly on the door and then slowly turned the handle. Emily was sitting in the high-backed armchair next to her bed. Her eyes were closed and they stayed closed as Lulu walked over and stood next to the bed. It was a hospital bed with sides that could be raised. Emily had fallen out of bed four months earlier. Luckily she hadn't broken anything but she had been badly bruised so the home had brought in the special bed for her. The cost – an extra hundred pounds a week – had been added to Emily's monthly bill. That seemed a little steep to Lulu; when she had googled the model she'd found similar beds available online for less than seven hundred pounds.

The staff had dressed Emily, probably after giving her a bath or at least a good wash, and brushed her hair. They usually took her down to the restaurant on the ground floor for breakfast. After breakfast she either returned to her room or went to sit out in the garden. Then she'd have lunch.